The Alternative

George McNeish

The Alternative by George McNeish
http://www.alternative.9li.ca/

Published by George McNeish 2015
http://www.georgemcneish.9li.ca/

Cover Design, Photography, and Artwork by George McNeish

Special thanks:

To my wife, Delta McNeish, for the inspiration to take on this project.

To Patricia Blonde for assistance with editing.

Copyright © 2015 by George McNeish

All rights reserved

Contact *george@9li.ca* for permission to quote.

ISBN: 1519127235

ISBN-13: 978-1519127235

Bible quotations from the King James version.

This book is part of the Sowing Peace Initiative

http://www.sowingpeace.ca/

Chapter		Page
	Introduction	v
1	"Bobby Johnson"	9
2	"Ruthie Lancer"	21
3	"A Roller Coaster Ride"	45
4	"A Miraculous Church Service"	65
5	"Krissy"	81
6	"The Monitory Value of Freedom"	103
7	"Accidentally Saving a Life"	117
8	"Pre-Approved"	135
9	"Becoming Free in Slave Territory"	153
10	"Wedding Plans"	167
11	"The Wedding"	179
12	"Progress"	185
13	"1845 Crop Destruction"	199
14	"Otis"	207
15	"Saving a Nation"	221
16	"Mississippi"	239
17	"Arson"	253
18	"Causes and Preparation for War"	273
19	"Meeting With the President"	279
	Epilogue	287

Introduction

In 1861 the USA would go to war. This would be the most devastating war they ever engaged in. In fact it would take until 1970 and the Vietnam war before the number of American casualties in all other wars the USA fought in exceeded the number of losses in this war. In 1861 the USA would meet its worst enemy. It would go to war with itself.

It seemed unbelievable that a democratic country could cause so much affliction to its own people. I began to uncover the reasons for this war. They all centered around one fact. The US laws allowed a horrendous crime to be perpetrated against people of African descent. These people had been stolen from their homelands and forced, as prisoners of war, to emigrate to a distant land where they could get no help. They were treated as livestock and refused any human rights. As property, their owners held the rights to do with them as they pleased. Property has no rights.

John Brown saw the plight of these wronged ones and went to war for them. He was executed for his role in fighting against injustice. He handed a prophetic note to a guard the day of his execution. He had written, "I, John Brown, am now quite certain that the crimes of this guilty land will never be purged away but with blood. I had, as I now think, vainly flattered myself that, without very much bloodshed, it might be done."

The Alternative

Thirteen months later the Civil War began.

Could this war have been averted? I began to toy with that idea. What if one ordinary person would have done things differently? I invented Bobby Johnson as that very ordinary person. What follows is pure fiction. The opposition that Bobby met was far greater than I anticipated and I began to doubt if he could, even in fiction, prevent a war. However, with the help of a fictionalized God, he accomplished great things. Although truth is stranger than fiction I wrote <u>The Alternative</u> to be a fiction that was more believable than the truth. I brought out the reasons for Bobby's desperation and revealed a very evil side of slavery. The events portrayed never happened but similar situations may have occurred. Many may argue that these evil atrocities occurred very infrequently, but the fact that the law allowed them to happen suggested to me that they likely happened more often than we would like to believe. For those who argue that such events were very rare I ask, "how often does a little girl need to be raped before it matters?" 40,000 would only represent about one percent of the slave population. Are we okay with that many rapes, murders, child abuses or other horrendous crimes? Bobby saw firsthand these appalling situations and could not live in a society that allowed them to continue unpunished.

Although they considered their human chattels as livestock, slave owners took advantage of the fact that slaves could be bred by themselves. I bring this behavior home when Ruthie, the daughter of such a slave owner not only realizes that she is a half sister of some of her father's slaves, but that her father had a preference for young girls. The anguish this fourteen year old faces when she realizes her best friend was impregnated by her father is one of the most emotional parts of the book. Yet how many young girls had to face these facts in real live. Ruthie became my most complex character.

The story took many surprising turns as I was writing it. At times I did not know what my characters would do next. I started out with a vague idea that I was writing an alternative to the civil war. My characters took on a life of their own as I set the challenge before them. It is they, and not I, that worked through the difficulties and solved the problems. I was completely unaware of how challenging this task would be.

Inspiration from History

My greatest inspiration was Fredrick Douglass. It was not enough for me to read his words or what others had written about him. I had to transport myself back in time so I could sit at his feet and listen to his stories. Although Fredrick Douglass was born a slave, I feel he was one of the most brilliant people in history. What he accomplished from such humble beginnings is unbelievable. Much of my observation of the time period I wrote about came from his perspective.

Much of the methodology used by my characters came from Booker T. Washington who was born a slave and was freed after the Civil War. This brilliant man went from being a slave to founding a university so impressive that the President of the United States paid a visit to it.

I also relied on the perspective given by Harriet Beecher Stowe in <u>Uncle Tom's Cabin</u>. Fredrick Douglass had met the author and read the book, so it was a must read for me.

Finally I give credit to Solomon Northup for his description of slavery in Louisiana. I chose a locale close to where <u>Twelve Years a Slave</u> was played out due to the knowledge I gained from his book. I borrowed his description of how slave labour was used on a cotton plantation. His report of the 1845 destruction of the cotton crop gave me an opportunity to use actual history as a turning point for my story. He and some characters from his book make cameo appearances in <u>The Alternative</u>.

Chapter One

Bobby Johnson

Bobby Johnson had all the opportunities that were open to a young man growing up on a southern plantation in the early 1800's. His father was a kind master and managed to get much work out of his slaves. Those who didn't perform well would be sold off, and kind masters were hard to come by in the south, so John Johnson's slaves would work very hard to stay on a plantation where they didn't get whipped and had better food than most slaves. The large plantation and the one hundred and seventeen slaves would one day become Bobby Johnson's property. He was the only child of John and Sara Johnson and therefore the only heir to the Johnson fortune.

The only problem with this is that Bobby Johnson did not want to be a slave owner. Being the only white child on the plantation, Bobby very naturally made friends with the slave children. When they were old enough for field work, Bobby went along with them. When Mr. Johnson found Bobby working with the slaves one day he realized that his son needed to learn the difference between the slave class and the master class. Bobby was nine years old when he was enrolled in school where it was hoped he would make some appropriate friends and learn about the distinction of the classes.

Bobby's best friend was Samson, one of his father's slaves who was about his own age. Samson was a weak and sickly boy and Mr. Johnson considered selling him as he was not much good for field work. However, with Bobby's insistence, Samson was kept mainly as a playmate for the young heir.

When Bobby was at home he would often play school with his friend and inadvertently, Samson learned to read and write. Bobby soon recognized the intelligence of his friend and one day would realize that Samson's strength was his mind. However, according to the southern slave laws, this mind could never be developed.

Bobby was also impressed with the older slaves. He realized their extensive knowledge of the cotton industry and learned much from them. His impressions of his darker companions were in direct opposition to the standards being taught to him in school and at church.

Most Sundays Mr. Johnson and his family would attend a church officiated by Reverend Ichabod Kempler. Reverend Kempler was born into a Jewish family living in a Christian town in the Southern USA. His friends would convince him to attend church with them and he soon became impressed with the pageantry of the church. He converted to Christianity at an early age and was mentored by the pro-slavery preachers of the south. Although he did little self study, he carried on the teachings of his mentors and became recognized as a preacher when he became a young adult. When the minister of the Hamburg church in Louisiana retired, Reverend Kempler naturally took his place.

Bobby's father considered himself a Christian but did not take religion very seriously. When the reverend would accuse him of being too kind to his slaves, he brushed it off. He found that kindness got better results than beatings and told the reverend so, but Reverend Kempler insisted that, if all slave owners took the same approach, no one would get any work out of a slave. "They work hard for you because they fear being sold." Kempler would insist. "If all were kind they would have no incentive to work. You are spoiling your slaves by not whipping them when they deserve it."

"That may be true," Mr. Johnson would brush off the accusation, "but they are my slaves to spoil and I will treat them as I please."

"That is a very unchristian attitude," Kempler would retort, then quoted chapter nine verses twenty-five and twenty-six from the Old testament book of Genesis. "And he said, Cursed be Canaan; a servant of servants shall he be unto his brethren. And he said, Blessed be the LORD God of Shem; and Canaan shall be his servant." Ichabod went on, "The Bible tells us that the Canaanites are to be our servants for all time. They are to be punished for the sin of Ham. It is wrong to treat these evil ones with kindness."

When Reverend Kempler could not get through to the older Johnson, he put pressure on the young Bobby so that he may see the errors of his father's way. Luke, chapter twelve, verse forty-seven would often be quoted. "And that servant, which knew his lord's will, and prepared not himself, neither did according to his will, shall be beaten with many stripes." Bobby took the Bible more seriously than his father. It troubled him why this verse should be in the Bible. There were endless stories of how Jesus was kind to all He met, yet this one verse seemed to contradict everything else the Bible taught.

Bobby's childhood was relatively uneventful. He was a brilliant child and the instructors at the school soon took advantage of his talents, having him explain lessons that some of the slower students would have trouble grasping. Bobby seemed to have a way to simplify complicated lessons so all could understand. His one drawback was the teasing he received. When his schoolmates found he had made friends with his father's slaves, he would be called a "nigger lover." Bobby learned that his darker skinned companions were his true friends and ignored the teasing, but he also learned it was not wise to talk about them in the presence of white people.

Higher education

Bobby's brilliant mind was hungry for knowledge. His greatest interest became religion and, at the age of twenty-one, he wanted to attend a bible college. He found it difficult to accept the teaching of the southern preachers, so he asked his father if he could study at a northern institution. He found that Brown University in Providence, Rhode Island had a very good religious society, so, with his father's blessings, he went there to study in September of 1821. He didn't want to leave his best friend behind and his father decided that it would be good to send Samson along as a servant for Bobby. "Samson's not much good around here anyway," Mr. Johnson commented. "You may as well take him with you." Bobby was provided with enough money to live the luxurious life style to which he was accustomed, plus enough to provide Samson with a slave's rations. Bobby could not tolerate having his best friend living a different lifestyle from himself, so he compromised and shared equally with Samson. They found a room together and cooked their own food. He even found enough money to enroll Samson in some classes at the university. In the south it was illegal to teach a black person, but they were in the north now. Besides the southerners did not need to know about this arrangement. Bobby and Samson shared an interest in religion, but Bobby leaned more toward philosophy while Samson wanted to study agriculture and technology.

Although Samson was met with opposition from both students and faculty, Bobby's friendship with him soon broke down barriers and within a month everyone seemed to have forgotten that Samson was black.

Both young men found the religious study classes very interesting. They began with a thorough study of the four gospels. One day they were studying the twelfth chapter of Luke. Eventually they read;

"Blessed is that servant, whom his lord when he

cometh shall find so doing. Of a truth I say unto you, that he will make him ruler over all that he hath. But and if that servant say in his heart, My lord delayeth his coming; and shall begin to beat the menservants and maidens, and to eat and drink, and to be drunken; The lord of that servant will come in a day when he looketh not for him, and at an hour when he is not aware, and will cut him asunder, and will appoint him his portion with the unbelievers. And that servant, which knew his lord's will, and prepared not himself, neither did according to his will, shall be beaten with many stripes. But he that knew not, and did commit things worthy of stripes, shall be beaten with few stripes. For unto whomsoever much is given, of him shall be much required: and to whom men have committed much, of him they will ask the more."

"In this passage," the instructor said, "the Lord Jesus Christ is telling us about his return. He tells us of great rewards for those of us who do His will, but severe punishment to those who do not. For those who know the Lord's will but ignore it, the worst punishment will come. For those who did not know, there will be a lesser punishment. The servant who knows but chooses to ignore it will be beaten with many stripes but the unknowing servant with fewer. Thus it is important that we learn the will of the Lord but even more important that we obey it."

Bobby and Samson looked at each other in astonishment. How often had they heard this scripture quoted in the south, but never in its true context. The south used this scripture as a licence to beat slaves, but the passage was meant for all of us. By "servants" was meant servants of God and by "his lord," it didn't mean the slave's master, but referred to Our Heavenly Father who we are instructed to obey. Now the Bible made sense. "We are all servants under God and equal in His sight," Bobby said. "That is so different from the Christianity taught in the slave states. Why is it that they can't see the Truth?"

Bobby couldn't wait until summer break of 1822 so he could tell Reverend Kempler about his recent enlightenment, but there was yet a couple of months before summer vacation. As he was thinking about ways he could break this to the reverend he remembered an experience he had when he brought up a verse in Exodus. He had second thoughts as he considered the minister's reaction to being challenged on his knowledge of the Good Book. No, Reverend Kempler was set in his ways and was not about to accept any new found knowledge from one of his students. "How could someone who had devoted his life to ministry be so blind to the Truth?" Bobby mused.

Then there was that verse from Exodus. What was it again? "And he that stealeth a man, and selleth him, or if he be found in his hand, he shall surely be put to death." Samson found Exodus twenty-one, verse sixteen and read it to Bobby. Now Bobby felt like a veil was being lifted. Meanings started to become clear and it was as though the Lord Jesus was speaking to his heart and revealing the Truth to him.

"Samson, I think we need to pray about this," Bobby said as he took Samson's hands. "Heavenly Father we pray to you that you show us the Truth. You know, God, how the preachers in the south have presented Your Word. If this is a corruption of the Truth, Lord, reveal that to us now. Show us, oh Creator, what you want us to do. We are Your humble servants and desire to do Your Will. Lord, take control of our lives and guide us on the true path."

"Amen," said Samson. "Bobby! What if this is talking about a spiritual death. Maybe it is not that the man stealers will be arrested and executed for their crime, but that they spiritually die when they steal a man."

"Yes, Samson. I think you are right. And when they buy a

man that has been stolen they buy the punishment with it. This is what has blinded them to the Truth. This is how they become so cruel. They are walking corpses devoid of real life."

"That would certainly explain why Ichabod Kempler is so blind to the Truth and why he gets so angry when he is challenged," Samson chimed in.

"Yes, but my dad is a slave owner. Does that mean he is spiritually dead?"

"Perhaps he is one that did not know the Lord's Will and therefore he has a lesser punishment. Your father has always been kind to us slaves, but I think even owning a slave is wrong, no matter how kind you are."

Both young men sat in silence as they contemplated and meditated on what they had said. Bobby remembered Reverend Kempler warning him that a slave who read the Bible would twist its meaning, but now he believed that the reverend had twisted the meaning and his darker skinned best friend had just saved his spiritual life by warning him of the consequences of slave owning. He knew now that he could never be a slave owner and he would try to convince his father to emancipate his slaves.

Summer Vacation

Time seemed to go quickly. Samson and Bobby were in such a state of joy. It was as though they had discovered a new world, a paradise were everyone was happy. Soon it was time for summer vacation and homecoming was a joyous occasion. Bobby was happy to see his parents and he gave both of them big hugs. The other slaves were anxious to hear of Samson's adventure. Word was that he had gone to help Bobby as his servant. Although nothing was said about his learning it soon became evident that Samson came back with more than an adventure.

It was a couple days before Bobby decided to talk to his

father about his new views on slavery.

"Dad, I read in the Bible that, if someone steals a man, he should be put to death."

"Yes, son, you have spoke of that before."

"Well, the African slaves were stolen from their homeland."

"I'm not sure I would use those terms, but they were captured and brought to America to be sold as slaves." Mr. Johnson observed, then added, "Are you suggesting I should be put to death because I own slaves?"

"No, dad. You have been very kind and have been a good master to your slaves, but I think even owning a slave is wrong."

"That may be," Mr. Johnson considered thoughtfully, "but the preachers in this area don't think so. Many of them are slave owners themselves. They even go so far as to tell me I will go to Hell for not whipping them."

Bobby was already aware of these facts. "I think they are wrong," he blurted out. "In fact I think the sentence of death has already been passed on them and they are all spiritually dead."

"Well, son, I'd suggest you keep those thoughts to yourself in these parts. Suggesting something like that could get you killed."

"Yes, Dad. I have already considered the consequences, but I can never be a slave owner."

"Son," his father began slowly. "You know I think religion is good because it helps some people to live honest lives, but you can take things too far and then it gets dangerous. I understand your interest in religion and I respect you for it. I even paid for your religious training, but there comes a time when you have to live in the real world." Mr. Johnson paused to let that sink in and then continued.

"I will retire in a few years and it will be your turn to run this plantation. If you think you can do that without slaves, more power to you. I would not own slaves if it was not necessary to make a profit. I don't know of any successful plantation owner that does not own slaves. I hope when it is time for you to run this plantation that you won't let your foolish ideas bring it to ruin."

Bobby could see that he would not be able to convince his father to free the slaves. He had not considered before the economic impact of such a move and he could now see his father's point of view. How would a plantation run without slaves. It had never been done to his knowledge and it may never be possible, but he was convinced slavery was against the Lord's will.

"What about Samson?" Bobby queried. "Could you at least give him his freedom?"

Mr. Johnson thought for a moment. "Well son," he finally began, "I have pretty much considered Samson to be your slave. If you want, I can make it official and you can do with him as you please. That way you can find out for yourself how long he hangs around to show his appreciation once you give him his freedom."

That very afternoon, Mr. Johnson signed papers transferring ownership of Samson to his son. Bobby was horrified at being a slave owner and immediately went into town to have emancipation papers drawn up. By the end of the day he held in his hand a paper declaring that Samson was a free man.

That evening, as soon as he had finished supper with his family, he went to the slave quarters to find Samson.

"Hi, Samson, I have something for you." He had a big smile on his face as he addressed his friend.

"What is it?" Samson asked as Bobby handed him an envelope.

"Open it and see." Bobby was beaming with delight.

Samson carefully opened the envelope and extracted the precious document. He looked it over carefully reading every word twice. "What is it, Bobby?" He couldn't believe his eyes and needed another opinion.

"It's your freedom papers." Bobby answered abruptly.

"But it says here that you set me free. I was your father's slave. How is that possible?"

"Well just this afternoon my father transferred your ownership to me. It was horrible. I was a slave owner and the slave I owned was my best friend. I couldn't stand the feeling that brought on and I had to remedy it as quick as I could."

Even though it seemed unmanly Samson threw his arms around Bobby and gave him a big hug. "Thank you, thank you, thank you," he said. "I cannot thank you enough."

"I suppose you will be leaving these parts now." Bobby commented.

"Leave?" Samson was shocked. "I have never lived any place else except when I went with you to college. I don't know where I would go. Oh, please Massa Bobby, don't send me away."

"Oh, no Samson. I would never send you away. You are my best friend and I was hoping you would stay. It's just that you are free now and you can go where you like and do as you please. In fact I was hoping we could continue school together in September. It will be so much better now that you are free."

It had been more than ten years since Samson had last addressed Bobby as "Massa." The shock of thinking he might be sent away caused him, during his first hour of freedom, to assume the role of a slave to his master. Bobby was very excited to have his friend on equal terms with him. He knew that Samson's strength was in his mind and was determined to help Samson develop his potential.

Samson was appreciative of the opportunity Bobby was giving him and the funding provided by Bobby's father, so he worked very hard for Mr. Johnson and asked nothing in return. He contented himself with slave rations, and slept in the slave's quarters. He put his study of agriculture and technology to use and was able to teach the slaves more productive ways to get their work done. He also invented tools to make their jobs easier. Soon they were able to complete all the work of the plantation and have much leisure time left over. Thus Samson became a hero among the slaves. Although many envied his freedom, they knew their turn would come. By this time it was well known on the Johnson plantation that Bobby Johnson would not be a slave owner. Since he was the only heir to the Johnson estate he would eventually inherit the plantation. At that time there would be no slave labour at this location.

One slight problem was soon remedied. Slaves were expected to work six days a week from early dawn until it got too dark to see. When the Johnson slaves began to have more free time, Mr. Johnson considered selling some of them. Samson and Bobby soon explained to him that such an action would reverse any advantage they had. "They now work hard because they know they will have a time of rest when they are done," Samson explained.

"Their greatest fear is being sold. If they think their hard work is going to get them sold they will soon go back to their old ways." Bobby put it to his father in such a way that Mr. Johnson would not think of parting with any of his loyal chattels.

Back to college

The next year at Brown University the two young men would see less of each other in class although they still shared a room and did their own cooking. Both became better cooks and would try to outdo each other in preparing a meal to share, so needless to say, they both ate well. Samson had lost some weight during the summer, but he soon gained it back.

Bobby dropped his other courses so he could concentrate on religious studies. In January of 1823, Bobby, then twenty-two met a young man of sixteen in a coffee shop. He was a newspaper reporter and had come to Providence because he heard that Brown University had a black student and he wanted to do a story about him. Bobby learned this young man's name was William Lloyd Garrison. He asked Bobby if he knew anything about this black student. Just then Samson walked in to meet Bobby as they had earlier arranged. "Well, Bill, this is Samson. We share a room together and have been best friends since we were children."

Mr. Garrison was soon filled in on the other aspects of their arrangement and how Samson got to be a free black studying at the prestigious Brown University. When they found out that Bill also believed that slavery should be abolished, they became very interested in his views. They had much in common and would stay in touch for many years.

Samson dropped his religious studies to pursue agriculture and technology on a full time basis. These were subjects he thought would be more useful to his future. Bobby could fill him in on what he had learned in religious studies, so there was no need for them to take the same classes. Both were anxious to complete their studies so they could pursue the work they were destined to do.

Chapter Two
Ruthie Lancer

The young ladies of Hamburg, Louisiana found Bobby to be an attractive young man, but living in slave territory with an antislavery attitude had its drawbacks. Bobby found the high society girls to be snobbish and they could not understand his friendship with Samson. The female slaves his father owned may have been a better choice, but there was nothing a slave would not do for her master's son, so he could never be sure they had sincere feelings for him. Bobby was not one to take advantage of such a situation and thought those who had sexual relations with their slaves were disgusting.

Bobby would often help his uncle at the general store in Hamburg. His uncle, Robert Taylor, was his mother's brother and owned the biggest store in the small town. Uncle Robert was always kind to his black customers, which drew the ire of some of the whites who would expect preferential treatment. They would get very angry when he served a black customer ahead of them.

When Uncle Robert had errands to run he was glad to leave Bobby in charge. One such day Bobby had the opportunity to serve a very beautiful young lady and her black companion. Bobby could not quite figure out the relationship between them. The young lady treated her companion with a degree of respect that was completely foreign to the typical slave owner. She even called this older companion, "Mom." Bobby knew some slaves were white due to the self breeding methods used by many slave owners, but this young lady did not dress or act like a slave. Bobby was courteous to both of them as he served them and placed their order in bags and boxes. His Uncle returned as he was finishing and watched them leave.

"I see you have met Ruthie Lancer," Uncle Robert commented.

"Who's Ruthie Lancer?"

"She's that young lady that you had your eyes glued to."

"Oh! Was it that obvious?"

"Well you may be in luck."

"What?"

"Mr. Lancer is not well and asked if we could deliver his slave rations for him. He is not able to make his usual pick up. Would you like to run them out there tomorrow?"

"Well... uh..." Bobby was embarrassed. He didn't want to say "no" but he didn't want to appear too eager to see the young lady again. "Who is Mr. Lancer?" he said at last, thinking that perhaps this young lady had a husband.

"Not to worry, Bobby, Mr. Lancer is Ruthie's father." Uncle Robert had guessed Bobby's concern. Then to add a little enticement and relieve Bobby of his embarrassment, his uncle added, "This may give you an opportunity to talk to some slaves that are not your father's." Although the south presented slavery as a benevolent institution Bobby was gathering evidence that slaves were not as content as the slave owners would have others believe.

Thus the deal was solidified and Bobby expected to make the delivery to the Lancer plantation the next day.

Ruthie Lancer's upbringing was nothing like Bobby Johnson's. Ruthie's mother died the day Ruthie was born and her father blamed her for the death. With no mother to take care of her, that duty was passed on to the slaves. Her father turned to alcohol to drown his sorrow and had little dealing with his daughter's upbringing. Thus Ruthie had a very troubled childhood. Whenever Mr. Lancer was able to detect his daughter's unhappiness through his alcohol distorted mind, he always blamed it on the slaves. The slave in charge would be severely beaten if he should find his daughter crying. Thus Ruthie's only parenting came from the slaves who were put in charge of her care. She soon learned that her slave mother was her servant and had to do what she wanted.

Once Ruthie was big enough to sit at a table her father would insist she joined him for evening meals. Mammy was the slave who looked after her up to that point and Ruthie insisted that her slave mother should eat with them. Mr. Lancer would rather have a dog sit at his table than to see a slave with that privilege. This was totally unacceptable and the slave that put that idea in his daughter's head must be punished. After a severe whipping Mammy found her duties were switched to field work and a younger slave, Sheila, who was nursing a child at the time was brought in to replace her as the house slave. Thus Ruthie got a new mother when she was three years old.

During those early years Ruthie would seldom see her father other than at supper time. As soon as they ate he would go to the slave quarters to check on the slaves and would not be back in the big house until after Ruthie was asleep.

Since Ruthie was the only white child on the plantation, she naturally made friends with her father's slaves and Krissy became her best friend. Krissy, like the other slaves, was hesitant to befriend the master's daughter, but the consequences of upsetting the daughter of a cruel master was unthinkable. Krissy soon realized the advantages of such a friendship and found Ruthie to be very kind, unlike her father.

To try to control the influence the slaves were having on Ruthie, Mr. Lancer enrolled her in a fine girls' school at the age of six. Academics were not considered to be important for girls so the main purpose of the school was to mold the young ladies to become fine wives for future husbands. Indeed, marriage was considered the only option for the ladies of the 1800's, and one who failed to find a husband was considered to be a complete failure.

Although Ruthie led the life of a spoiled but neglected child, she started developing feelings for those who cared for her and when she was eight years old she could no longer tolerate her father whipping her care giver. When Sheila didn't immediately give Ruthie a cookie as they were coming out of the oven, Ruthie began to throw her usual tantrum just as her father walked in. That called for an immediate whipping but Ruthie felt bad about the situation she had caused and ran between her father and Sheila just as the whip was being applied. When he saw her, Mr. Lancer tried to pull back, but the tip of the whip left a gash in his daughter's right cheek. She would have a scar for the rest of her life. Sheila was terrified that she would be blamed for the injury and for sure Mr. Lancer would blame no one else, but Ruthie would no longer allow her father to whip Sheila and the young girl stuck by the side of her slave mother to protect her from ever receiving another beating. After that incident Ruthie and Sheila developed a relationship that more closely resembled a mother/daughter relationship. Sheila became the one she would run to for advice or protection.

Ruthie was born on December 22nd, 1805 and since no one knew the exact date that Krissy was born, they would celebrate their birthdays together. When they were fourteen it started to become obvious that Krissy was pregnant. Although Krissy had a very good reason to keep this from her friend, it was beginning to show and she could no longer deny her situation. Ruthie tried to find out who the father was.

"You don't want to know," Krissy said.

"Come on, you can tell me. I won't tell no one."

"I can't tell you."

"You mean you don't know?" Ruthie was shocked.

"You've been with that many guys that you don't know who the father is."

Krissy was hurt. "No, I know who it is, I just can't tell you."

"I'll bet it was that Sam. He's kinda cute."

"Ya, you're right," Krissy lied.

"Well you are quite a tramp getting yourself knocked up at fourteen. Didn't you know any better. S'possin' being a nigger you wouldn't." Ruthie stomped off and went to see Sheila leaving Krissy crying uncontrollably.

When she got to Sheila she told her what had happened. "You know I really liked Krissy, I didn't know she would turn out to be such a tramp."

"You don't know the half of it," Sheila replied. "You should be kind to Krissy. You don't know what happened."

"It was that nigger Sam. Krissy told me."

"Well Krissy lied to protect you."

"What do ya' mean."

"Well I suppose you think I am a tramp since I had Willy and I have no husband."

"I never thought about that, but I suppose you had a good reason."

"The same reason as Krissy."

"What do ya' mean."

Sheila was trying to put this as gently as possible, but she decided this could no longer be kept from Ruthie.

"Well Willy will be a half-brother to Krissy's baby."

"What?"

"And.... and..." Sheila was struggling." You, Ruthie, are their half-sister."

Now the big nasty secret was out.

"You mean." Ruthie was struggling to make sense of it. "You mean." She said again but couldn't continue. Her brain was searching for an answer. Any answer but the obvious one because that could not possibly be true.

"Yes Ruthie," Sheila helped out, "your father is the father of Willy and the father of Krissy's baby.

"You lyin' nigger," Ruthie shouted. "My father may not be the nicest person but he loved my mother very much. He has often told me that he could never love another."

"T'ain't no love in it," Sheila said calmly. "Your father never showed us any love. We was no better'n a toilet for him to relieve himself. T'was never 'bout love."

"I ain't never gonna believe that," Ruthie was forgetting her finishing school training. "You just made that up 'cause you's unhappy here. 'Spos'n you wanta git sold."

Sheila was calm. She knew this was difficult for Ruthie and she knew that she didn't mean the hurtful things she was saying. "Willy, come here," she commanded.

Willy was born when Ruthie was three, just before Sheila took over Ruthie's care. Ruthie had watched him grow and become a young man of eleven, but there was a lot she hadn't noticed.

"Ruthie, I want you to look into Willy's eyes and tell me what you see."

The two children stared at each other for a while. Then Ruthie began to notice. Willy's face bore resemblance to her father, but those eyes.... those eyes. "Father?" she queried mesmerized.

"Father!" she shouted surprised.

"Father!!!" she screamed angrily.

She stood up and started pacing back and forth, not knowing what to do or were to go. Her young mind was trying to fathom the impact of what she has just learned, but it was too much for her. She felt disgust for the man who was her father. She felt shame that she was his child. And then...

"Oh, Sheila. I am so sorry. I am sorry I didn't believe you. And... And I am so sorry for what Father has done to you."

"Oh, Krissy," she continued hysterically. "I was so cruel to her. Do you think she will ever forgive me?"

Krissy had come to the door of the kitchen where they were conversing. She had heard the commotion and had guessed what it was about. She wasn't sure if she should make her presence known or quietly slip away, but just then Ruthie in her angry pacing had moved toward the open door and caught a glimpse of her. She ran to Krissy and threw her arms around her.

"Oh, Krissy," she sobbed. "I am so sorry. I didn't know. I didn't know. I am so sorry."

Krissy could not answer. She was chocked up with tears. She felt relief that her nasty secret was out. But now what? What could be done about it? Could things be the same between her and Ruthie now that she knew? Being raised as a slave she was accustomed to hardship, shame and brutal beatings, but this love that her master's daughter was pouring out was strange to her. She did not know what to do.

Ruthie stopped crying long enough to tell Krissy. "I will never be mean to you again as long as I live. Please forgive me, I am so sorry for what I said."

Krissy was too choked up to respond. She tried to express her forgiveness, but words would not come out of her mouth.

Ruthie stood and looked at Krissy for a while, then her sorrow and shame gave way to anger.

"Father!" she shouted. "Father, how could you do this to my best friend? She is just a child like me. How could you?" she stormed out of the room.

"Not a word of this to your father," Sheila shouted after her in fear. "If he finds out I told you he will kill me."

"I will kill him first," Ruthie shouted back as she ran to find her father. The kitchen was at the back of the house. Her father was on the front porch drowning his sorrows as usual.

"Father! How could you?" Ruthie screamed when she saw him. "My best friend and a child my age. How could you?"

"Oh Jeannette! Jeanette don't be angry with me. I will do better. I'm sorry," he muttered. Many times when he was in a drunken stupor he would mistaken his daughter for his wife.

"Father! This is me. You should be glad that Mother didn't live to see this day."

"Oh Jeanette, don't be mad. I will shape up." He suddenly held his stomach and doubled over in apparent pain. Ruthie ran to him.

"Father are you all right?" she gasped.

Fred looked up and finally recognized his daughter. "Ruthie, is that you? I was just talking to your mother."

"Mother's dead!" Ruthie retorted angrily. "How could you do that to my best friend?"

"I don't feel too good," her father gasped having obvious difficulty breathing. He tried to stand up and fell unconscious on the porch.

"Don't think you're going to get off that easily? I'm not done with you yet, you can't die now." Ruthie said angrily. She looked at her father with contempt. He disgusted her in every way. He had shamed her and embarrassed her. She wanted to make him pay. As she watched him lie there she screamed at him. "You will pay for this. I will never forgive you. You are a filthy low life and don't deserve to be anybody's father."

Suddenly she realized her father wasn't responding. "Oh, no, I've killed him," she gasped. She remembered her angry retort to Sheila. "I didn't mean it," she said out loud to herself. She ran to her father being torn between the love that comes natural between a father and his daughter and the extreme anger and shame she felt for what he had done. Her father didn't look well and she feared he might already be dead. Not knowing what to do she ran to get the only person she knew would have the answers she desperately needed. "Sheila," she screamed hysterically. As she ran to the door, Sheila was already coming out of the house.

"He's probably just passed out from drink'n," she said trying to calm the situation. She ran to her master and started checking for a pulse. Willy had followed her. "Willy, run and get Mammy," she commanded.

Mammy was the only person on the plantation that knew a little about doctoring. She would know what to do. Soon Willy came back with Mammy. She calmly went to her master and checked his pulse. It was weak but she found one. His breathing was shallow and irregular. "He needs a doctor," she said without emotion. "'Course, if he died, no one would care much," she added, then realizing Ruthie was present, "Oh I'm sorry child, I didn't mean to sound uncare'n."

One of the slaves was quickly dispatched to fetch the doctor. It was a few hours before he returned. No one had thought about giving him a pass and patrollers had detained him. Finally convincing them that his master needed a doctor, one of them escorted him home to check out his story while the other continued to fetch the doctor. Another half hour passed before the doctor arrived.

"How long has he been like this?" Doctor Smyth asked as he began to attend the patient. The brief history of what was known was conveyed to him as he checked for vital signs and injected him with some medicine. "We need to get him to a hospital," he said finally.

A couple of the slaves picked him up to put him in the doctor's buggy. "I hope he dies," one said when he thought they were out of earshot, but Ruthie was close enough to hear as she followed her father.

"Shh... d'ya want ta get us killed," the other slave rebuked.

Ruthie was so distraught that nothing seemed to register, but the things she heard that night would go into her memory. She had experienced every emotion known to a fourteen year old that night. She was no longer in any shape to make sense of it. She blankly watched as the doctor left with her father. Mammy and Sheila did what they could to comfort the young lady. Sheila filled Mammy in on what led up to the incident. At Ruthie's insistence they came into the parlour where she and Sheila took the sofa while Mammy sat in the armchair. Other than for cleaning purposes they had never dared to enter the parlour and to sit on furniture reserved for the master's family was unthinkable. But tonight Ruthie needed them and the master would not be back for some time. As Sheila sat, Ruthie curled up in a fetal position with her head on Sheila's lap. She laid there and sobbed while Sheila gently caressed her soft hair. Finally merciful sleep took over and the worst day in the life of a young teenager came to an end, but everything had changed. The innocence of youth was now gone. Now she knew. She knew what no daughter should ever have to know about her father. It disgusted her. It tormented her. It robbed her of innocent joy.

Was It a Nightmare?

Ruthie woke up with a start as morning's dawn was starting to brighten the room. Did she have the most horrible dream or did these things really happen? She found herself in the parlour, and something seemed strange about the cushion she was using. She looked up and saw she was lying on Sheila's lap. This was strange to her, but it seemed to confirm that her horrible experience was not a dream. Sheila, being wakened by her movements was just beginning to stir. Ruthie got up and ran towards her father's room. "Father, father, were are you?" she cried. She opened the door to his room and found it empty. "No, no," she whimpered. "It can't be true. It was just a horrible dream."

Sheila got up and run to her aide. "Ruthie, Ruthie, It'll be alright. You have gone through quite an ordeal, but the worst is over."

"Where is father?" Ruthie questioned. "What happened to father?" she further queried.

"Don't you remember?" Sheila interjected. "Doc Smyth took him to the hospital last night."

"Then it's true." Ruthie was sobbing. "It wasn't a dream. It's all true."

"Yes Ruthie, it really happened."

"But that means I was so cruel to you. I didn't believe you when you told me the truth."

"It was hard for you to believe," Sheila reassured. "But now the truth is out in the open. I am so sorry I had to tell you, but I couldn't allow you to be mad at Krissy for something that wasn't her fault."

"Oh and Willy. Why didn't you tell me before?" Ruthie appeared to be in a semi-conscious state.

"Oh, Ruthie, you don't know how many times I wanted to tell you, but you were so young and you were not ready to know the truth. I had to protect you so you could enjoy your childhood."

Ruthie sat back down on the sofa. Zombie like, she just stared into space. Sheila came and put her arms around her. Slowly Ruthie returned the embrace. They just sat there silently for almost half an hour.

"Sheila. You are a mother to me. I never knew my real mom, but you have been the best mother anyone could have. I love you so much."

"I love you to," Sheila whispered and kissed Ruthie's forehead.

Just then the sound of a horse approaching made them aware of the outside world. They went to the door to see who it was. Perhaps it was the doctor with news of her father, but Ruthie looked out as a stranger dismounted. She felt as though she should know him. Perhaps in another life.

"Hello, hello," said the stranger. "You must be Ruthie. Well you certainly grew into a fine young lady and the splitting image of your mother."

"Who are you?" Ruthie puzzled.

"Oh, yes. I don't suppose you would remember me. I'm your Uncle Jack. Jack Adams at your service."

"Uncle Jack?" Ruthie was confused. Somewhere in the back of her mind she seemed to recall her mother had a brother named Jack, but he had never come to visit.

"Oh yes, you were about one year old the last time I was here. I do say you look so much like my sister it's uncanny."

"What brings you here today?" Sheila inquired. Jack was taken back by the boldness of a slave who would dare to speak to a white man without first being spoken to." Sheila realized her mistake and kept silent.

"Yeh! How come you show up now after all these years?" It was Ruthie's turn to ask.

"Well, I heard your papa was sick and came to see if you needed anything."

"No, we's," Ruthie remembered her finishing school training and corrected herself. "We are quite fine, thank you."

"Well, can I come in and sit a spell? I stopped by the hospital and I have some news of your father."

"Come on in," said Ruthie directing him to the door. "How is father doing?"

"The doctor said he is recovering quite well and should be back home in a day or two."

"Well, that's good news." They entered the house. Ruthie directed her uncle to the armchair and took the sofa. Sheila went immediately to the kitchen and began preparing some tea.

"Did Doc Smyth say what caused it?" she fearfully asked expecting it was her behaviour that made her father sick.

"Yes he did." Uncle Jack piped in. "And that is one of the reasons I am here."

Ruthie shuddered. Did they know how she had screamed at her dad and wished he was dead? Was she to be arrested for attempted murder? She stared at her uncle in disbelief.

Ruthie's reaction puzzled Uncle Jack, but he went on. "It appears that your father's drinking has got the better of him. Doc says if he takes another drink it could kill him. We need to go through the house and make sure there is no alcohol here before he comes home."

Ruthie was relieved by this announcement. So her father's illness was not her fault. Sheila came in with tea and biscuits. She offered them first to the guest and then to Ruthie, then quickly left the room.

"These are good," Jack commented. "You'll have to lend me your slave so she can teach mine how to cook."

"So, Uncle Jack. Why has it been so many years since you have called on us?" Ruthie wanted to know.

"We used to visit all the time when your mother was alive and we came often to see you when you were first born," Uncle Jack stated, "but after your mother died your father didn't make us feel very welcome. Yes me and your Aunt Sue, Uncle George and Aunt Frieda would come often. We kept coming to watch you grow, but after a while.... well we just didn't feel like your father wanted us here. It seemed as though he thought we blamed him for our sister's death. We didn't. We know that these things happen and we missed our sister very much, but we really wanted to spend time with our brother-in-law and our precious niece. But your dad was so mean to us we had to stop coming."

"Why was that?"

"He kept insinuating that we were only coming to torment

him, so we just stopped coming. But we never stopped thinking about you and wondering how you were doing."

"Oh! Why would father think you blamed him for mother's death? How did she die?"

"You haven't heard? Well it was a complication from the pregnancy. When you were born you were coming out the wrong way. Doc Smyth, he was just starting his practice then, had been called to an emergency in another town and he didn't get here until the next day and by that time it was much too late. Mammy got you turned around and we thought you were going to die for a while. Mammy had a hard time getting you to breath, but finally she got you going. During this time no one noticed that your mama was bleeding. With no doctor around nobody knew how to stop it. It was less than an hour before she bled out. There wasn't anything anyone could do about it."

After what she had learned the day before this was too much for young Ruthie to take. She sat there in shock for a while, blankly staring into space. Uncle Jack never thought of how this may affect his niece. Now he looked at her blank expression. "Are you alright?" he inquired.

Ruthie slowly turned her head until her blank stare met Uncle Jack's eyes. She began to whimper. Then she began to sob uncontrollably. Sheila defied protocol and sat by Ruthie and held her. Ruthie turned to her and between her tears she said, "Oh, Sheila, I killed mommy."

She Is Just a Slave

It took Uncle Jack and Sheila some time to get Ruthie calmed down and assured that her mother's death was not her fault. Uncle Jack was not comfortable with Sheila being so familiar with his niece, but he was glad for the help. He hadn't considered how his words might affect his sister's daughter and he was sorry he had not been more gentle in his approach. He wasn't sure that he should have said anything about how

Jeanette died, but Ruthie deserved to know and it was obvious her father had said nothing. Uncle Jack was not sure when he would get another chance to speak to his niece. He let the day's work slide so he could spend time with her.

Once Ruthie was more calm she said, "I guess that is why I always felt that father was angry with me. He must have blamed me for mother's death."

"I think you are right," Sheila piped in. "I never thought that man treated you right."

Uncle Jack clearly was not comfortable with this slave's boldness. "You may be excused," he said to Sheila. "I want to have a few words with my niece." Then he turned his attention to the young lady. "Ruthie, Ruthie, Ruthie," he repeated the name with sympathy in his tone. "I can see that you have not had a very good upbringing. You must learn to keep your slaves in their place. You are much too familiar with them. If you keep it up they will forget they are servants and you will have nothing but trouble with them."

This was nothing new to Ruthie. The teachers at the finishing school she attended tried everything in their power to drive a wedge between her and her father's chattels. Her white friends chided her for being a "nigger lover," but how could Ruthie turn her back on those who had been a mother to her when she had no mother. In fact, with her father being drunk most of the time, the only parenting she got was from his servants. Learning that she was a half-sister to at least one of those slaves caused her to feel even closer to her black friends. Then she remembered Krissy and how she had gotten so angry with her father. She was not completely convinced that her anger had not brought on her father's illness.

"Uncle Jack," she began. "I was very angry with father when he got sick."

"Why was that child?"

"I had just found out that he got Krissy pregnant."

"Who is Krissy?" Uncle Jack inquired.

"Krissy is my best friend in the whole world."

Uncle Jack was horrified. "What does her father have to say about that?"

"I don't rightly know who her father is."

"Well! Where does she live."

"Right here on the plantation."

"What? You mean your friend lives with you?"

"No, she stays in the slave quarters."

"Oh, she's a slave," Uncle Jack was relieved. "Ruthie, you mustn't be so attached to the slaves. Krissy isn't your friend. She is your father's slave. He has the right to do whatever he wants with her."

Ruthie didn't get the expected sympathy from her uncle. "You mean that you think what father did is okay?" she queried.

"Ruthie! A slave is a slave. They do not have rights," her uncle tried to explain. "They are not like us and they are used to such treatment. But no, I do not think it is okay. In fact I think it is disgusting that a man would have sex with his own slave, it's like having sex with a dog. But it is his slave and he can do what he wants with her. No one has the right to interfere with that."

"But Krissy is just fourteen. She will be due soon. She was only thirteen when it happened. She is just a child. How could he do that to a child."

"There you go again thinking that a slave is a regular person." Uncle Jack interjected. "She is not a child. She is a slave. Even if she was two years old it would be the same. She is property owned by a man who can do anything he wants with her. If you go on identifying with these creatures you are bound to continue being hurt. If you keep it up you will be no better off than they are." Uncle Jack was clearly getting agitated.

Ruthie got up and ran for her support system. "Sheila, did

The Alternative

you hear what Uncle Jack said." Sheila did. She had just been in the next room. Uncle Jack did not care if she heard or not. To talk about a slave in her presence was no different than talking about a dog when it was within earshot.

Uncle Jack followed Ruthie to the kitchen. "Look, young lady," he said sternly. "You must abandon this behaviour. Now come away from that nigger so we can continue our conversation."

Ruthie and Sheila turned to face Uncle Jack. They each had one hand on the other's shoulder. They both stood defiantly in front of their adversary. It was Sheila, emboldened by Ruthie's actions, who spoke first. "I think you should leave Mr. Adams."

Uncle Jack was furious. How dare this chattel address him in such a way. He was about to reproach her and had his hand raised to strike her when Ruthie added calmly, "Yes, Uncle Jack, please leave us alone. You've done enough damage for one day."

The gentleman's rage grew to a frenzied pitch. "How dare you, young lady. How dare you side up with a common nigger and defy your own uncle. You will get yours for this. If you like those dammed animals so much you might as well go and live with them. You are acting like a nigger so you might as well be treated like one. I tried to save you from a live of misery, but you are digging yourself in." He then turned to Sheila, "And for you, you black bitch. I will report your actions to your master. I wouldn't be surprised if he will whip you to death. Don't think you can get off with that kind of behaviour in front of Jack Adams."

As Uncle Jack ran down the porch steps he tripped and fell. He got up and brushed himself off and, trying to appear dignified, he attempted to mount his horse. He missed the stirrup and kicked the horse in its side. The horse reared and ran. Uncle Jack was holding the reigns and the horse dragged him until he had to let go. He got up and brushed himself off again and went chasing after his horse, all the time yelling and cursing. The last Ruthie and Sheila saw of him he was chasing his horse down the road. They could still hear his cursing when he disappeared from sight, but that also faded away. Sheila and Ruthie looked at each other and laughed harder than either one had ever done before. This was the comic relief that Ruthie needed to heal. Her troubles where forgotten for the moment as she watched her uncle depart. She held her mother, Sheila, in her embrace and that was all that mattered.

"Mom, can we get something to eat?" Ruthie asked still laughing.

"Child, your mother is dead. Surely you don't expect her to answer."

"No, Sheila. My mother is not dead. You are my mother. I will not call you 'Sheila' any more. From now on you are Mom and I expect you to answer when I call you by that name."

Sheila burst into tears of joy. "Well, child, I'm not sure if it is wise but I've always tried to be the best mother I could to you and it is amazing to hear you address me as such. For sure we will dine and celebrate this moment. When your father returns home we may have to pay the price, but for now, let us enjoy ourselves."

"Oh, Mother, you don't have to worry. Father would never whip my mom. I will see to that."

Worried About Father

When Mr. Lancer came home from the hospital he found that all strong drink had been removed from the plantation. He was aware of the doctor's diagnosis and knew this was a condition of him coming home. He remembered that his daughter was angry with him before the doctor took him to the hospital but his clouded mind could not recall why. Sometimes his cravings took him to fits of anger worse than the drunken rages he experienced in the past, but gradually they came less often and conditions on the Lancer plantation became the happiest they had been since the death of Mrs. Lancer.

If a slave did not produce enough to satisfy his quota, he would get a beating, but Mr. Lancer no longer took any pleasure in this and left the punishment up to the overseers whenever he could. The domestic help would never see another beating, partly because Ruthie was always present to protect them and partly because Mr. Lancer no longer took pleasure in indiscriminate beatings.

Ruthie now spent more time with her dad as he no longer went out to "check on the slaves." Ruthie now realized the truth of what was happening when her dad was conducting such checks and she began to search the faces of all the younger slaves to look for resemblances to her father. When she thought of these past actions she was filled with shame for the one she called father, but she was happy with his reform and forgiveness was forthcoming.

As Ruthie turned into a beautiful young woman the subject of finding a suitable husband would come up. The scar on her cheek was slight and actually seemed to enhance the beauty of her face. She wanted nothing to do with the white boys who called her "nigger lover" and the young black men steered clear of her because to be caught with a white woman usually meant death to the slave who would be so bold.

Ruthie longed to meet the perfect man who would make her his wife. All her education was towards this one goal and she was taught that it was a complete failure for a woman not to fulfill this only purpose for the female human. Ruthie wasn't sure she agreed with these principles. She found that protecting her father's slaves from her father's wrath had been rewarding and she surmised that, if there was no man on earth that could fulfill the role of her husband, she would get along just fine on her own. However her heart still yearned for a mate who could understand her.

In the fall of 1824 Ruthie had occasion to accompany her mother, Sheila, to a store in Hamburg. Sheila was familiar with the gentleman that owned this store, but this day they were served by a younger man who Ruthie later learned was the owner's nephew. He seemed vaguely familiar to Ruthie. He was very handsome and he was extremely kind and courteous, not only to her but also to Sheila. This young man was different from any she had ever met. She longed to get to know him but feared she would never see him again.

On their way home Sheila ventured to ask Ruthie, "What did you think of Bobby?" From the way Ruthie had looked at him and the way she acted in his presence, the answer seemed obvious, but she wanted to hear Ruthie's thoughts.

"Bobby?" Ruthie inquired.

"The young man who served us at Robert's store. He's his nephew you know."

"Oh, him. Well he's kind a cute and I think I've seen him before."

"Oh? You have previously met?" Sheila inquired.

"No." Ruthie was straining her memory trying to think were she had seen this handsome young man. Suddenly it came to her. "About five years ago I saw him walking past the girls' school just as we were leaving class." She smiled at her recollection.

"So you never actually met."

"No. I would have remembered if we had." She paused for a moment then giggled as she added, "He's really cute." Another pause and then, "Mom, have you met him before?"

"He often looks after the store for his uncle when Robert has some place he has to go. He has served me a few times." Sheila answered.

"Oh Mother, do tell me. Is he always so kind and considerate?"

"Oh yes. He is not like other white people. That is one reason I like to go to Robert Taylor's store. Both Robert and his nephew treat me as an equal and they are always honest with me. They never try to cheat me. Most think we are stupid and don't know how to count our change so they seldom give us back what they should."

"Oh Mother, do you think....?" Ruthie could not finish her question but a mother knows what her daughter is feeling and Sheila was mother enough to this young lady to guess what she wanted to know.

"Yes Ruthie. Judging from the way he was looking at you I do think he could be the one."

"Are you sure Mother? Do you really think he liked me? I am so afraid I will never see him again."

"We can never be sure about these things, Ruthie. Time will tell. Just be patient. If it is in the good Lord's will, He will make a way for you to get to know Bobby Johnson."

"Oh Mother, you must bring me along every time you go to that store. I so much want to see Bobby again."

They continued to talk for the remainder of their trip. Ruthie had never before been so excited. She asked Sheila all sorts of questions about boys. What should she do if Bobby asked her out? Should she say yes right away or would that make her seem too eager?

That night Ruthie's dreams were filled with romance. However, the events of the next morning would cause her to forget. Fred Lancer had not consumed alcohol for about four and a half years. While Ruthie was dreaming, he discovered some of his slaves had a supply of homemade whisky. Instead of punishing them for this he gave into his cravings. He reasoned that the alcohol from his heavy drinking days before he got sick would have been flushed from his system and just one little drink would not harm him. He underestimated the power that his addiction still had on him and was not able to stop. He could not be sure how much he drank that night but after raising his second glass to toast the slaves who had supplied him he had no recollection until he woke up in bed the next morning with Doc Smyth by his side.

"Well Fred. You defied the gods and lived through this one. Your liver is severely damaged and the extra damage you did to it last night will likely mean you will never recover. I can help you cope with your illness, but alcohol will certainly kill you. I fear your liver is already too far gone and we may not be able to save you, but another drink will surely finish you off."

The horrors of addiction screamed in Fred Lancer's brain. He knew the doctor had warned him that his next drink may be his last, yet he was powerless to resist. He wondered how he was going to be able to face Ruthie. He was not deserving to be a father. These thoughts were going through his tormented brain as Ruthie came in.

"Oh, Father, Father are you alright?" Then turning to Doc Smyth she inquired, "Is he going to live?"

"Ruthie," the doctor answered as gently as he could. "There is severe liver damage and, barring a miracle, it will eventually lead to death. However, if we can keep the alcohol away from him he may have a couple of years left before he is completely gone. He will have difficulties and he will need to avoid stress and take it easy, but I think he will be around for a little while yet."

Ruthie ran to her father and held him in her embrace. "Father, Father, don't die on me," she sobbed.

Doc Smyth interrupted, "Ruthie, we need to let him rest now. He should be up and around in a couple of days but bed rest and a strict diet is what I prescribe for him. I have let Sheila know what he can eat. I will come back tomorrow to check on him. Send for me if he gets any worse."

Ruthie walked with Doc Smyth to his carriage. The Doctor stated, "your father will be out of commission for a little while.

If you need any help I can find someone to come out and lend you a hand."

"Oh," Ruthie suddenly realized. "The slave rations should come today and father usually divides everything up to be ready for distribution tomorrow."

"I can stop by Robert's store and get him to divide everything for you before he delivers it. I will ask him to send his man to deliver it tomorrow so he can help with the distribution."

"That would be great," Ruthie answered. "I am so worried about Father."

Chapter Three

A Roller Coaster Ride

The courtship between Bobby and Ruthie was a rocky one. Bobby felt like he was on an emotional roller coaster. One day he was sure God had destined that Ruthie would be his wife and the next day he would be filled with doubt. The day he met her in his uncle's store was a happy one. He was excited about meeting her the next day but when he talked to his father, he said he remembered meeting a Fred Lancer who was an alcoholic. Bobby couldn't imagine that Ruthie would come from such stock but the next day he found out the delivery date had changed and they needed to divide the order into slave rations because Mr. Lancer was not well. Doc Smyth knew nothing about confidentiality and told the whole story so there was no doubt about Mr. Lancer's drinking problem now.

After starting the day in a jubilant mood, Bobby went home that night confused and disappointed. Surely this was not because of one day delay.

"No mom," Bobby replied to his mother's question then turned to his dad. "You were right. Mr. Lancer is an alcoholic. Doc Smyth says he nearly killed himself with drink last night." Bobby exaggerated the facts beyond what he knew."

The following day he made the delivery and he made a point of watching Ruthie on her own turf. How did she relate to the slaves? Was she snobby like the other white girls he had met? Did she treat the help as though they were animals. Turns out that Ruthie was just as anxious to get to know him. They were so busy watching each other and trying to impress each other as they worked that, inevitably, they collided while reaching for the same parcel. Bobby's strong arms grabbed Ruthie and saved her from a fall. He held her longer than necessary and Ruthie did not seem to mind. He saw her right cheek close up and noticed the slight scar in the shape of a cross. This surely was a sign from God. Ruthie was the one God had chosen for him. Bobby was now sure of it.

Ruthie invited the young Bobby to the porch of the big house for tea when the job was done. Sheila had predicted this and had tea and snacks ready for Ruthie and her guest. Although they had a chance to talk they were interrupted when Mr. Lancer came out in a jovial mood. He thanked Bobby for the delivery and asked if he could come back the next day to get an order for household supplies. Bobby was happy to have another chance to see Ruthie and readily agreed. Bobby's life had always been a happy and tranquil one. He knew nothing of the life that Ruthie was living.

"Well Ruthie, I see you've made yourself a friend," Fred Lancer addressed his daughter after their guest had left.

"What do you mean father?"

"You don't normally invite the delivery boy to tea."

"I was just trying to be polite. He helped us so much today."

"So that was just a reward for extra service?" Mr. Lancer queried. "He looked like a fine young man. I thought perhaps you were interested."

"Well yes Father. I thought it would be nice to get to know him. I don't get out much you know."

"I am sure you can do better than a delivery boy."

"He's not a delivery boy. That was Robert Taylor's nephew and his father owns a large plantation the other side of Hamburg."

"Oh? You seem to know quite a bit about him. Have you known him for a while?"

"I just met him a couple of days ago when I went with

The Alternative

Sheila to Robert Taylor's store. He looks after the store for his uncle sometimes. Sheila told me about that."

"Well you best proceed with caution. There is only one thing a young buck like that wants and if you go throwing yourself at him he will get the wrong idea."

"I'm not throwing myself at him. Besides Bobby appears to be quite a gentleman. He is very kind and courteous."

"I suppose you learned that from watching him give out provisions to niggers."

"Well, yes father. He was very kind to our help. He is kind to all people."

"Young lady, when are you gonna learn that niggers aren't people. They're just stupid work animals. If you go takin' up with some nigger lover you'll get nowhere. You can't run a plantation on love. You need hard work and discipline and you don't get that by bein' kind to the work animals."

Ruthie sat sullenly and let her father's words sink in. She had heard this so many times before. She had stood up to her father many times. But he was sick and the doctor said he needed to avoid stress. Ruthie sensed his anger and needed to get him calmed down.

"Father, we can talk about this later. Doc says you need to rest. Why don't you go and lay down. I will get Mom to bring you some food." Ruthie didn't usually call Sheila "Mom" in front of her dad but it slipped out this time. She hoped he hadn't noticed.

"Look young lady. I am still your father and I deserve respect. Your mother died the day you were born. That nigger is not your mom."

"Mr. Lancer. Let's see if we can get you back to your room." Sheila came in and tried to calm the situation. She wasn't sure it was wise but Ruthie needed her help and she had to try.

"You dammed nigger. I'll teach you for twisting my daughter's mind. I'll show you both what it means to be a nigger," Fred Lancer grabbed his whip from the wall and began to swing it wildly.

Ruthie ran to place herself between this wild man and the woman she considered her mom. "You'll have to whip me before you can whip my mom," Ruthie said defiantly.

"Have it your way. If you are going to act like a nigger perhaps you should be treated like one. If you would rather be a nigger than your father's daughter I'll whip that notion out of you." Mr. Lancer was coming at both of them swinging his whip. Suddenly he doubled over and fell to the floor.

Ruthie ran to him. "Father, are you alright?" The anger of a few seconds ago turned to concern for her father's health.

"Jeanette, I seem to have lost my balance. I don't feel very well. Can you help me to my bed, Jeanette."

Ruthie helped her father stand up and led him to his bed. She made no attempt to correct his delusion. When he laid down she drew the blanket over him and tucked him in as though he was her child. She stood back and looked at the pitiful site. This man who was her father reduced to a quivering delusional child. Tears began to form in her eyes as she left the room. She went to the parlour and sat on the sofa exhausted. All was so hopeless she didn't even have the energy to cry.

Sheila came to comfort her and sat next to her. "Oh Mom," Ruthie said as she buried her face on Sheila's shoulder. "I don't know what to do. I killed my mother and now it seems that I am killing my father, but he is so unreasonable. Sometimes I wish he was dead."

Sheila was wise and knew when to be silent. She sat and listened as the young lady poured out her heart. Sheila knew Ruthie just needed to get it out so she sat silently with an occasional "yes dear" to let Ruthie know she was listening.

The night's rest did Fred Lancer some good and he was

The Alternative

feeling much better the next day. Sheila and Ruthie put together the list of items needed for the family meals. It was about ten in the morning when Bobby stopped by. Mr. Lancer kept a careful eye on him and he had no chance to speak to Ruthie. Mr. Lancer insisted on handing the list to Bobby after he looked it over and approved it. He met Bobby's eyes with a glare as Bobby politely took the sheet of paper. Mr. Lancer demanded, "When will you bring these items?"

"If we have them in stock I can bring them back this afternoon."

"Well take a look at the list. Do you have those items in stock? What's wrong? Can't you read?"

Bobby glanced over the list. "Yes Mr. Lancer, I believe we do have these items."

"Don't you know what you have in stock, boy. What kind of grocery boy are you if you don't even know what you have?" Mr. Lancer spoke gruffly and attempted to treat Bobby as rudely as he could.

Ruthie was at the other side of the room. Her father's actions embarrassed her. She glanced over toward Bobby thinking that she would never see him again after today. When Bobby looked her way she quickly turned being much too embarrassed to meet his gaze.

"You don't need to be lookin' around for my daughter. Ain't gonna be no social time today. Just go get those things and bring 'em back pronto. If yer a real good delivery boy ya may even git a tip."

Bobby left to fulfill his errand.

Ruthie took a step toward her father intending to rebuke him for his rude conduct, but remembering the events of the previous evening thought it best to leave it alone. She was sure she would never find a husband so long as her father was alive and she wished he would hurry up and die.

"I need a drink." Mr. Lancer was raving. "Did you put

whisky on that list? I suppose you didn't. I'll go see if those damn niggers got any hidden. They can't hide it from me. I can sniff that stuff out a mile away."

Mr. Lancer headed for the slave quarters. They would all be in the fields so he could ransack their dwellings without hindrance. Ruthie stared after him. She started to become alarmed. "Sheila, what should we do? I was just wishing father was dead and now it looks like he is going to kill himself."

"We can't stop him. Maybe Doc Smyth will know what to do. Why don't you ride to town and get him."

"What if father comes back and whips you when I'm gone. You better come with me."

"No child, I'll have to take my chances here. I'll get Mammy out of the field in case he needs doctoring before you get back."

Willy went directly to get the horse hitched to the small carriage as soon as he heard Ruthie would be needing it. By the time Ruthie grabbed her jacket and her purse Willy was already bringing the carriage out of the shed.

"Don't worry Ruthie. Doc made sure all the whiskey was removed after the last time. There is nothing for your father to find." Willy tried to reassure Ruthie.

"Oh Willy, won't you come with me?"

"I better not. If I left without Massa Lancer's permission I'd get a beating for sure. If he found out I left with you he'd likely kill me."

Even though Willy was her brother, Fred Lancer saw him only as another slave. In his distorted mind he may very well think that Willy was acting inappropriately to his daughter if they were seen together. "You are likely right," Ruthie stated as she climbed in the carriage.

Although she had driven the carriage around the plantation, this was the first time she was going into town alone. She was afraid to drive her horse too fast and proceeded into town at a trot. When she got to Doc Smyth's house she found he was out on his rounds. "He will be back shortly," his assistant stated. "I can send him out to your place when he gets here."

Ruthie wanted to talk to the Doctor and explain her father's behaviour to him, so she opted to wait. The doctor must have had some problems as he didn't return at the expected time. Ruthie had waited about an hour and a half when she saw the doctor's carriage approaching.

"Ruthie Lancer what brings you here. Is your father alright? I had planned to see him tomorrow."

Ruthie quickly went over the events of the night before and how her father had collapsed, then his raving today and his quest to find whisky.

"That is very typical of an alcoholic. It is a very difficult habit to break. That is why it is important to keep all alcohol out of his reach. I made sure the slaves got rid of their stash so he won't likely find any. Eventually he will give up and lay down. Your father is going through a really rough time. Things will get better when he gets over it."

Ruthie started to cry. "Doc, I wished he was dead. Am I an awful person to wish my own father was dead?"

"Now, now, Ruthie. You mustn't blame yourself. When there is a alcoholic in the family the whole family suffers. You've had a pretty rough time as well. Perhaps I can give you something to calm your nerves. Here take these pills. They should help you to feel better."

Sherry, the Doctors assistant, brought a glass of water and Ruthie took the pills.

Doc Smyth continued. "Now you just sit here as long as you need to. Sherry will stay with you. I will go out and check on your father."

The doctor left his office, climbed into his carriage and proceeded in the direction of the Lancer plantation. Ruthie sat until she felt herself calming down. She regained her composure and bid Sherry goodbye. She took her time as she was in no hurry to get home. When she passed Robert Taylor's store she suddenly thought of Bobby, so she turned around and parked her carriage. She climbed down and entered the store. Bobby was not in sight so she made inquiries.

"He's headed out to your place with your order." Mr. Taylor stated. "If we'd known you would be in town we could have given it to you."

Ruthie thanked Mr. Taylor and proceeded home. She watched for Bobby along the road but did not see him. "Perhaps he is still at the plantation," she thought as she drove up the long laneway. Willy was waiting at the house to take the carriage. She went directly into the kitchen as the doctor was coming from her father's bedroom.

"Ruthie, you made it back. Are you feeling better now?" the doctor inquired.

"Yes I am fine, thanks, but how is Father?"

"Have a seat and I will tell you about it."

Ruthie was worried. Did the doctor have bad news for her and therefore wanted her to sit to receive it? "Is he going to live?" she asked as they both took seats at the kitchen table.

"Oh yes, he will be fine. It is just the stress that got him down. I gave him something for that and he is resting now. He should sleep until morning."

"Oh thank you so much Doctor Smyth. Is there something I should do to help him?"

"Just do your best to keep him calm. Avoid talking about anything that may get him upset. But that is not why I asked you to sit."

"Oh Doctor, I'm just so worried about father."

"Yes Ruthie. That is what we need to talk about. This has been very hard on you. I am concerned about your health."

"I'm not sick Doc. It's father that needs your help."

"Yes, but too much worry can make you sick. We need to come up with some strategy to help you cope. Maybe you should get away for a while?"

"How can I leave now when father needs me?"

"That's just one possibility. Your servants can look after your father and there may be less stress for him if you are away for a while."

"You mean you think I am causing my father's illness?"

"No, Ruthie. Your father brought this on himself by drinking, but you are going through a difficult time in your life and your father's problems just add to that. A teenager's life can be stressful even in the very best of circumstances. I just think that it may be better for both of you if you spend some time away from each other. Is there some place you could go for a few days?"

Ruthie thought for a while. She had only met her Uncle Jack the one time and that didn't go well so she was quite sure he wouldn't want her. She didn't even know her Uncle George and she was quite sure Uncle Jack would have given him a bad report, so that was out of the question. The only friends she had were her father's slaves. "There really isn't any place for me to go," Ruthie said sadly with tears in her eyes.

"Well, perhaps you can come to my office and help out some times. That would at least get you away for a few hours and it would do you some good. Any time you want, just come to the office. If I'm not there Sherry will keep you company and if you like, she can give you something to do to take your mind off your troubles."

"I may take you up on that Doctor. I will see how father feels about it. If he wants me to go I will come to see you." Ruthie was thankful for the doctor's concern, but she felt she could manage at home, however having the option to go someplace for a few hours was not a bad backup plan. She still felt she needed to protect Sheila from her father's wrath. She didn't want to abandon her mom, but she thanked the doctor for his kind offer and bid him adieu.

It would be some time before Bobby would again see Ruthie. He was hopeful that he would have a chance to talk to her when he delivered the order, but she was nowhere in sight. Mr. Lancer had obviously taken a turn for the worse and the doctor had been called. Doc Smyth had come in an emergency and had to break other appointments. He asked Bobby if he would deliver messages to the patients that were expecting him. This took Bobby on a different road when he returned to town.

Bobby's Dilemma

Bobby Johnson was a handsome young man and heir to a sizable plantation. This made him very desirable to the young ladies in the Hamburg area. However, when they heard his anti-slavery views, most wondered if he would be able to keep the plantation running when he inherited it. Bobby found the young ladies snobbish and intolerant of his friends. When he met Ruthie, he could tell right away that she was different. It seemed like love at first sight, but Bobby was in for the roller coaster ride of his life.

Already love had played with his heart, and he had just barely met her. The joy he felt when they first met was heightened by the anticipation of seeing her the next day. He was saddened by doubt when he found out she had an alcoholic father. He got to see her in action when they passed out the slave rations and an invitation to tea made his day, but his inability to connect with her on subsequent visits again threw his heart in the dumps. As time wore on, he did his best to put her out of his mind.

Bobby was dealing with a bigger problem. He was not sure he could support himself and needed to sort things out before he considered taking on a wife. It was true that he was heir to a

The Alternative

large fortune but it was also true that most of that fortune was tied up in slaves. The land and buildings he would inherit were worth about $2,000, but the one hundred and seventeen slaves were worth approximately $180,000. Bobby prayed about his problem. He felt he could not be a slave owner and his father was considering selling the plantation so Bobby would not bring it to ruin. "Perhaps that would be best," Bobby thought, but when he considered what may happen to his friends if they got sold to a stranger he began to wonder if they would be better off with himself as their master. To take ninety-nine percent of his inheritance and turn them loose seemed very irresponsible. He had thought God had chosen Ruthie to be his wife, and that did not seem likely to happen. Perhaps he was also wrong about the slavery issue. Slavery had been practiced in the south for over 200 years. It seems unlikely that it could ever be stopped. But yet it just didn't seem right. Surely God would not tolerate its continuance. Although Bobby was not sure what he should do He knew that God would make a way if it was His will.

Indeed God was making a way. Samson was well aware of Bobby's dilemma and he had a plan he felt would work. Having been a slave, Samson saw firsthand the drawbacks to slavery and felt he could make a plantation more profitable without slaves. The changes he was initiating on the Johnson plantation were already showing results. The slaves were assured they would obtain their freedom when Bobby took over and Samson stressed the importance of making the operation work. His goal was to use the Johnson plantation as an example so other plantations would follow when they found it could be more profitable to run their operations without slaves. Already the Johnson plantation was producing larger quantities of higher grade cotton. Neighbors and strangers alike were attempting to find out Mr. Johnson's secret. They were taken aback when Mr. Johnson referred them to Samson. Many thought he was too busy or too lazy to answer their inquiries and therefore referred them to a slave. Many did not know that Samson was a free black man. The fact that Samson was the brains behind the success was not even suspected. However Samson was most anxious to get his ideas out and occasionally would get himself hired to teach his methods on other plantations. Samson had experimented with crop rotation as well as new methods of weed and pest control. Plus he was very inventive and made many new tools to complete the work faster and more efficiently.

One invention was a seed drill that could be pulled with one mule and seated one operator. The usual method had required three slaves and two mules to plant a row of cotton. Ridges were formed six feet apart and a plough was drawn by a mule to make a drill to put the seeds in. Then a slave, usually female, carrying a bag of seed around her neck, dropped seed into the drill. Another mule pulled a harrow behind to cover the seed. With Samson's invention, the seed was placed in a hopper and automatically dropped into the drill through a mechanism that controlled the rate. The faster Samson's seed drill was pulled, the faster the seeds were dropped meaning that the mule could pull the drill much faster than walking speed. A harrow was attached at the back to cover the seed. All the operator had to do was steer the mule and keep an eye on the hopper to be sure the seed was flowing and to refill it when necessary. Thus one operator and one mule did the work of three slaves and two mules. The operation went faster and the seed was dropped more evenly, so there was less waste.

"When Bobby takes over we will all be free," Samson told the slaves at the Johnson plantation. "If we can prove to be more efficient, other plantations will follow and we can make the whole south free." This was Samson's dream. While Bobby worried about one plantation, Samson had a plan to free the south. Samson assumed that Bobby knew what he was doing. After all it is what Bobby wanted. Bobby followed Samson's progress but it didn't occur to him that this was the answer to his dilemma. He knew Samson was making the operation more efficient, but his father was still using slave labour. Would it work with paid labour? Bobby didn't know.

Samson was one that concentrated all his efforts on results and did not let emotions get in the way. When Bobby told him about Ruthie, his advice was very straight forward and practical. Bobby thought that God had chosen Ruthie as a mate for him and Samson simply said to leave it in God's hands and, if it is meant to be, it will happen with the Lord's timing.

Meanwhile, with Fred Lancer's health deteriorating, he was in desperate need of an overseer that could run the plantation. He felt that he needed one that would whip his help back into shape, but Ruthie would not hear of it. She had heard rumors of a free black man that could run things and get good results without a whip and arrangements were soon made to employ Samson to run the plantation during planting season.

Bobby knew that Samson had a job but did not know who his employer was. When Samson was introduced to Ruthie, the owner's daughter, his mind was totally on business and he did not think of the Ruthie that had played with Bobby's heart.

Before Samson went to work for Mr. Lancer, he had set up a system on the Johnson plantation that ran itself. Key persons were selected for their ability to organize and each had an area of responsibility. They would meet daily and plan the day's activities, assigning workers to the jobs that needed to be done. The atmosphere was relaxed and the workers accomplished their tasks efficiently and stress free. Samson planned to visit the Johnson plantation every second Sunday to check on progress and so he could attend church with his friend.

Two weeks into planting season Samson would make his first visit back to the Johnson plantation. He arrived late on a Saturday night with plans to attend Church the next day. On Sunday morning he talked with the supervisors and other workers on the plantation and found, as he expected, that all was going well. No work was done on Sundays so all gathered

A Roller Coaster Ride

around Samson to inquire about his new job. Samson explained that God had been good to him and the work he was now doing was progressing better than expected. When someone shouted "hallelujah" the meeting began to appear as a southern gospel meeting. Samson, being the most knowledgeable of the Bible, led the group in song and prayer and gave them an inspiring message of hope and salvation. Bobby, being attracted by the sounds of rejoicing in the Lord, soon joined them. When Samson finished his discourse the group focused their attention on Bobby and with the urging, "Massa Bobby, tell us 'bout the Lawd," Bobby was compelled to give an impromptu sermon. He spoke of equality of all of God's people and how all were important in the sight of God. After more singing and praying the group turned to feasting on their meagre provisions. Sunday was a day they could sit and eat together and many would find some way of providing treats to share that were not available throughout the week. As the festivities continued Bobby and Samson had an opportunity to talk.

"Bobby," Samson inquired, "I thought we might go to church together today."

"Well Samson, I think we just had church and if we left now we would be quite late for the service in town."

"I suppose we did have church. And a rip roaring service it was."

"Yah, we should do this more often." And that is just what they did. From then on a church service was held every Sunday at the Johnson plantation. As word got out the slaves from neighbouring plantations would join them. Bobby would lead the services each week and, when Samson was home he would take part. The spiritual revival brought even more joy to the workers on the plantation and the week's work seemed to pass quickly as they anticipated the next Sunday service.

In the excitement of starting a new church Bobby didn't get much information on Samson's new job. Samson simply said everything was going well and they went right back to talking church. Bobby was still unaware of which plantation Samson was working on. If he had heard that the plantation owner had a daughter named Ruthie that would have certainly got his attention, but this never came up in their conversation that Sunday.

In the evening, while Bobby was having dinner with his family, Samson slipped off on the ten mile trip to his work.

Do You Know Bobby?

Monday morning at the Lancer plantation saw much progress. The two weeks of training had paid off and everyone was familiar with their new roles. Some were inclined to go back to the old ways as they feared a whipping if they didn't do things the way "Massa Lancer" wanted, but Samson assured them that there would be no more whippings and the reluctant ones soon saw the advantages of the new methods.

Next Samson wanted to interview each of the workers to see if they had any ideas on how things could be further improved. Samson was aware that what worked on one plantation might not on another. The workers, when encouraged to think for themselves, would come up with the best plans. They did need to get used to the new tools and the new way of doing things before they could make suggestion, but with two weeks of work already done Samson felt the time to make regular inquiries had come. He observed carefully. If someone was struggling to complete a task he would ask how it could be made easier. If someone excelled at a task he was asked if he had any ideas that he could share with others. Thus Samson would systematically interview every worker, and, when he was done, he would start over again.

This first day of interviews didn't yield many results. It was difficult for workers, who were told how to do something and were punished if they didn't do it that exact way, now be trained to think for themselves. Samson knew it would take time to build up trust so he didn't push for results. He didn't expect much for the first while, but he knew that, by continually asking for their input, many of the workers would give him good ideas that he could implement now and in the future.

Samson had only conducted a few interviews when he saw Ruthie coming. He saw nervousness among the slaves as they saw their owner's daughter approach. Ruthie was leading a small girl about four years old by the hand and both seemed to be filled with joy.

"Good morning Ruthie. What brings you out here today?" Samson inquired with a smile.

"Hello Samson. This is Ella," she said as an introduction. "Say Hi to Samson, Ella," she instructed the young child.

"Hewoe Misser Samson," said the child.

"Ella wanted to see her mommy," Ruthie added, however it was Ruthie who wanted to see Samson and the child made a good excuse. "Could we interrupt Krissy's work for a moment?" Ruthie asked to show respect for Samson's position.

"That is alright by me," said Samson, "but I am not sure who Krissy is so I can't help you find her."

Just then Ella spotted a young woman carrying a bag of cotton seed. "Mommy," she cried as she pulled away from Ruthie and ran to her mom.

"Oh Ella," they heard Krissy say. "Mommy's working, she doesn't have time for you now."

"It's okay Krissy," Samson called over to her. "You can take a few minutes break to be with your child." He then turned his attention to Ruthie.

"Krissy is my best friend and I really enjoy taking care of Ella for her," Ruthie confided, but she felt it would not be wise at this moment to confess that Ella was her half sister.

"Oh. I've been conducting interviews with the workers and

The Alternative

I believe Krissy can be next," said Samson, pleased that Ruthie would consider a black lady her best friend. Samson began to realize there was nothing typical about Ruthie. He remembered his best friend, Bobby, talking about a young lady with a similar view. What was her name now? He began to recall conversations he had four months previous. Why I think it was "Ruthie!" He vocalized the name as he thought.

"Yes Samson," Ruthie answered.

Samson stared at her in amazement. Was this Ruthie the same young lady his best friend had met last fall? The one he thought he would never see again? Could this be true? He remembered his conversation with Ruthie the previous week when she said she had known somebody who wanted to free their slaves. Was she talking about Bobby?

"Yes Samson," Ruthie repeated. "Are you all right? Why are you looking at me like that?"

"Bobby," Samson burst out. "Was that friend you talked about last week named Bobby?" he got the question out with much excitement.

"I did know a Bobby very briefly," Ruthie considered. "Maybe I mentioned him."

"Remember you said you once knew someone who wanted to free his slaves, was that Bobby?" Samson could hardly contain himself.

"Why yes, I believe that was his name. Bobby Johnson it was. Do you know him?"

"Know him?" Samson now laughed hysterically. "Bobby Johnson is my best friend. We grew up together on his father's plantation and he is the one that gave me my freedom."

"What?" It was Ruthie's turn to be amazed. "You know Bobby Johnson? Did he tell you how my father treated him? I don't blame him for never wanting to see me again after that."

"Oh he definitely wanted to see you again." Samson was

about to divulge all his friend's secrets but had second thoughts. He simply added, "He thought your father would never permit it."

"Oh Samson, not a word of this to my father. He'd probably send you packing it he found out you know Bobby Johnson. But please, next time you see Bobby, apologize for me. I was so embarrassed by the way my father treated him and I would very much like to see him again, but if my father knew he would be upset. I would have to meet him somewhere." Ruthie felt her depression of the last few months lifting. Was it really possible that she would see Bobby Johnson again? The thought of such a possibility caused her heart to pound.

"What are you two so excited about?" Krissy came over with Ella in tow.

"Krissy, you won't believe this. Samson is Bobby Johnson's best friend."

"Are you serious?" Krissy and Ruthie bantered back and forth only as teenage girls who are best friends can do. Samson could not understand anything they were saying but it was all done in the utmost happiness so he stood by and watched in amusement.

Finally Krissy became intelligible. "Well you must see him again, Ruthie."

"I don't know if he will want to after the way father treated him," Ruthie ignored Samson's assertion to the contrary a few moments before.

"Samson," Krissy pleaded for her friend. "could you set it up so Ruthie could see Bobby someplace away from here.

"Well ... certainly," Samson pondered this for a moment, then after a slight hesitation said. "We are starting church services on the Johnson plantation every Sunday. Why don't both of you go there about ten o'clock Sunday morning. You can just tell your father you are going to church. I think I will let it be a surprise to Bobby. I won't tell him you are coming. I can

The Alternative

give you directions."

"That sounds wonderful." Krissy and Samson solidified the deal without consulting Ruthie. If she were to have any objection Krissy would be sure to talk her out of it, so they didn't give her a chance to weigh in her opinion.

As Ruthie took Ella and headed back to the big house, Samson began his interview with Krissy. This interview took much longer than it should have and the conversation often strayed from the business at hand, but Samson covered all the mandatory questions and Krissy had some good ideas about planting procedures. In Ruthie's absence Samson would confess what he knew of Bobby's reaction to meeting Ruthie and Krissy would tell all about her best friend's confessions of her feelings for Bobby.

"We really got to get them together," they both agreed.

Samson completed his day with a few more interviews, he talked to the work force as a group at the end of the day inviting everyone to come to him with any problems or suggestions. Throughout the rest of the week it was much the same procedure although he would also work alongside the other workers and offer suggestions when he saw someone struggling. When he saw someone watching out for the approach of an overseer he gently reaffirmed that no one was going to come and whip them. Gradually confidence was gained as Samson worked patiently with slaves who had seen abuse. Slowly the fear of the whip slid out of their conscious minds and took its place in their long term memories. Although Samson had not planned to return to the Johnson plantation so soon he again took the ten mile trip, about one hour on horseback, on that Saturday night. He wanted to be there when Krissy and Ruthie showed up for church.

Mr. Lancer had been glad to see his daughter's spirits improve that week. He thought it was because the work of the plantation was proceeding well and no one was being whipped.

When he heard his daughter wanted to go to church he was glad. He apologized that he was not well enough to go with her but suggested that she take Krissy along for company. It sounds amazing when everything works out but Samson was not remiss in his prayers and he was accustomed to seeing his prayers answered. Krissy and Ruthie set out in their carriage in plenty of time to reach the Johnson plantation by ten that Sunday morning.

Chapter Four
A Miraculous Church Service

Sunday March 21st, 1824 saw much excitement at the Johnson farm. When Bobby headed for the clearing where they would hold their church meeting his father's slaves were already preparing for a large revival. News had spread to neighbouring plantations and many slaves were beginning to congregate. Some had passes from their owners, others had snuck away to attend the Sunday service. Those who had arrived early were helping the Johnson's slaves to roll in large logs, stones and anything else in the area that could be used for seating. Many would have to stand or sit on the ground, but all were thrilled to be there. They had heard about the impromptu meeting of the previous week and were excited to see it repeated. Many had heard of Bobby Johnson and his views on slavery and they wanted to hear his refreshing message that would be so different from the messages of the slaveholding preachers.

When Bobby saw the commotion he pitched in and did what he could, even bringing chairs from the house. His parents, John and Sara Johnson, were curious about the happenings. Bobby had informed them of his plans to hold church meetings and they readily consented, but they were surprised to see the reaction it was creating.

As Bobby worked he noticed Samson directing the activities. He immediately went to him.

"Samson, I thought you were not going to join us until next week. You are back so soon."

"I was really excited about this meeting and I couldn't stay away. I feel that amazing things are going to happen." Samson

A Miraculous Church Service

knew that Bobby would be excited to see Ruthie but he wanted that to be a surprise, so he didn't let on, but he hinted, "You may be surprised at who shows up today."

"I am already surprised Samson. I didn't expect so many people. I am really glad you are here to help."

Samson showed Bobby the place he would speak from. Logs and stones were placed in front of his position for the congregation to sit and a gradual hill rose behind these make shift seats to provide more seating. The shed behind Bobby would help to reflect his voice out to the crowd that was already forming. One of the chairs from the house were placed at the front for Bobby to rest when he needed to and the remaining chairs that were brought out for the occasion were placed beside the logs and stones. As John and Sara Johnson decided to join them they were given seats of honour on chairs near the front. More and more people were coming and the work was being accompanied by sudden bursts of song. Many of the old hymns and the spirituals common among the black population were sung as they worked. Everything was in place by nine thirty and the singing continued with more intensity. As ten o'clock approached they began to sing, "Go down, Moses, way down to Egypt land. Tell ole Pharaoh to let my people go."

After that Bobby was called up to speak.

"Yes, Moses went to Egypt to free the Jewish slaves that the Egyptians had imprisoned for four hundred years. Your time is coming."

"Hallelujah," the congregation responded.

"Yes, your time is coming. Perhaps one day all the south will be free."

"You are our Moses," someone shouted.

"Maybe," Bobby continued, "But Moses was a Jew and he led his own people to freedom. I think it will be one of your own who lead you. But the true leader is the Almighty God and His Son, Christ Jesus. This is where we must turn for guidance.

The Alternative

When He sets you free you will be free indeed."

Bobby continued his sermon for a few minutes and then, as the congregation jumped up and started singing again, Bobby noticed a familiar face in the back rows. "Could it be? Is it Possible? It is!!!" were the thoughts running through his head as he recognized Ruthie. He wanted to run to her, but the congregation was watching him. None was watching as close as Samson who followed his friend's gaze and knew he had made eye contact. He saw the excitement of his friend as he tried to continue the service, but Bobby was now having difficulty stringing two coherent words together. This meeting now seemed miraculous which inspired him to say. "A miracle is about to happen and all God's children will be free."

Again the crowd responded with "Hallelujahs" while Bobby was fighting to stay in control of his emotions. Samson approached him and Bobby took the opportunity to turn the service over. Being thus relieved of his duties, his first impulse was to run to Ruthie, but he was unaware that Ruthie had come to see him and he didn't want to make a fool of himself in front of the congregation, so he sat in the chair provided for him and tried to listen to his friend's discourse.

Samson began by saying, "Yes this is a great day where we will witness the will of God in action. Last fall my best friend Bobby met a young lady who he thought he had lost contact with. God has brought her and her friend to us today. Ruthie and Krissy, could you come forward." Samson knew the service could not continue with the current suspense, so he brought it to a close in a way Bobby would remember forever. Samson introduced the two young ladies to the congregation adding that they had come ten miles from the Lancer Plantation. The crowd applauded and shouted more hallelujahs as Ruthie turned toward Bobby. After a moment they simultaneously threw their arms around each other and for the first time in their lives they shared an embrace before a crowd of close to two hundred people. Caught in the spirit of the moment, Krissy

A Miraculous Church Service

gave Samson a hug as well.

When Mrs. Johnson had first seen the crowd coming she instructed her house staff to prepare food for them all and they were now bringing the food out to makeshift tables. Mr. Johnson shouted over the excited crowd. "We have food for everyone. Please help yourselves." Then he and his wife joined their son.

"So this is Ruthie," said Mr. Johnson as he approached.

"Welcome, Ruthie, to our home," said Sara Johnson. "Bobby has said so much about you. I am glad we can finally meet you."

Ruthie began to feel like a welcome and honoured guest. This was so different from her father's treatment of Bobby. Ruthie thought about this as she shook hands with both the older Johnsons.

Later the Johnsons ushered Ruthie to their house. A big grand house it was reflecting the love of those who inhabited it. As Ruthie entered her mind was flooded with thoughts. How different the Johnsons were from her father. They sat in a church service with their slaves and slaves of their neighbors yet they treated them as friends. When Bobby spoke it was as though all truly admired him, nothing like the forced respect that was expected from a slave to a member of his master's class. Bobby was so different from her and his whole world was different from the one she knew. Could it ever be possible that they would accept her in their world? She admired them so much and the love she felt for Bobby was causing her heart to throb so hard she feared those around her would hear it. She felt so much joy and happiness at the moment, but would that all be taken away from her again. She had to sneak away from her father to see Bobby and she wanted to take advantage of every moment for she feared she may never see him again. She must express her love for him today because there may never again be a chance. As these thoughts and more flooded her mind it was more than she could handle. The Johnsons showed her to the parlour and as she sat on the comfortable sofa next to Bobby she broke down and cried.

The Johnsons were puzzled. One moment she was expressing absolute joy and the next she was crying. Had they done something to offend her.

"Whatever is the matter?" Mrs. Johnson was the first to inquire.

"Oh, you must think I am horrible," said Ruthie. "You are all so nice to me, but it is so different from what I am used to." Ruthie was suddenly afraid and decided she better act immediately on her thoughts of a moment ago. It could be taken from her at any second, so she turned to Bobby and confessed, "Bobby, I love you so much. You probably think I am being to forward in saying that, but I didn't get the chance to say it before and I fear I will never get another chance to let you know. So I just want you to know that I love you. That way, even if we never see each other again you will know what you mean to me."

Needless to say, all three Johnsons were shocked at this confession and didn't quite know how to react. It was obvious to all that this young lady had affection for the young Bobby, but for a young lady to confess such a thing in front of others was unheard of. The awkward pause seemed longer than the few seconds it would take Ruthie to continue.

"Now you must think I am a really horrible person to say such a thing. But you see I had to sneak here today because I wanted to see Bobby. I told Father we were going to church. He knows nothing about me coming to see Bobby. And Father is so sick, the doctor says I mustn't stress him. Whenever he thinks I am interested in a man he gets stressed and I fear that stress could kill him. My mom died giving birth to me and I don't want to be responsible for my father's death. It just seems like I am such an awful person and you are all so nice. I don't deserve

A Miraculous Church Service

to have such friends as you and I don't blame you if you never want to see me again. Oh how I wish I could have had a live like yours. You are so happy and kind. I never met anyone like you before."

Bobby held Ruthie close to himself. "Don't worry Ruthie it will all work out some way."

Mrs. Johnson took a position on the other side of Ruthie and joined in the hug. "Yes dear. You mustn't worry. God will make a way." Her son's faith was beginning to affect her and she felt the Almighty God had a plan.

Bobby looked to his mother approvingly and included her in his embrace. As Ruthie felt the bodies of a mother and son pressing against her she again burst into tears.

"Oh you poor child," Mrs. Johnson said in a motherly way. "What can we do to help."

"You are doing it," Ruthie sobbed. "These are now tears of joy. I love you all so much."

As they sat there Mr. Johnson joined them on the sofa and put his arm around his wife. After a few moments silence Ruthie regained her composer and spoke quietly.

"My mother died when I was born. I was raised by my father's slaves. Mammy looked after me until I was three then Sheila took over. They tried to be good mothers to me and I even started to call Sheila 'Mom,' but this is the first time in my life I have experienced a real mother's love." Again tears took over as she finished her sentence.

They sat silently for a few moments more, then Ruthie gently pushed against the bodies that were embracing her. At first they were warm and comforting but now she was beginning to feel hot. "I am much better now," She said calmly. "I am sorry for being such a cry baby."

"Not at all," said Mrs. Johnson. "We are quite happy that you shared your story with us. We feel we know you much better now." She reached over and rung the bell to summon the maid. When Anna entered she said, "Could you bring us some tea."

Ruthie jumped up and said, "Oh, can I help in the kitchen. I don't want your servants to have to work on a Sunday."

"Yes, why not, we can all work together. Bobby knows his way around a kitchen as well." Mrs. Johnson made the announcement as she gave the servant the rest of the day off.

Mr. Johnson added wood to the fireplace outside the kitchen door and soon had some water boiling. Mrs. Johnson gathered some herbs from her garden to make a nice blend of herbal tea. Bobby gathered up some snacks, some of which he had baked himself in their outdoor oven. Ruthie added the boiling water to the teapot with the herbs and when the tea was ready she poured it into cups. After the elder Johnsons had done their part they were urged to relax in the parlour. When everything was ready, Bobby brought in the tea while Ruthie carried the snacks.

As they sat and had tea, Bobby had a few confessions of his own. "Ruthie," he began. "I've never met anyone like you and last fall when we first met I was sure that God had chosen you for me. The day we were handing out the rations and I bumped into you I saw the cross on your face and I thought God had placed His mark on you as a sign for me."

"What do you mean?" Ruthie inquired.

"That scar on your face is in the shape of a cross," Bobby stated then addressed his parents. "Mom, Dad, do you see it."

"You are looking at my scar?" Ruthie inquired indignantly.

"But Ruthie," Bobby tried to explain, "it is a sign from God. He has put the sign of the cross on your face."

Ruthie laughed uncontrollably. "God didn't put that there. My father did." She explained how she had gotten the scar.

"I know my father did not mean to do it but he never whipped my mom again after that day. Whenever he tried I would get in between and make sure he saw the scar he put on my face. He would back right down and leave us alone." Ruthie laughed as though she thought this was a joke.

"As I was saying," Bobby continued, "I thought God had chosen you and if I had gotten the chance I would have spent time with you, but when things didn't work out I thought I must have been wrong. Until you showed up today I thought I would never see you again. Now that you are here I am not as sure, but I definitely want to get to know you better. I now realize the challenges you've gone through and I admire you very much for being strong enough to endure them. I also realize how fortunate I have been and I know that if you are the one God has chosen for me, we will live a very happy life together. For now all I ask is for a chance to get to know you better."

Ruthie listened intently to this speech and she replied, "There is nothing I would like better than to spend time with you Bobby Johnson, but I fear that will be impossible. I admire you for your faith in God, but I have had to live in the real world and I have not had a God to help me. If your God can make a way I am all for it, but my fear is that it will never be." Then she suddenly added, "Now I must be on my way. I didn't notice the passing of time and I told father we went to church. He will be wondering about such a long church service and it will still take us an hour to get back home."

While Bobby was getting to know Ruthie in the big house, Samson and Krissy were getting acquainted in a social setting. Krissy, learning from her friend's experience, did not hesitate to let Samson know she admired him. Samson, with much less emotion, indicated he would like to continue a friendship but was afraid it may be awkward as he was hired to supervise the plantation where Krissy was a slave. Krissy assured him that she would expect no special favours while working but wanted to spend her free time with him whenever possible.

Fred Lancer was sleeping when Ruthie returned home and she had a chance to tell Sheila about her adventure. When her father awoke she told him there was a social after church with lots of food. Mr. Lancer accepted this explanation for her tardiness and was truly glad his daughter was happy. He recognized her need to get out and was happy to learn it had gone well. The following Sunday he surprised Ruthie by asking to go to church with her. They attended one in Hamburg and Ruthie was completely embarrassed by her father's behaviour as he shouted hallelujah and amen at inappropriate times and generally made a nuisance of himself. They were shunned by the congregation at the end of the service and Mr. Lancer wondered at the lack of friendliness.

"I thought you would have made a few friends last week," he stated.

"We went to a different church last week."

"Why didn't you go to the same one today?"

"Last week I had Krissy with me, so we went to one were her friends would be. I didn't think you would want to go to that one."

"You know me well, daughter of mine. You will never find me worshiping God with niggers."

Meanwhile, Bobby's rollercoaster ride was about to get bumpier. William Garrison had written a letter to Samson and himself and he used that as an excuse to go to the Lancer plantation were he hoped he would have a chance to see Ruthie. He got his chance when Mr. Lancer sent Ruthie out to the field to find out who had come to the plantation and gone out there. Ruthie, although happy to see Bobby, warned him to never come again. She sealed her warning with a kiss then stated that this would be his last one if he did not heed her warning. She then sent him across the field to avoid going by the big house where her father would be sure to recognize him. She told her father that the intruder was a messenger with a message for Samson and had to hurry off to deliver more messages.

Again being cut off from seeing Ruthie, Bobby was torn.

A Miraculous Church Service

Samson would carry letters between them when he went home every second week and Ruthie would go to the church service when she could, but did not want to do that too often as it may arouse her father's suspicion. How could she explain her sudden interest in church? She would also drop into Robert Taylor's store and tried to let Bobby know in her letters when she would be there, but these plans would often be upset by her unpredictable father so she seldom made it at the appointed times. Sometimes she would get to the store to learn that Bobby had just left. Other times Bobby would arrive to find she had just been there.

Bobby talked to his friend about this problem and Samson assured Bobby that if he put everything in God's hands it would all work out. One night Bobby dreamt that he asked Mr. Lancer for permission to see his daughter. Mr. Lancer just laughed at him and then he saw he was with his daughter picking out a wedding dress. "What do you think this dream means?" he asked.

"Perhaps you should ask Mr. Lancer for permission as you did in the dream and you will find out," Samson answered with a grin.

"How can I do that when Ruthie has forbidden me to visit her father's plantation?" Bobby queried.

"God will make a way," Samson answered with complete conviction.

"I guess I will have to leave that in God's hands." Bobby admired his friend's faith.

By June, Samson's contract with the Lancers had terminated. Most Sundays he would still take a trip to the Lancer plantation to pick up Krissy for church so Bobby still had the opportunity to correspond with Ruthie. June 18th, 1824 was Bobby's twenty-fourth birthday. Bobby was working at his uncle's store when God sent him an unexpected birthday present. Mr. Lancer came into the store in an exceptionally

The Alternative

good mood. "God will make a way." Bobby heard his friend's voice echo in his mind. This was the opportunity he needed and, for Bobby, it was all or nothing. He would have to ask Mr. Lancer's permission now or give up his idea forever.

"Good afternoon Mr. Lancer." Bobby said with a smile.

"Do I know you?" Mr. Lancer strained his clouded memory.

"I made some deliveries to you last fall." Bobby reminded him.

"Oh, yes." The clouds began to peel away. "I believe my daughter took a liking to you."

"That is just what I would like to talk to you about."

"What's that?" Mr. Lancer seemed puzzled.

"I would very much like it if you would give me permission to see your daughter again." There, Bobby had blurted it out. Now the reaction was in God's hands. How would this man handle such an announcement was anyone's guess.

"Aren't you the delivery boy? I know my daughter is of marrying age, but I think she can do better than a delivery boy."

"My uncle owns this store and I help him out sometimes. I do need to confess that I volunteered to make those deliveries in the hope of seeing your daughter after I had met her in this very store."

"And you have not forgotten after all this time." Mr. Lancer was impressed but continued his interrogation. "What does your father do?"

"He owns a plantation about five miles east of here."

"How many slaves does he own?" Thus came the inevitable question to determine social standing.

Although Bobby resented this question he answered politely. "About one hundred."

Mr. Lancer's plantation had about fifty slaves so the Johnson's operation was twice the size of his. Perhaps this young man could look after his daughter when he was gone. Although the thought of his daughter getting married troubled him, the thought that he may die before she married troubled him more. For a while Mr. Lancer appeared as a disturbed man as each thought flashed through his head resulting in facial expressions changing from joy, fear, anger and back to joy. Finally he put on the biggest smile he was capable of and offered his hand to Bobby. "I appreciate your courage and respect in asking my permission. If it is still my daughter's wish to see you I give you my permission. I will let her know your intentions tonight."

As Bobby took the hand of his future father-in-law he breathed a sigh of relief and thanked the good Mr. Lancer. At that moment he felt the presence of God as he had never before felt it. "Thank you Heavenly Father," he whispered a prayer.

"What, speak up boy, I don't hear as good as a used to." Mr. Lancer interjected.

"Oh, I was just thanking God for this wonderful opportunity. I am very thankful I was able to talk with you today." Bobby was very cordial to his guest. "Now what was it you came in for?"

Mr. Lancer told Bobby what he needed and after measuring out generous proportions of each item he told Mr. Lancer that he would be grateful if he would be allowed to pay for it as a gift. Mr. Lancer was never one to turn down something for free so he happily walked off with free supplies. Thus Bobby's birthday on eighteenth day of June 1824 ended as one of the happiest in his memory.

Ruthie was all the family Mr. Lancer had and, after losing his wife, he was now terrified of losing his daughter. Therefore he did not want her to get married and leave him. As a drunk he was a very selfish man and now, as a dry alcoholic, he was not much better. However, as the effects of the alcohol gradually left his body, he began to get more concerned about his daughter's future. Knowing he would not live much longer he thought it wise if he could see his daughter married before he died. Thus, when Bobby approached him with his request, Mr. Lancer was torn and confused. The news that his daughter may have a compatible suitor caused both terror and joy. There was no reconciliation available for how he felt. He had extra money in his pocket due to Bobby's generosity and he sought a way to drown his sorrow or celebrate his joy in the only way an alcoholic knows. Since the solution was the same, it did not matter if it was sorrow or joy that he was dealing with as he headed to the local bar for a drink.

The bars in town had been issued a warning not to serve Mr. Lancer and he had not been there for some time, so the man at the bar did not immediately recognize him. Mr. Lancer had already bought a few rounds for everyone before the owner came in and informed the bar tender that Mr. Lancer should not be allowed to purchase alcohol. However the friends he had made decided to return the favour and provided a few more rounds before Mr. Lancer had to be forcibly removed from the bar. As he fell into his carriage, a bootlegger slipped him a bottle of moonshine and indicated he could keep him supplied.

Ruthie saw her father's carriage approaching and ran out to greet him. He was in a semiconscious state when she watched him fall out of the carriage. Sheila and Willy were there to help him up. Mr. Lancer looked at his daughter in his drunken state and said, "Jeannette, I am glad you are here. I have wonderful news. Our little girl is getting married."

"And just who is she marrying?" Ruthie didn't try to prevent the delusion.

"Oh she will marry a fine young man. Bobby Johnson. His father owns a huge plantation the other side of Hamburg. He'll be a fine husband for her." Mr. Lancer's speech was slurred and, while stressing the word "huge," he almost passed out.

"Who told you this?" Ruthie pumped her father for as much

A Miraculous Church Service

information as she could.

"Oh the young man came to me himself and asked to marry her. He is a fine young man and he will......" Mr. Lancer completely passed out. He was put into his bed a left there to sober up. A half bottle of home brew whisky was found in the carriage. This was removed and destroyed.

Ruthie rushed to her room, closed the door and laid down on her bed and cried. How could Bobby do this to her. Going behind her back and asking for her hand in marriage, she could not imagine that she could have been attracted to such a low life. Blaming Bobby for her father's intoxication she was so outraged that all she could do is cry. She thought for once she had made a true friend but he had betrayed her. Thus she judged Bobby on the word of her drunken father without inquiring of the true facts. It was evidence enough that it was he who had approached her father since his drunken mind was still able to recall his name. This was all the proof she needed to know that Bobby Johnson could not be trusted and she must sever all ties with him.

Morning arrived and Mr. Lancer was suffering from the worst hangover. He went to the shed and searched his carriage for the only remedy he knew, but the bottle was missing. Since his memory of the previous evening was hazy he wasn't sure it had ever existed, so he went back to his bedroom and covered his head with a pillow until the pounding began to subside a few hours later.

He ventured out of his bedroom in the middle of the afternoon and Sheila was waiting for him with coffee and food. As he sat down to eat, Ruthie joined him but no one spoke. Finally, as Mr. Lancer finished his meal he looked at his daughter apologetically. Although he could not remember drinking he knew from the way he felt that he must have had a drink. "I'm so sorry," he blubbered.

"Doc said this is to be expected," Ruthie answered

nonchalantly.

"Oh Ruthie, I have been such a horrible father to you, but I have some good news."

Ruthie remained silent and sat patiently with her father. Then, after a few moments she blurted, "Father, you must never do this again. I will stay here and look after you but that liquor will kill you. I don't want you to die."

"Oh, Ruthie. I am not deserving of such a daughter as you. But I have some good news for you."

"Oh, father." Ruthie was not ready for a repeat of the news she had heard the night before. "You are all the good news I need. Just keep yourself healthy so I can look after you. That is all the good news I need."

"But Ruthie, a young man came to me yesterday..."

Ruthie interrupted. "I don't want to hear about any young man. I told you father that I will stay here and be your loyal daughter as long as I can."

"Well, I did tell him it would be up to you, so if your mind is made up we will let it rest."

"Yes, father, my mind is made up. If I had any interest in a young man it is ended now. If you see that young man again you can tell him for me that I never want to see him again."

Ruthie ended the discussion. Mr. Lancer did not remember the conversation he had with his dead wife the night before and was unaware that Ruthie may have obtained misinformation. He tried to tell his daughter that a young man wished to see her, but she seemed determined not to have anything to do with it. In his drunken state he had believed that the young man had asked for her hand in marriage but none of that even entered his mind once the alcohol ceased to have effect. For a short time he had dreamt of seeing his daughter married. Now he was content with her expression of undying devotion to him. Yet somehow a spark had been ignited, and knowing that his time was limited, he was concerned about her future.

Chapter Five

Krissy

Whether or not there was a relationship between Samson and Krissy would depend on who you asked. Samson liked Krissy, but he was busy saving the world and had no time for a relationship. As a slave, Krissy worked from sunup to sundown six days a week and only had her Sundays free. She thought that Samson would understand this and devote much of his Sundays to her. However Samson was very involved in the church meetings at the Johnson's. If Krissy helped him in this, he was happy to have her around but time alone with her was not in his schedule. Thus Krissy was often left by herself on Sundays and she was getting very impatient.

Bobby knew that Krissy was Ruthie's best friend and, when he found her after the Church service one day, he decided to find out what she knew. He wanted to know why Ruthie was avoiding him. He had sent many letters to Ruthie but was no longer getting replies.

"Hi, Krissy, How are things."

"Everything is fine." Krissy smiled in such a way that Bobby was momentarily distracted from his purpose.

When Bobby recovered he said, "How is Ruthie?"

"She is doing well." Krissy's pleasant smile disappeared.

"Did she say why she won't see me?"

"Yes, she said you went behind her back and asked her father for her hand in marriage."

"I had asked for permission to see her. That is all I did."

"Well, she heard differently and now she wants nothing to do with you."

"Maybe you could straighten it out for me."

"Perhaps, but she was pretty well convinced that you had no business talking to her father at all, so I doubt that it would do any good."

"What should I do?" This was a dangerous question to ask Krissy in her present state of mind.

"If I knew who my father was I would have been very pleased if you had asked him for permission to see me." She giggled.

Bobby was stunned. He always admired Krissy, but Krissy was Samson's friend. He was not sure of how their relationship was going as he had been preoccupied with his own troubles, but this obvious flirting must mean that there was nothing between them.

"Why don't you show me around." Krissy broke the awkward pause.

Bobby walked with Krissy as he pointed out various features of the plantation. At one point they crossed paths with Samson who was conversing with neighbours. He seemed to barely notice his friends coming and when Bobby told him he would show Krissy the big house he readily consented.

Once in the big house Bobby had planned to introduce her to his parents but found they were resting in their room and thought it best not to disturb them. He showed Krissy the parlour and the dining room, then to the kitchen. Krissy was paying more attention to Bobby than the things he was showing her. Finally they went up the stairs and Bobby showed Krissy his room. He was surprised when Krissy walked in and, when he followed her, she closed the door and put her arms around him.

"Whoa, not so fast." Bobby was confused by her actions and was not sure of her intentions.

"I just want a chance to get to know you Bobby," Krissy explained. "I am sorry if I come across as being too bold, but when one is a slave one has to seize opportunities when they come."

"But I thought you and Samson...?"

"We are just friends and he ignores me most of the time." Krissy didn't allow Bobby to finish his question. "Now if you will sit with me and hold me I promise I will not take advantage of you." Krissy laughed at her own joke.

As they sat and held each other, Bobby felt the warmth of this beautiful black lady. They embraced and he felt his lips touch hers. At that moment he felt such desire that he momentarily forgot about God, but as he gently pulled Krissy into a reclining position, he caught a glimpse of his Bible.

"Now who is going too fast." Krissy was first to struggle back to a sitting position. "I don't want you to get the wrong idea about me. I hold Christian values and I know you do as well. I would love to let you have your way with me, but that is something we would both regret, so slow down big man and we can do this properly. Let's just get to know each other first."

"You are absolutely right," Bobby agreed, "but we need to get out of here before someone draws the wrong conclusion." They immediately left the room and Bobby ushered Krissy down the stairway to the front hall. His parents, now rising from their Sunday nap, saw them.

"Hi, Mom, Dad. This is Krissy. She is a friend of Ruthie and Samson. I was just showing her around." Bobby appeared a bit sheepish as though he had been caught in an embarrassing act.

"Yes, we have met. Would you like to join us for tea?" Mrs. Johnson politely asked.

"I would love to have tea with you, but I don't know when Samson will be ready to go," Krissy replied.

"Not to worry, I told Samson we were going to the big house. He will come to get you when he is ready," Bobby chimed in.

We can have the servants bring the tea out to the porch," Mr. Johnson suggested.

"Sounds wonderful," said Krissy anticipating being served tea for the first time in her life. Bobby was pleased as Krissy spoke elegantly to his parents. She could not have made a better impression. When the servant brought her tea Krissy was met with a glare. The servants had brought snacks and tea for Samson before, but how dare this black stranger seat herself with white folks. This was too much for them to comprehend. Krissy was very pleasant and cordial as she accepted the tea. When Ruthie was in finishing school she would practice her lessons with Krissy and in this Krissy played perfectly the role of a mistress being served by a slave. Although this was amusing to the white people present it did not go well with the serving class.

Soon Samson arrived to take Krissy home. Krissy took the opportunity to give heartfelt thanks for Bobby's kindness in a way that was designed to make a boyfriend jealous, however Samson did not react and so Bobby assumed that meant his friend had no interest in the beautiful Krissy.

As Samson and Krissy rode home, they were silent for a while, then Krissy brought up the subject that was annoying her.

"Samson; I appreciate you picking me up for church, but you always seem so busy. We never seem to have any time for just us."

"Bobby and I started this church and I need to socialize with the congregation," Samson replied.

"It's just that I only have a few hours on Sundays when I don't have to work. Bobby seemed to have found enough time to show me around today."

"I noticed. Did you enjoy yourself?"

"Yes. Bobby is quite a gentleman and he doesn't take a girl

for granted."

They rode on in silence for a few more miles, each deep in thought, then Samson explained. "I've got a lot of things to do currently. I am working on a plan that will end slavery and make living conditions better for us. Once I get things worked out, I will have more time."

"If you are too busy to pick me up for church you could ask Bobby to do it," was Krissy's curt reply. "I'm sure he won't mind."

"That would allow me a couple more hours each week. If you are sure you won't mind I think I will ask him."

Krissy smiled. "That would be wonderful." Her attempts to provoke a jealous reaction from Samson had failed. Perhaps he did not have an interest in her. She wore a pleasant smile on her face as she contemplated spending her Sundays with Bobby.

Ruthie's Desperation

Mr. Lancer had some good days and some bad days. Sunday August 15th, 1824 was not a good day. He was resisting his cravings and he had the shakes, but Ruthie stayed with him to help him through. After lunch they sat on the front porch and talked. Jeanette Lancer had passed away on December 22nd, 1805 and Fred Lancer reacted by drowning his sorrows. Now, with severe health issues as a result of his drinking he was finally sobering up enough to deal with his grief. He told his daughter, who was born on the day of his wife's demise, about his undying love and how he missed the one he had fallen in love with. "Although I knew it was not your fault," he addressed Ruthie, "I couldn't help but put the blame on you and I am afraid I did not treat you very well; but now you have turned out so much like your mother that you are a real comfort to me." There were tears in Mr. Lancer's eyes as he spoke. "And then I became so greedy. I didn't want to lose you. You have turned out to be a fine young woman and I pray I will see you married before I die, but I was afraid of you going away, so I didn't want you to meet any eligible bachelors." He paused and sobbed as he tried to control the shaking. "I hope it is not too late," he went on. "I'm not sure how much longer I'll be with you and we need to think about your future. The plantation will support you but you need a strong man to run it for you. One that has experience driving slaves and who is not afraid to apply the lash when needed."

Ruthie was listening intently and her agitation at this last remark could not be hidden from her father. She did not want to get her father upset, but could he not see how Samson had gotten more work out of the slaves without using the whip? She did not voice her opinion, but her fidgeting gave her away as she cleared her throat several time as though she was about to speak.

Finally her father continued. "You are much too soft Ruthie. You are so much like your mom. She seemed to think that slaves were regular people. They are work animals that we own. If you want a horse to run faster you have to use a whip. But don't feel so bad. They are not like us. They are used to it and it doesn't hurt them like it would us. When they are lazy they expect to be whipped. If it bothered them they would just work harder."

Ruthie realized that everything about this statement was a lie. Her father was simply using the things he had been told to try to justify the cruelty of slavery. She would never see things as her father did and Mr. Lancer was far too set in his ways to allow reality to change his perception.

"Father, you mustn't get yourself upset," Ruthie began. "Samson did an amazing job at planting and he organized things so that the work of the plantation continues. The slaves are happier than they have ever been and they seem to be getting everything done. Perhaps we should hire Samson back for the harvest." Ruthie did have some ulterior motives to get Samson back. Although she would see him when he came to pick up Krissy on Sundays she wanted to see him more often. She did not trust her father's statement that he wanted to see her married and was sure he would drive away any suitors who came calling, but with Samson to run the plantation and to get some affection from the male slaves, she would get by. Her father went to the slaves to satisfy his sexual desires, so why shouldn't she. She knew that southern society would not see things her way, but if she was to become the plantation owner then the slaves would belong to her and they would have to do as she asked. She would be careful not to let anyone know who the father of her children would be as she didn't want any lynching on her behalf.

She admired Samson and she desired to be with him. Since Krissy seemed to like him, that was a problem, but she could use that to her advantage. Since he was in a relationship with her best friend, no one would suspect him of fathering her child.

As these thoughts were going through her head a wagon was approaching. She and her father watched as Samson and Krissy rode by on their way to the slaves' quarters.

"I think I'll go and see how Krissy is doing," Ruthie suggested. "Is there anything you need before I go?"

"I'll be okay. I'll call for Sheila if I need anything," Fred Lancer answered. "Perhaps you can check if Samson will be available for harvest time while you are back there?"

"Yes, I will do that," Ruthie smiled. She had planned to find an excuse to talk to Samson and her father just gave that to her. If he had known what she was thinking he would not have been so anxious to put his daughter in contact with this free black man.

By the time Ruthie got back to the slave area, Krissy was nowhere in sight and Samson was heading to the shed with his wagon. She went towards the shed to intercept Samson. It appeared as if he planned on spending the night. Perhaps things were heating up between him and Krissy. That may make her mission more difficult but she was sure any member of the male sex could be persuaded to cheat on his partner.

When Ruthie reached the shed, Samson was unhitching the horse. "Planning to spend the night with Krissy?" was Ruthie's inquiry.

"Not exactly. I won't be coming back for a while and I thought I would stick around until morning to see if the field work is progressing properly."

"So you won't be picking up Krissy next Sunday?"

"She told me she would rather have Bobby pick her up."

Ruthie felt her heart jump. For a moment, nothing made sense. Why was her Bobby going to be picking up Krissy? Oh, that's right. It was no longer her Bobby. But why did her heart jump at the mention of his name? What happened between Krissy and Samson? She should be delighted that Samson was available, but what about that two timing Bobby? Oh, why should she care what he does, she was done with him, and Samson was available. All these thoughts were going through Ruthie's head at the same time and she became dizzy. She was about to faint when Samson dropped the reins he was holding and prevented her fall.

"Are you okay?" he inquired.

"I'm alright. Just a little dizzy."

"Have a seat on this stool. I will get someone to take you to the house."

Ruthie looked at the dirty stool. "No, I'm okay now."

"Are you sure? Perhaps you should sit a spell." Samson spread his cloak on the stool to make it more inviting and Ruthie finally agreed to sit.

"Are things okay between you and Krissy?" she asked when she got settled.

"Oh yes. It is just that I don't have time for her and she seems to have taken a liking to Bobby." Samson had second thoughts about the second part of his statement, but it was too late. He had already said it. "That doesn't bother you, does it?"

"Oh no, Bobby and I are history." Ruthie didn't know why this statement made her feel uneasy. "You seem to be taking it well. I mean Krissy leaving you for Bobby."

"We are just friends. I don't have time to be involved in a relationship right now and I am happy if Krissy finds someone she likes."

Ruthie stood up and took a step towards Samson. "But everyone needs a little affection now and again." She reached out to Samson and attempted a hug, but Samson stepped back and avoided her.

"I suppose they do, but I have big plans in the works and I don't have time."

"Oh, Samson. I have the perfect solution for you." Ruthie managed to take Samson's hands in hers. "I can give you what you need and I don't want any commitment."

"What?" Samson became very uncomfortable and pulled away from Ruthie.

Ruthie began to cry. "Oh, Samson. I don't want much. But I don't believe I will ever marry. I just want to have a child. I want to have your child. Just think, Samson. Your child would be born free. If Krissy had your baby, it would be my father's property, but I am not a slave so I could bear a free child for you. And don't worry. I would never tell anyone about you."

"Are you crazy? Don't you know what they would do to a black man that takes advantage of a white woman? You are making me very uncomfortable."

"But Samson, no one would need to know."

"I would know and you would know." Samson began to pity this young girl's desperation. He reached out to Ruthie and put his arm around her while watching through the doorway for any sign of intruders. "Ruthie. I admire you very much. If it were not for slavery and the attitudes of the south, things may have been very different but I pray to God every day and He answers my prayers. I cannot do what I am doing without the help of our Heavenly Father, so I could never consent to having a child outside of marriage. You know it would be impossible for us to be married."

"Oh, Samson. You must think I am horrible coming on to you like this."

"No, Ruthie. You have had a hard life and you are going through a rough time. I understand and I will pray for you."

"I have never had much luck with God. I don't think He cares about me."

"He does and he has the perfect man picked out for you."

Ruthie laughed. "Surely you don't mean Bobby. It sounds like it didn't take much to get him chasing after Krissy."

"I wasn't thinking about Bobby in particular, but it could be Bobby. He loves you very much."

Ruthie roared with laughter. "You must be joking. Didn't you just tell me he took an interest in Krissy?"

"No, I believe I said Krissy took an interest in him. If he has any interest in Krissy it is only because you completely rejected him."

Ruthie's laughter suddenly turned to anger. "Can you blame me after what he did to me?" With that Ruthie stomped off to the house angry and embarrassed. She did not give Samson a chance to reply.

As Ruthie entered the kitchen she was still in an agitated state. Sheila and her father were there to greet her.

"Did you ask Samson if we could hire him for the harvest?" Her father was sipping an herbal tea and his shaking had subsided.

"No I didn't." Ruthie had forgotten about that part of her mission and now grasped for an excuse. "I don't think we should hire him."

Mr. Lancer noticed his daughter's agitation and wondered at her sudden change of mind. "Why's that? Did that dirty nigger come on to you? Did he touch you?"

"Oh, no, father, it was nothing like that." Ruthie suddenly realised the danger she was putting on Samson. What had actually happened wasn't much better than what her father suspected so it wouldn't do to tell the truth. She had to come up with another reason fast or Samson's life would be at stake. "It's just that him and Krissy broke up and I don't think Krissy would want him around."

"Well I don't give a damn what one nigger thinks about another nigger. If Krissy gives you a problem we will sell her. I can't understand why you have such feelings for these creatures. You come in all upset because a couple of damn niggers broke up. If anyone should be upset it should be me. Krissy is good breeding stock and I would benefit if she got pregnant." Mr. Lancer was getting himself worked into a rage. Ruthie was too agitated to care. All the pent up feeling she had subdued for the past few months were coming to the surface.

She had just made a desperate attempt at seduction and had failed. She had been willing to sacrifice self honour, yet the price she was willing to pay had been refused. She had been made to second guess herself as to her treatment of Bobby. Her best friend was going after the love she had spurned. Now her father whose habit of checking on the slaves had got some of them pregnant was criticizing her. It was too much to bear. She turned to her father and screamed. "How dare you criticize me. And don't worry, if you can't get stud service you can always breed your own stock. Or have you lost that ability?"

Ruthie stormed to her room, slammed the door and fell on her bed. She cried bitterly for hours. Sheila was left with the task of calming her master. Mr. Lancer was on the brink of collapse and Sheila tried to help him get settled.

"Get your filthy hands off me you damn nigger." He pushed Sheila away and fell to the floor. His sudden exertion had caused him to lose consciousness. Sheila did not know what she should do. Should she go to Ruthie and try to comfort her? It did not seem likely that would do much good. Should she try to make her master more comfortable? His last instruction was to keep her hands off him. Should she send for a doctor? There was no one to write a pass and it was too dangerous for a slave to venture out without one. Plus what did she care if her master died. There was always a chance she would get a worse master, but she had just heard this one call her people down to the state of livestock. She was left with one option. To do nothing.

She then began to worry about her master dying in her presence while she stood by. What if someone should stop by and see her there. She best leave and spend the night in the slave quarters. She could claim she knew nothing if she was asked.

When Samson had heard the yelling coming from the house, he was afraid. Ruthie was upset when she left and he had been alone with her. He thought of running, but that would only make him appear guilty. Then he remembered his promise to pray for Ruthie. He knelt down in that shed and prayed. He was not sure how long he prayed, but when he stopped he saw Sheila coming from the house. He walked to meet her.

"Oh Samson, You don't want to go to that house tonight," Sheila said to the approaching man when she had recognized him in the failing light.

"Is it bad?" Samson blurted his question.

"It's not bad. It is just better that you don't see what is there."

"I heard yelling and I was afraid."

"Not to worry. Ruthie defended your honour. But I would be more careful in the future if I were you." Sheila had guessed that there was more to the story than Ruthie had told. Although Ruthie had explained her state of mind to the satisfaction of her father, Sheila knew that a girl did not get that upset over a friend's breakup. "Just stay far away from the big house until morning," Sheila reiterated her warning.

A Prayer Answered

When Ruthie woke up the morning of Monday August 16, 1824, she did not want to get out of bed. She realized that she had almost gotten Samson killed and wasn't sure he was out of danger. If her father had any idea of the feelings she had towards Samson he would be sure to have Samson lynched. No matter how unfair this was, it was the way of the south and nothing could be done about it. How she dreaded facing another day. She remembered Samson's kindness as he tried to comfort her after she had made such a fool of herself. By doing this he had increased the danger to his own life. She found herself admiring Samson as a man. He isn't just a nigger. He is a real man. She had never before thought of a black person on equal terms with humans, but Samson now appeared to her more human than any white man she knew.

Krissy was Ruthie's best friend, but one thing that made this friendship attractive to Ruthie is that Krissy, being her father's slave, had to do whatever she said. Yes, Krissy was a good nigger and more like a favourite pet to Ruthie than a human being. Now she began to wonder, if Krissy was human and an equal to herself? If that is so then slavery is wrong and the whole south is wrong. How could this be? Everything she had been taught from childhood was wrong. The whole society she lived in was wrong. "That's ludicrous," she said out loud in reply to her thoughts. "There must be some other explanation."

Ruthie finally gathered the courage to face the world and ventured from her room to the kitchen where she assumed Sheila would have a pot of coffee waiting. "Now there's another good nigger." She thought adding to her bedroom contemplations.

When she reached the kitchen, Ruthie was alarmed. There was her father lying slumped on the floor. Why was he there? Was he alive? Where was Sheila? Alarmed and confused, she ran to her father. He was still breathing and he moaned when she touched him. She tugged on his body to get him straightened into a more comfortable position. Mr. Lancer began to regain consciousness and moaning asked, "What happened?"

"Oh! Father, are you alright?"

"I think I'm okay. Did I get drunk again? I don't remember touching a drop."

"No Father. We had an argument last night and you were upset with me. Oh! Father. I am so sorry. I didn't even think about you. I was so wrapped up in my own selfish problems that I forgot how sick you are. Please forgive me Father, and don't die on me."

Mr. Lancer struggled to his feet. He had only half heard what his daughter had said. He was busy trying to make sense of his own condition. As he slumped on to a chair he said, "That's funny. I don't remember touching a drop but I'm waking up with the worse hangover I ever had. Are you sure I didn't get drunk?"

"Where is Sheila? How could that damn nigger let this happen?" Ruthie spoke out of character in her anger.

"Oh! Honey, your language." Even in his diminished state her father was shocked. "I have never heard you talk like that before. You don't want to pick up my bad habits. They're not fit for a lady."

Just then Sheila came in carrying a basket of eggs from the henhouse. Ruthie turned to her and screamed, "Where were you, you stupid nigger. I found my father lying on the floor this morning. How could you let that happen."

Sheila was not accustomed to Ruthie addressing her in such a tone. She stumbled for an excuse. "Well, when I tried to help

The Alternative

him he told me to keep my hands off him so I left and spent the night in the slave quarters. Can I help it if he fell after I left?" Sheila spoke in half truths.

"Why weren't you here this morning to put the coffee on for us?" Ruthie had not calmed down at all.

"Well, I....I...." This was going to be harder to explain. She had hoped that Mr. Lancer would be dead by morning and didn't want to be the one to discover him. Now she realised that leaving him for Ruthie to discover was not such a good idea. Thankfully he was alive. If he had died things would have been much worse. "I....I musta slept in," was the only excuse Sheila could come up with on short notice. This is not an excuse a slave wants to use very often because it is usually followed by a severe whipping that is designed to give her the incentive to never sleep in again.

"Well you damn nigger," Ruthie was sounding more like her father as she expressed her anger. "It sounds like you're getting to uppity for your class. Suppose you need a reminder of your place. Maybe I've been wrong to protect you. I have a notion to send you to the sheriff for a public whipping myself."

"No, please Miss Ruthie. It will never happen again. I'll be right dedicated to you an' Massa. I'll do anything you want. Please don't send me to the whipping post."

The public whipping post is one place no slave wants to go. Many would prefer a much more severe beating on the plantation rather than endure the humiliation of a public whipping. In the latter case one was stripped naked before strangers and tied to the whipping post were all could see. Then a man who knew nothing about her, but was hired for his ability to inflict the greatest punishment, both physically and mentally, would apply the prescribed number of lashes in the most painful and embarrassing way he could. Often, just a threat of a public whipping would be enough to solicit cooperation from even the most uncooperative slave. This is exactly the effect it was having on Sheila. She could not believe that Ruthie would subject her to such humiliation, but she was not about to take that chance. Ruthie had the right to do it and could do it. It was in Sheila's best interest to completely humiliate herself to this young lady that she had mothered for many years. Just as a dog rolls over in submission to a more powerful dog, she must humble herself to these animals that have the power to cause her so much anguish.

Ruthie now calmed down and turned her attention to her father. "Are you okay father. Should I send for the doctor.

"No, I think I'll be okay. I just need a cup of coffee."

Ruthie glared at Sheila who got the message and went to work frantically to make a pot of coffee. Within moments, not giving near enough time for Sheila to complete the task she shouted. "Why's that coffee taking so long?" As they watched Sheila's actions becoming more frantic, Ruthie turned to her father and smiled. She was glad he was okay, but more than this she was beginning to enjoy the power her class had over the serving class. She began to understand her father's obsession with it. Yes, one could easily become addicted to such power.

Mr. Lancer smiled back at his daughter. Had she finally overcome the weakness she had inherited from her mother? She was certainly acting more like her father's child at the moment, but she had no experience in such matters and he was worried she would go too far. He, himself, knew the limits for pushing a slave, but if one goes too far, the system can backfire. Slaves were not like other animals and could completely shut down and be no good to anyone if pushed beyond their endurance. For now, he was amused at his daughter's ability to humiliate this slave, the same slave that she had protected from him in the past, the slave that was responsible for the scar on her cheek when she got between Sheila and his whip. Now, watching Sheila's humiliation before his daughter, it was sweet retribution for all the times he had wanted to punish her.

The Alternative

"Well, dad, how about we go into town for a coffee. It may be faster than getting one here and I can see the sheriff while we're there."

"Oh, no Miss Ruthie. I has it ready now. I's comin' with it directly." With that Sheila rushed with two cups of coffee, but tripped over a stool and spilled them both. Now she was in tears, believing there was no hope for her. "It's okay," she cried. I made a pot. I'll get two more cups."

This was too much for Ruthie and she suddenly felt sorry for Sheila. "That's okay mom," she used the more endearing term for Sheila. "Take your time. I will come and help you." She got to Sheila on time to pick up a cup of coffee that was poured for her father and took it for him. Sheila poured another cup and followed.

When Ruthie got to her father she urged him. "Come, father. Let's get you to your bedroom. You can have your coffee there." She felt a sudden urge to make amends with Sheila, but did not want to do it in her father's presence. Her exhibit of power had pleased her father. Her suddenly becoming soft would not, but she felt Sheila had endured enough and she now needed to change rolls from mistress to friend.

She got her father settled as best she could and went back to the kitchen to confront Sheila.

When Sheila saw her approach she began to cry. "I's so sorry Miss Ruthie. I don't know what got into me. I shoulda had your coffee ready an' I makes such a mess spillin' everythin'."

Ruthie grabbed an empty cup and went through the door to the outdoor fireplace where the coffee pot was being kept hot. She filled the cup and brought it back for Sheila setting it on the table, she picked up her own cup and took a sip. "Come, mom. Have a coffee with me."

"Are you sure? I's been such a bad nigger. I's not deservin' of any coffee."

"Come, mother, and join me. I'm sorry for the way I treated you. I was just upset about father, but he's okay. It's just that he could have died and no one was here to help him."

Sheila was not about to admit that she knew Mr. Lancer had fallen but she also knew that a slave's excuse was never accepted by a white master or mistress. "I'm so sorry I didn't come back to check on him. I don't know what got into me to be so foolish."

"Don't worry about it, mom." Ruthie spoke calmly and sincerely. "You couldn't have known. The reason I was so upset is that I didn't bother to check on him either. He's my own father and he could have died while I did nothing. I suppose I blamed you because I could not own up to my own mistake. I'm just glad that father is okay. If I had let him die I don't know what I would do."

It had taken years for Sheila to learn to trust Ruthie. Slaves were always very careful of what they said to the white people among them. If they didn't respond correctly a severe beating could result. Whether or not the statement was true did not matter. If the truth would result in a beating a lie was regarded as a wiser choice. Over the years Sheila had begun to trust Ruthie enough to be truthful with her. The threat of a public whipping removed all that trust. Ruthie, who had been both friend and daughter to her was now her mistress who had power to do her harm. Never before had she considered the possibility that Ruthie would exercise such power, but now it was abundantly clear that it could happen. Worse than that, she now had a secret that she could never confess.

Ruthie tried desperately to get her mom back. Ever since she had found out what happened to her biological mother she had considered Sheila as her mom. Having a mother that was a slave gave many advantages to a young girl, but Ruthie still loved her as a mother. Over the years trust had been built, but now a moment of anger had ruined all of that. Ruthie desperately wanted Sheila to respond as a mother, but, for now,

Sheila was clearly responding as a slave.

"I's so sorry Miss Ruthie. Would be better I died than Massa. He's always so good to me. I don't know what got into me that I didn't check on him."

Now Ruthie knew this was an outright lie. She also knew it was a typical response of a slave to her mistress. She felt her anger build at the lie but it was her anger that got her in this mess. She desperately sought the advice of her mother, but she felt like she had just killed another mother. What was she to do? She sat and began to sob. Surely her mom would come to rescue her but Sheila just sat by and watched her cry. Finally she ran to her room and jumped into her bed, burying her head in her pillow. She cried herself to sleep. She did not come out of her room all day. Except for brief visits to the outhouse, she would remain in her room that night and all the next day. When her father came to her room on the Tuesday evening she told him to leave her alone. She did not want to face the world. This world she lived in was cruel and Godless. At that thought it reminded her of Bobby. Then she remembered Samson saying he would pray for her. As the sun came up that Wednesday her Father heard her screaming as though she had gone mad. He had Sheila make her some breakfast as she hadn't had a meal since Sunday and was bringing it to her room when he heard her.

"Where are you God?" she screamed as though she thought her voice must reach heaven. "Don't you care about me? I have no one I can turn to." As she made the last statement, Bobby came to her mind, and again Samson's assurance that he would pray for her. She began to feel better as she poured her heart out to a God she did not believe in. Having eaten nothing since Sunday she suddenly felt so hungry she could barely stand it. "God, if you are there you will send me some food."

Just then she heard a knock on her door. "Who is it?" she said.

"I'm just coming to bring you some breakfast," her father answered. "Please try to eat something. I am so worried about you."

Ruthie was astonished. Had God actually answered her prayer? Perhaps it was just coincidence.

"Come on in, father," she said and when he opened the door she picked up a bell by her bed and rung it loudly. "Set it there on the table and pull up a chair." She instructed her father. "I am famished. Surely this is not enough for both of us."

"I left mine in the kitchen. I just thought I should bring this to you before you starved to death."

"Well I sure do appreciate that but I would also like some company." Ruthie stated just as Sheila arrived in answer to the bell. "Please bring Father's breakfast. We will be dining in my room."

As Ruthie began to dig in to a delicious meal she quizzed her father. "What made you bring this to me just now?"

"I was worried about you. You hadn't eaten since Sunday and I was afraid you would starve."

"But why now? Why not last night?"

"I didn't think about it last night, but something told me I needed to bring you food this morning."

"Why didn't you just send Sheila with it?" Ruthie asked just as Sheila arrived with her father's meal. "Thanks mom." Ruthie was not concerned about her father hearing her use that term. She desperately desired Sheila to resume acting as her mother and was willing to break all the rules to win her back.

Mr. Lancer ignored Sheila as he took a sip of coffee then answered his daughter's question. "I don't know. I just had a feeling I should bring it. I was afraid you wouldn't accept it from Sheila."

"Father, I hate to say it, but God has been speaking to you."

"What do you mean?"

"Well I had just prayed to God to send me some food and you showed up with breakfast."

"It's more like you were screaming at God. I thought you had gone mad."

"No, father. I am not crazy. I may have been mad all my life but I believe that I am now finally sane." As she finished her meal she gave her father a big hug. "I love you so much, dad. We must do this more often. Never before have I seen you do something that you could get a slave to do. It was so sweet of you to bring breakfast to me in bed. Perhaps tomorrow I will treat you to breakfast in your room."

Chapter Six
The Monitory Value of Freedom

To say Bobby was an impulsive person may be an understatement. He managed to embarrass himself the following week by picking up Krissy on horseback. He was so anxious to get to the Lancer plantation early he did not think of hooking up a carriage. By the time he completed an uncomfortable ten mile ride with Krissy behind him on the horse, he was in no mood to take more than a minor role in the Sunday service. The combination of seeing Bobby with Krissy who usually came with Samson and Bobby's limited involvement in the service got the congregation talking. Did a girl come between the best friends that were co-preachers at these services? The ladies tend to see these things before gentlemen do and Krissy immediately noticed the reaction of the crowd and went into damage control. When the service was over she went immediately to the food tables to help with serving. When Bobby followed her she told him that he must stay with Samson and talk to the congregation. Later, while Bobby went to get the carriage hooked up, she spent time working the crowd with Samson herself. She wanted to show that they were all still friends, and it seemed to be working. She had also asked Bobby to invite his parents along for the ride when she went home so it would not look so much like she was Bobby's date.

    Mrs. Johnson also noticed the congregations reaction, so the ride home was an interesting one for the lovebirds. The Johnson's, however, did not realize the cause of the reaction to

The Monitory Value of Freedom

the degree that Krissy did. Black and white couples were unheard of in 1824. The Johnson's thought this the only cause of the controversy as they admonished their son with, "Do you know what you are doing?"

Krissy, knowing the true cause answered, "When we show them we are all still friends, they will accept us."

The conversation very quickly turned to a discussion on the children of a slave mother. "You do realize that any children Krissy has will be the property of Mr. Lancer." Mr. Johnson advised his son.

"Yes," Krissy concurred. "If you are serious about me you will need to buy me." The discussion continued. Krissy was a young slave in the prime of her youth and could produce many slave children for her master, so she would not go cheaply. Bobby had not had the best luck in his relationships and it occurred to him that Krissy may be using him to get her freedom. He was not so sure she would stay with him and he weighed these possibilities as he thought about the right thing to do. If he bought Krissy's freedom, then that would no longer be an excuse and he would find out if she really liked him. Also, no one deserved to be a slave and certainly not Krissy, so yes, to his parents dismay he consented to trying to buy her freedom. He was not sure if he could, but he would try and he assured Krissy that this would not obligate her to him in any way.

Bobby was having second thoughts as he began pulling his recourses together to make an offer. His parents were against the transaction so he needed to do this himself. He found he could raise about five hundred dollars, so he would go make that offer. It would likely be turned down anyway, but he had said he would try, so that would meet his obligation. This was a big step to take and he needed to consult the two people he always turned to for advice before following through.

"How do you think Krissy will feel when she finds out that you offered five?" Uncle Robert inquired.

The Alternative

"I never thought about that. I suppose she will think I don't value her very highly. But that is all I have."

"What about your horse. You could sell that."

"But how would I get around?"

"So your horse is more important than Krissy's freedom."

"Well.... No..."

"I'll tell you what I'll do. You can sell your horse to me and I will loan it to you until you can afford to buy it back, plus I can advance some wages. But first, go to Mr. Lancer and negotiate your best price. Just tell him you will think about it, then let me know how much you need and we will talk about it."

Next, Bobby brought his problem to Samson who he was sure would see things his way. He had given Samson his freedom and felt that he would be supportive. "It's your money," Samson stated bluntly. "You can do as you please, but I think you are wasting it."

"Don't you think Krissy deserves her freedom?"

"Of course she does. Everyone does. Are you going to buy the freedom of all the slaves in the south?"

"I'm not sure I can even afford one."

Bobby was very confused when he went to the Lancer plantation. Placing a monetary value on a person was repulsive to him, but he had made a promise and he had to follow through.

The only predictable thing about Mr. Lancer was that he was never predictable. Bobby not only got the shock of his life that day, but he got a crash course on how the other side lives.

"Hello Mr. Lancer. I'm Bobby Johnson. My uncle sent this for you." Bobby handed him a prescription from his Uncle's store.

"Yes I remember you Bobby. I'm not sure were Ruthie is, but I'll send one of the young slaves to fetch her."

"No need to do that. I didn't come to see Ruthie."

"Surely you didn't come all this way just to bring my prescription?"

"No, I have a business matter to discuss."

"Oh! What is that?"

"I would like to talk to you about purchasing one of your slaves."

"So your short of help on your plantation. What makes you think I would have a slave to spare?"

"No. It's not like that. There is one particular slave I am interested in."

"Which one is that."

"Her name is Krissy."

"Oh! she is a fine slave. A hard worker and a good breeder. She is worth a lot of dough. Why do you want her."

"I met her at our church services. I would just like to purchase her." Bobby was being as evasive as he could. He was afraid that revealing his true purpose could affect the price.

Mr. Lancer studied Bobby for a while. He noticed Bobby's nervousness as he fidgeted and moved back and forth. "Where's my manners?" Mr. Lancer spoke. "Come and sit and we will discuss this." As Bobby took a seat Mr. Lancer burst out laughing. "Why you little rascal. You ain't even married my daughter yet and your already lookin' for a little on the side. No wonder you didn't want to see Ruthie."

Bobby was speechless. How could Mr. Lancer make such an assumption. He wanted to set the older gentleman straight but Mr. Lancer didn't let him speak.

"Well Bobby Johnson. I won't sell Krissy to you but I'll tell you what I will do. I'll give her to you." At this Fred Lancer laughed so hard he grabbed his stomach to ease the pain. When he got himself under control he continued, "I'll give her to you as a wedding present when you marry my daughter." More laughter. "You just gotta promise that you will treat my

The Alternative

daughter real good. Now get out of here before Ruthie comes. This will be our little secret. Next time you come around you better have a big bouquet of flowers for my daughter." He continued to laugh as he waved Bobby away.

Bobby could see that there was no reasoning with him. He could not imagine a man so crude as this. As he rode off he thought aloud to see if it would make any sense. "He thinks I'm going to marry his daughter but he will give me a slave so I can have a little on the side." Bobby knew some of the plantation owners did this, but he was surprised that Mr. Lancer would be so open about it and even think it was okay concerning his own daughter's future husband. How could one so pure as Ruthie come from this crude stock. Perhaps Ruthie was not as she seemed. Maybe that is why God was keeping her away from him. All the way home he thought about Ruthie. His mission had been for Krissy's sake, but he seemed to have forgotten that.

When Bobby got home he went straight to his room and prayed. Then he would read his Bible and pray some more. When he was called for supper he said he wasn't hungry and he continued to fast and pray, seeking an answer and trying to make sense of what happened. When he finally fell asleep, he dreamed. He was a knight trying to save a damsel in distress. A huge dragon kept driving him back. He saw the damsel calling out to him for help. It was Ruthie. He tried to get to her but the dragon wouldn't let him. An angel cried out, "you forgot your armour." He searched for his armour and found his Bible. "Put it on," the angel called. "It is the only way to get by the dragon."

Bobby woke up with a start. He lit his lamp and read his Bible until day break. Then he went down the stairs to have breakfast with his parents.

The Monitory Value of Freedom

Did You Say You Had a Plan to End Slavery?

Mr. and Mrs. Johnson were worried about their son. He had gone to see Mr. Lancer about purchasing Krissy but had gone straight to his room when he came home. He didn't come down for his evening meal with them. They chatted at the breakfast table as they waited for Bobby. Mauve served them coffee.

"Something must have gone wrong yesterday," Mrs. Johnson said to her husband.

"It's not like Bobby to skip supper," Mr. Johnson replied. "I hope he is okay."

"He's had a bit of a rough go lately. But he always seems to be able to bounce back."

"I hope he hasn't gone and wasted all his money. He's a good worker but not much of a business man."

They heard Bobby coming down the stairs. They looked to him expectantly as he approached the breakfast table.

Bobby took a seat in silence. He was in no mood to talk. He knew his parents expected a report on the previous day's business, but he did not want to talk about it.

"Well, what happened?" Mr. Johnson asked.

"Not much." Bobby answered evasively.

"I take it things did not go to well." Mrs. Johnson said with concern. "Did the deal fall through?"

"I'm just a little confused." Bobby stated.

"Confused?" Mr. Johnson was puzzled. When someone goes to buy a slave, many things can happen but he could not see how any of them could be confusing. "Are you now a slave owner?" He asked to break the suspense.

"No, we did not complete any deal."

"But you came to an agreement?" Mr. Johnson inquired. "Or did you decide to back out and not waste your money."

"You heard what I told Krissy. I can't back down on a

promise."

"Oh! So you made a low offer and Mr. Lancer refused. That would get you out of your obligation but how are you going to break that to Krissy?" Mrs. Johnson joined in on the guessing game.

"Well, mom, I thought about doing that but Uncle Robert reminded me of how that might affect Krissy, so I just went to get a price."

"And..." Both the older Johnsons said together.

"He refused to sell Krissy."

"That's not surprising and it gets you off the hook." Mr. Johnson was relieved.

"He said he would give her to me."

Now all three Johnsons were confused. No one just gives away a slave without conditions. "There must be some conditions." Mrs. Johnson voiced the concern.

"That's the problem. I don't think I can meet the conditions." Bobby thought he better start from the beginning. "Mr. Lancer seems to be of the opinion that I am going to marry Ruthie. He accused me of looking for a little on the side when I told him I wanted to buy Krissy."

"He must have been furious." Mrs. Johnson interjected.

"That's what confuses me. He wasn't upset at all. He seemed to condone it. He was perfectly willing to give Krissy to me, as a sex slave I suppose, so long as I married Ruthie and kept her happy. I have heard of such practices but I didn't expect anyone to be so open about it. I find it totally shocking that he would give his future son-in-law a slave for such purposes."

"Well, I suppose you straitened him out." Bobby's mother spoke.

"I tried to, but he wouldn't listen. He is expecting me to marry his daughter." Bobby was having difficulty explaining.

"The thing is that I would do it if I could. It is Ruthie that I love, but she won't have anything to do with me."

"Are you saying you would be willing to go through with the deal and accept your gift of a sex slave?" Mr. Johnson asked in jest. He was aware of his son's high moral standards.

"Only so long as I don't actually have to have sex with her. I would not own her for long. I would get freedom papers for her as quick as I could."

"Son," Mrs. Johnson spoke with compassion, "I know you have a strong faith in God. I'm not sure I share that faith but I do know that love will find a way. If you really think that Ruthie is the one for you, then don't give up. Be patient. It will all work out."

"Now Sara," Mr. Johnson interjected. Don't be getting the boy's hopes up too high. We all know that things can change. We may be convinced that we are in love with one person one day and the next day we meet someone new and everything changes."

"Is that what happened between you and Suzie."

"I had forgotten all about her but I believe you are right. I had completely fallen for her and was so upset when she started dating Darren Longfellow, but then you came along and I never thought of her again." Mr. Johnson sensed a trap and choose his words carefully, then to divert attention he turned to his son. "Just hang in there Bobby. Everything will work out in the end."

Once breakfast was over Bobby headed into town to talk to his uncle. He thanked Uncle Robert again for his good advice and, having recounted the story to his parents, he was a little less embarrassed to tell his uncle the happenings of the previous day.

"So, if I got this straight, it is really Ruthie that you want to marry." Uncle Robert stated "The fact that she is still on your mind indicates that you were not really committed to Krissy."

Bobby's next stop was to get the advice of his best friend. Samson was wise to the ways of the south and would be able to make more sense of what happened. As he approached the field where Samson was working, his friend addressed the young ladies working there.

"Bobby is coming out to give us a hand. I don't want any of you ladies chasing him away. We can really use his help." When they heard about him and Krissy many of the female slaves saw Bobby as a ticket to freedom and would try to be friendly to him.

Bobby picked up an unused hoe and examined its edge, he found a file in the toolbox and gave the hoe a few strokes to sharpen it, then he went over to were Samson was.

"Hi, Samson."

"Hello Bobby."

"Samson," Bobby began, "I want to talk to you about what happened yesterday." Bobby looked around and found most of the workforce moving towards his position as they worked. "But it's kind of personal." He added.

"We have a lot to do today. If you help out I can leave early and then we can talk."

"Yes, come to the house for supper. We will talk then."

Cynthia had managed to get within earshot and had overheard the last part. "I would be happy to have supper with you in the big house," she said. Samson glared at her. "Yes, Massa Samson. I'll get right back to work."

"If you work here nobody will get anything done," Samson reflected. "I have a crew hoeing the corn field over there." Samson pointed out the field. "They can use your help."

Bobby went immediately and found a crew of his father's older slaves. He always enjoyed working with them as they would reminisce about the old days. Sometimes they would repeat stories about Africa that they had heard as children. By

The Monitory Value of Freedom

now the slaves were comfortable with Bobby's presence and would often talk about things that they would not ordinarily talk about in the presence of a white person. Sometimes it was as though they forgot Bobby was white and their master's son. Bobby felt a great deal of pride being thus accepted into their society. He found the conversation that afternoon both informative and relaxing. It did much to get his mind off of his troubles.

Normally slaves would work until it got too dark to see. With the new system on the Johnson farm they could often quit early, but lately the weather had not been cooperative so, this being the first good day in a while, everyone was poised to put in a full day. However Samson remembered his promise to stop early to have a talk, so he went to get Bobby about seven that evening. "If you want to come now the rest of the crew can finish up here."

Bobby looked around and saw they were almost done with the field. He was enjoying the work and the comradery far too much to leave so he said, "I think I will finish up with the crew. We can talk later."

Thus with Bobby's loyalty to them the crew worked even harder than they had all day and the field was soon finished. They still had enough daylight left to put their tools away and make it back to their quarters.

Bobby and Samson made their way to the big house, stopping by the well, they pumped up enough water to wash off the field dust, then proceeded to the house. The elder Johnson's were just finishing their meal. "Sorry, Bobby. We didn't know when you would be in, so we went ahead without you."

"That's alright. Samson will be dining with me tonight. Can you get Mauve to bring our food to the porch."

Mauve had heard this request. "I will bring it out directly. Tonight I have fried chicken just the way you like it." Word of Bobby's troubles had gotten around and all were doing their part to cheer him up. However Bobby was quickly coming to terms with the difficult decisions he had to make. His faith in the Almighty was growing stronger and the assurance of his loved ones was having its effect. Although he was confused he knew the Almighty God was in control and everything would work out.

As they ate, Bobby recounted his experience to his friend. When he finished Samson said, "So I see you have had a crash course on how the other side lives."

"That's exactly what I was thinking. I can't believe that people actually think that is okay."

"It definitely happens more often than you think. It is more common among the ones who don't go to church, but I even know of a Christian minister who preaches high morals on Sundays but has sexual relations with his slaves during the week. It seems he thinks this is okay because he owns them. As long as his extramarital sex does not extent to white women, he feels his virtue is intact." Samson made this explanation to his friend.

"I guess that is because most of the white people around here, at least the ones I know, either consider black people as less than human or as an inferior breed of human."

"What do you think, Bobby?" Although such a question may appear as an insult when coming from a friend who should know his position, Samson merely wanted Bobby to clarify his thoughts in his own head.

"I think you already know the answer to that. You are certainly proof enough of what a black person can do if given the opportunity. I can't understand half the experiments that you do and I would never have been able to organize the workforce as you have."

"That's because your talents lie in a different area. I would never have been able to do what I have without you. You have a talent for recognizing talent in others and encouraging it. The main problem with slavery is that the talents of the black people are not recognized and therefore not developed. When all people can work together cooperatively, society will advance at a rate never before imagined. Within a few years we would have inventions that we cannot even imagine now."

"Do you think slavery is okay if we recognize each other's talents?" It was Bobby's turn to ask an insulting question.

Samson looked at Bobby in disbelieve and waited until Bobby got a sense of how inappropriate this question was before he answered, then he said emphatically, "Slavery is the reason we do not recognize each other's talents. It is impossible to hold someone as a slave and consider him your equal. Once the white people recognize the talents of the blacks, slavery will have to end. That's why what we are doing here and at the Lancer's is so important, but this will not be fully realised until you free your slaves. It is working to a degree now because I have told the workers they are working towards freedom but when your slaves are free we will have a working model of a free plantation. When people realize that slavery is not economical, and that they can earn more money without it, they will be glad to give up their human chattels."

"Whoa, your losing me. Did you just say you have a plan to end slavery?"

"Yes, Bobby. I thought you knew."

"Samson, I have been racking my brains trying to figure out how to run one plantation without slaves and compete in a market where everyone else uses slaves. I never even dreamt it was possible to end slavery altogether."

"Your part will be easy. You see, with the changes so far, the plantation has made more money than it did before. This will be more fully realised when your workers are free. Then other plantations will want to know why we are successful and gradually everyone will have to give up their slaves to remain competitive."

"Samson! If this plan works you are a genius. I will definitely be paying more attention to what you are doing. For now, although my troubles seem small in comparison I need to figure out what to do about Krissy and Ruthie."

"God has a way of making everything work out for the best," Samson replied. "You may be surprised at how easily it is all resolved. When you pick up Krissy on Sunday, and don't forget the carriage, you should have a talk with her and explain what happened with Mr. Lancer. When you see how she takes it you will know what to do."

Chapter Seven

Accidentally Saving a Life

As it turns out, Krissy already knew about the deal her master had made with Bobby even before the boys talked about it. Mr. Lancer would break it to his slave the same day Bobby asked to buy her in a way she would not soon forget.

When Krissy got the message that the master wanted to see her right away, her heart jumped. Often a slave was whisked off to a new owner in this way. There was no opportunity to say goodbye to friends and family. If a mother and child were to be separated it was considered more prudent to do so without prior knowledge and when they were not in proximity of each other. With this knowledge Krissy took an unauthorized detour to see her daughter. She prayed that it would be Bobby she was being turned over to, but a slave had no choice in these matters and anything was possible.

"Oh! Ella, dear. Come give mommy a hug," Krissy cried as she tried to say goodbye to her child.

"What's wrong Mommy?"

"It's nothing dear. It's just that mommy may have to go away for a while and mommy will miss Ella when she goes. But don't worry. Mommy will send for Ella as soon as she can."

Ella cried. "No mommy, don't go. Don't leave me here."

"Hush child. I'm not sure if they are going to send me away, but if they do mommy will come back and get you real soon." Krissy tried to sound convincing to her child. She hoped what she was saying was the truth but it was completely out of her power to change whatever was in store for her. If Bobby was able to buy her, then perhaps she could convince him to also buy Ella. At this point she didn't know. Her master may have made a deal with someone else. When the master was also the father it was not unusual for him to sell off either mother or child once the child was old enough to be nurtured by other slaves.

"Now Mommy has to go see master. I will try to come back, but if I can't, Ruthie will take good care of you. You be good for Ruthie and mind what she says."

Krissy pulled herself from her clinging child with the help of an older slave that looked after the small children. She hoped that her delay had not been too long and that no one noticed her detour. When she got to the big house she was directed to Mr. Lancer's room. Having never been in that part of the big house before, she assumed this was where the transaction was occurring. When she got to the door, Mr. Lancer quickly whisked her inside. When he closed the door, all was dark. She had eerie reminders of a night five years previous. She heard the lock turn and then a single candle on the nightstand was lit. The shutters of all the windows had been closed and the late afternoon sun struggled to find cracks to enter.

"Your friend Bobby was here and wanted to buy you," Mr. Lancer said, toying with her. Since a slave is not to speak unless asked a question Krissy remained silent. At least it was Bobby, but something wasn't right. She had no ideas about the dealings of a white man but she was very uncomfortable being in a darkened locked room with the same man who had previously raped her. That had happened in the slaves quarters. Now she was in the big house and completely away from anything that was familiar to her.

"I told him I would not sell you. You are much too valuable to me."

The Alternative

Krissy was already scared, now she was terrified and began desperately to look for a way out. This reaction delighted Fred Lancer and he laughed whole heartedly.

"I did tell him I would give you to him," Mr. Lancer continued. "But for me to lose such a valuable slave I need something in return. I need you to give me another slave. Now get your clothes off and lie down here with me so we can get started."

Krissy ran to the door and tried to open it. She shook it and hollered. "Help, get me out of here."

"Are you refusing an order from your master? Stop that hollering and obey me at once or it will be a public whipping for you." Mr. Lancer remembered how this threat from his daughter had worked on Sheila and expected a similar response, but Krissy screamed even louder. Mr. Lancer grabbed her, putting his hand over her mouth to silence her and dragged her to his bed. Then suddenly he released her and, clutching his chest, he fell limp. Krissy ran back to the door and yelled for help. She suddenly realized her master was no longer trying to prevent her and saw his body clumped motionless on the bed. Her first thought was that he died, but this thought only served as an opportunity to take out her anger. She went at him and punched him in the chest as hard and fast as her cotton picking callused hands would go.

Suddenly she heard Ruthie and Sheila at the door. "What's wrong Krissy?" Ruthie shouted. "Why is the door locked.

"I think the old man is dead." Krissy answered. "He was trying to rape me and he collapsed."

"I'll go get the spare key in the kitchen." Ruthie run to the kitchen and rummaged for the key, but there was no key to be found. Obviously her father had taken that with him to assure privacy. Just then Willy was coming in. "Quick, go and break down father's door." Ruthie shouted.

Willy hesitated to be sure he heard properly.

"Hurry. Father has locked himself inside and may be dying."

As Willy ran to the door, Ruthie found paper and pencil and quickly scribbled, "Willy to get Doctor, Father collapsed. Ruthie Lancer." She heard the door give way and ran back to the room. She handed Willy the note. "Here's your pass. Go get Doc as quick as you can."

Willy could saddle a horse faster than anyone on the plantation, but he was also good at riding bareback, so he unhitched the reins of the first horse he came to and sped off to the doctor's house.

Ruthie ran to her father. Being aware of what he was trying to do she thought it would serve him right if he died, yet it was her father and she would attempt to save him. She shook her father and he moaned, "Oh, Jeanette, I was trying to get to you, but you were so far away. The more I ran towards you, the further away you got. I'm so glad you found me Jeanette. I thought I had lost you forever."

"Father, this is Ruthie. Mother is dead. Father, do you understand me."

"Ruthie, Ruthie. Am I still alive? I thought I had died and gone to Hell. I saw your mother in Heaven but I couldn't get to her. Is it too late Ruthie? You said you found God. Can you find Him for me?"

Mr. Lancer appeared quite delusional. He would alternate between talking to his dead wife and Ruthie while complaining of a severe chest pain. Ruthie helped him to lay on his side and, within an hour, Willy was back with the doctor.

Doc Smyth recognized immediately what had happened and put some medicine in a syringe then injected his patient. "That should help him to rest. I would take him to the hospital but I don't think it is advisable to move him now. I will stay here until my nurse arrives. He must be closely watched for a while."

The Alternative

"What was it Doc?" Ruthie asked.

"He had a severe heart attack. He would have died if someone hadn't given him chest compressions. Now they left a bit of bruising and I can teach a better way to do it. Do you know who it was that saved his life?"

"He was locked in the room with Krissy. She must have done it." Ruthie was puzzled.

"Isn't Krissy a slave?" Doc asked. "How would she know about chest compressions? Well, anyway, she must have saved his life"

If anyone was going to save Mr. Lancer's life, Krissy was a very unlikely candidate. Ruthie could not think of anyone who would be more likely to want her father dead. Now where was Krissy? In all the excitement she had slipped away. Seeing that her father was resting and the doctor was watching him she went to find her friend.

Ruthie found Krissy near the slave quarters clinging to her daughter who was asleep on her lap. She was crying bitterly. When she saw Ruthie approach she cried out, "Oh! Please Miss Ruthie. I didn't mean to kill him. I was just so angry. Please have mercy on me. You know what he did to me."

"Father's not dead." Ruthie said calmly.

Krissy was relieved but now feared being punished for hitting her master. If he remembered, it could be very bad for her. A slave who would strike a master was often put to death.

"Did you punch father in the chest?"

Krissy was alarmed. How did Ruthie know. She thought of lying in an attempt to save her life, but she believed in God and a worse punishment than death if she lied.

"Y..y..yes Miss Ruthie. Please look after Ella for me when I'm gone. Please; she's just an innocent babe."

"I don't think you will be going anyplace soon, unless you want to go and be with Bobby. You can have anything you want and take Ella with you if you want. You saved my father's life and I will be forever grateful to you."

"But Miss Ruthie. I was so angry with him I wanted him dead."

"It's okay Krissy. God works in mysterious ways. You wanting him dead is what saved his life. Doc says if he hadn't got the chest compressions when he did, he would have died. You saved his live."

Krissy was confused. A few seconds ago she thought she had killed her master and was considering her own life as a price to be paid to rid the world of such a low life. Now she was facing the news that her actions had saved his life and she did not know how she should feel about that. This evil man was her best friend's father, but surely the world would be a better place without the likes of him. She sat, hugging her daughter and crying bitterly. What if the same thing should happen to Ella. She would have gladly given her life to prevent it, but now she was being called a hero for saving the life of one who would hurt such a child. None of this made any sense. Ruthie said a silent prayer and knew just what to do. She sat down beside Krissy and but her arm around her. "I know what you're feeling," she said. "When I found out what he had done to you five years ago, I wanted to kill him myself. Tonight, when I found out what he tried to do, I was hoping he had died. But I think something has changed. The doc says he is not out of danger and still might die, but he would already be dead if you hadn't saved him. When they ask you why you did it just say the Lord made you do it. That is what I believe happened. You don't need to say anything about your anger."

An Unintentional Hero

Ruthie's faith was being tested. Her father's behaviour and her father's health were both weighing heavy on her. In the past she would have been devastated but now she seemed to be experiencing a kind of serenity. Her father may die, and perhaps the world would be better off if he did. His aggression toward Krissy was completely inappropriate and showed that he had not changed his ways. The doctor was watching her father and there was little she could do while he rested. She decided to put everything in God's hands as she retired for the night. She prayed, but considering the circumstances, she could not bring herself to pray for her father's recovery. God knew best, so she simply asked God to do His Will and help her to accept the outcome.

The day's events had been overwhelming. They were erased from her mind as she fell into a restful sleep, but in her dreams she would again have to deal with chaos. She was trapped in a castle surrounded by dragons. A knight on a white horse was trying to rescue her. She saw the knight was not wearing any armour and she yelled out to him, "where is your armour?" He picked up a book and started to read. As he did he advanced toward her. Whenever a dragon got in his way he would read something out loud and the dragon would become a little worm and slither away. When he got to her she saw the book he was reading was the Bible. When he lowered the book to reveal his face she saw it was Bobby. He pulled her up behind him on his horse and they rode away leaving the horrible castle behind. "When we return the dragons will no longer have any power over this place." Ruthie heard a voice and it seemed to be coming from Bobby.

Ruthie woke up. Surely this dream must mean her chaotic life was about to change. She went to check on her father. The doctor was struggling to stay awake.

"Ruthie, it's good that you have come. It seems your father is out of danger, but we just need to be sure. Could you watch him while I take a nap? I can barely stay awake."

"Of course I will Doc Smyth. What should I be watching for?"

"If he stops breathing or if he wakes up then let me know right away. So long as he is resting comfortably we can't do anymore. I believe he will pull through okay, but his heart is weakened and he must not get stressed."

Ruthie took over the watch. She wished she had a Bible to read. That was something she needed to acquire. She prayed the best she could. She thanked God for healing her father and prayed that he had learned something from his experience. She kept up her prayer vigil until the early morning sun began to peep through the windows. The shutters were still closed in her father's room. She heard Sheila working in the kitchen and Willy talking in a low voice. She tip toed to the kitchen and asked Willy to quietly open the shutters to let in some light. She went back to her father's room and adjusted the curtains so the light would not be overwhelming. When she got back to her father's side she found he had awakened.

"Are you alright Father?"

"I think so, but I have so much pain in my chest."

"I'll get the doctor. He said I should call him."

"Ruthie! What happened?"

"You had a heart attack. I'll get the doc."

Doc Smyth had just awakened and met Ruthie outside her father's door. "How are you feeling this morning Mr. Lancer?" he asked when he found his patient awake.

"My chest; my chest really hurts."

"That's not surprising. You had a massive heart attack. It appears your heart had stopped for a few moments, but one of your slaves revived you or you would have been dead before I arrived. Now let's have a look."

The doctor examined his patients chest and placed his stethoscope in various positions. Mr. Lancer moaned as the instrument came in contact with certain areas of his chest. "Your heart is doing nicely, but that slave needs to learn how to do proper chest compressions. I'm afraid she caused quite a bit of bruising. That's going to hurt for a while but if she hadn't acted, you would be dead."

The sound of horse hooves was heard outside and soon Sheila ushered in a robust woman in a uniform. She had a large doll with her.

"Nurse Mackenzie," Doc Smyth greeted her. "I'm glad you could make it. And I see you brought Tommy," he was indicating the doll. "Nurse Mackenzie will stay with Mr. Lancer today. She and Tommy are going to show you how to do proper chest compressions. Fred's heart is not strong and if it stops again someone will have to get it going. I want someone who knows how to do the compressions with him at all times for the next week or so. Someone must watch him at least through the next few nights. Later he should be okay but someone must be close by and be with him while he is awake."

"Now, Mr. Lancer," the doctor turned his attention to his patient. "I will give you something to help with the pain but I'm afraid it will make you sleep. You will be doing a lot of sleeping for the next few days." The doctor injected some medicine into his arm and within moments Mr. Lancer fell asleep.

"When he wakes up he will be hungry. I have a list here of what he can eat and foods he needs to avoid. Please be sure to have a proper meal ready for him. You may want to go over the list to be sure you have everything on hand." Doc Smyth addressed Ruthie and the slaves who were present. Ruthie took the list. Although Sheila could read a little she would have to go over the list with her.

Krissy, having received no instructions to the contrary, went to the fields as normal at the break of day. She again was becoming a subject of gossip and she took steps to curb it before it got out of hand. As they were using Samson's system there were no overseers watching them and they knew that, so long as they kept up with the work, an overseer would not be required to drive them with a whip, so they were very conscientious about getting everything done on schedule. If anyone was not doing his or her share of the work, he or she was reminded of the alternative. Another benefit of not having an overseer is that they could relax once the work was done. Thus the work was performed better and faster than when they worked under the eye of an overseer.

If anything was troubling anyone they had been encouraged to talk about it before a small problem got bigger. Krissy was aware that gossip and rumors provoked by the events of the previous evening would affect productivity, so she called a meeting. Some were hesitant to join as they still hadn't gotten used to the idea that no one would whip them for not going immediately to work, but most gathered around Krissy to hear what she had to say.

"Many of you may have already heard that Massa had a heart attack last night and you will probably hear that I saved his life. That is the official story and when you are around them," she glanced in the direction of the big house, "that is all anyone should say, but I don't want you to be angry with me so I will tell you what really happened."

"You all know Bobby that picked me up for church last week." There was laughter as they remembered her getting on the horse behind him. "Well he approached Massa to buy me and that is why I was called to the big house yesterday. For some reason, I don't know why, Massa decided he would give me to Bobby, but he wanted me to produce another slave to replace myself. I don't have to explain what that means. Well, the short of it is that his heart could not handle it and it stopped beating. Now I don't want any of you to think I revived him out of the goodness of my heart. I was furious and I wanted to make sure he was dead, so I began punching him as hard as I could. It seems my punches got his heart going again so I apologize to all of you, but it seems I unintentionally saved Massa's life. Ruthie knows the truth but if anyone else hears it you know you will find me hanging from a tree, so not a word about it to anyone. I hope this stops the gossip and you won't be too mad at me."

Someone said, "Krissy, we know if anyone had a reason to want Massa dead, well you had more reason than any of us." With that everyone turned to the work they had for that day. Throughout the day many would express their sympathies to Krissy. They knew all too well the habits of their master. "Maybe he won't live much longer," would be added to their sympathies as a word of encouragement.

Later that day, Krissy was again called to the big house where Nurse Mackenzie would greet her as a hero and show her the proper way to do chest compressions.

That's Great, I'm Not in Love With You Either

While Bobby was praying in his room late that Tuesday afternoon, Mr. Lancer was attempting to rape Krissy. Of course, since Krissy was his slave, in the eyes of the law he had committed no crime. When Bobby slept that night and dreamt that Ruthie was a damsel in distress, Ruthie was dreaming that Bobby was her valiant knight. As Bobby and Samson talked about ending slavery and Bobby's dilemma, Ruthie was nursing her father back to health and Krissy was explaining how she had saved her master's life. If Bobby and Samson had realized the turmoil that their friends were going through, they would not have thought Bobby's relationship problems were worth discussing, but they didn't know. Bobby decided to help out with the field work for the rest of that week. Uncle Robert stopped by on Thursday evening and brought the news that Mr. Lancer had suffered a heart attack but was recovering. Bobby wanted to run to Ruthie to offer comfort, but he knew she did not want to see him, so he continued to pass his time by working in the fields until Sunday August twenty-ninth arrived. He asked Waldo to ready the carriage early that morning. As soon as he finished breakfast Waldo drove him to the Lancer

Accidentally Saving a Life

plantation were they picked up Krissy in style.

When they arrived, Ruthie and Krissy were sitting on a log in the yard having a best friend conversation. Since Krissy had saved her father, Ruthie began feeling even closer to her and her attitude that Krissy was of a lower class had vanished. They were now friends on equal terms. As Bobby held the door for Krissy, Ruthie said, "It's nice to see you Bobby."

"Likewise," Bobby replied. His heart began beating hard as he thought, "She spoke to me!" Remembering her father he asked, "How is Mr. Lancer? I heard he had a heart attack."

"He's doing quite well thanks to Krissy. But don't let me hold you up. I'm sure Krissy will fill you in on your way."

Ruthie stood and watched as her valiant knight rode off with her best friend.

Bobby found himself in an awkward position. Ruthie had talked to him and he started thinking of the possibilities of getting back together with her, but he was now in a carriage riding with Krissy and he did not know what she expected.

"Hello dreamer, real world calling." Krissy brought Bobby out of his daydream.

"Oh, sorry, I was just thinking," Bobby explained. "What did she mean by thanks to you."

"Well I kinda saved my masters life."

"Kinda? How do you kinda save someone."

Krissy was on the verge of crying and she fought back tears as she remembered that awful day. "It was a horrible experience and I don't want to talk about it. You've never been a slave so you wouldn't understand," Krissy stated and then added, "There is one thing I don't understand though, and maybe you could shed some light on it."

"What's that?"

"Why would Mr. Lancer want to give me to you?"

Bobby blushed as he tried to think of the best way to break

this to Krissy. "Well I don't really understand it either but somehow Mr. Lancer got it in his head that I am going to marry his daughter."

"Oh!"

"And you were supposed to be his wedding present to me." Bobby was panicking. "Now please understand, I think the whole idea is absurd. I was going to talk to you about it today. I don't know what I should do."

"So you agreed to this arrangement?"

"No. He didn't give me any say in it. He just assumed I was going to marry Ruthie and accused me of wanting a little on the side." Bobby was quick to add, "This is so far from the truth. I never have heard of such a thing before. I do want you to have your freedom but it is all so confusing."

"Do you want to marry Ruthie?"

Now Bobby went silent. He was put on the spot. He didn't want to hurt Krissy but he knew he couldn't lie. Finally he said, "Ruthie doesn't want anything to do with me, but that brings up another thing I want to talk to you about. I really like you, Krissy, as a friend and I would very much like to remain friends with you, but I don't think I am in love with you."

There has been talk of a silence so thick you could cut it with a knife. The two young people sitting in that carriage as it bumped along the rocky road that Sunday morning shared a silence that would require a machete. As they sat, they studied each other, each awaiting a reaction from the other. Finally Krissy broke the silence.

"That is only because you don't know me yet," she smiled pleasantly and Bobby began to wonder if he could ever get Ruthie off his mind and accept Krissy as a life partner. "If you really knew me," Krissy continued, "you wouldn't even want me for a friend."

Bobby suddenly looked at Krissy with surprise. Krissy was laughing as though she was telling a big joke. Krissy saw his puzzled look and continued. "I have done both you and Samson a big wrong. I didn't realize it at the time but I think I was coming on to you just to try to make Samson notice me. Now don't get me wrong Bobby, I really like you as a friend and you would make a great second choice, but last week when we were showing the congregation we were still friends with Samson, well I really enjoyed the time I spent talking to the people with him. I started to understand what he was doing and why he did it. I was upset because he wasn't spending time with me, but I realised I could really enjoy spending time with him. Bobby, I am so happy that we are just friends and I will always cherish you in my heart."

"Wow!" Bobby exclaimed. "I didn't see that coming. I was so worried about hurting you Krissy. Whatever happens I will always remember you and pray for you."

"Bobby, you can never know what hurt is until you've lived the life of a slave. You are very special to me and you are the first white man that ever considered how I felt, so I know the Lord will bless you for that."

"Thank you Krissy. You are so kind." Both of them suddenly grabbed each other and they shared a hug so intimate that they put the greatest of lovers to shame. However it was a hug between friends much as a brother and sister might share during a time of great joy.

Bobby's face suddenly became sad. "I don't know why I can't get Ruthie off my mind. She has shown me that she wants absolutely nothing to do with me. I don't know what I did to turn her against me."

"You did nothing wrong Bobby. The funny thing is that my attempt to get a jealous reaction from Samson totally backfired. He did not seem to even notice. But Ruthie! That's another story. She noticed. I see a change in her. Seeing us together has triggered something in her and I think she is ready to give you another chance." Suddenly Krissy had a brilliant idea. "Bobby!

Do you have an extra Bible?"

"Yes, I always have a few extras."

"Bring one with you when you take me home. Ruthie told me she wants one."

"That's great. I will give you one to take to her."

"No, I think you should give it to her yourself."

"Hmmm. Mr. Lancer said I should bring a big bouquet of flowers."

"First see if she will take the Bible from you. Next time you can take flowers."

They were just arriving at the Johnson plantation where everyone was getting ready for the outdoor church service. The guests were beginning to arrive on foot, horseback or wagon and Waldo pulled into the receiving line to drop off his two special passengers.

"Hi, Bobby. Do you want to do the message today?" Samson greeted his friend with a question.

"Why not. You did it last week. I will do it today." Bobby found a quiet place to sit down with his Bible and reflect on what he would say. Krissy remained with Samson greeting the people as they arrived.

While the guests were arriving the singing had already started. One person would start a hymn and soon everybody else would join in. Then another would start one of his or her favorites. As they sang they gathered on the logs, tree stumps, inverted buckets and whatever else was provided for seating and when those seats were taken others would sit on the little hill that rose from the stage area. A few chairs were placed at the front for the benefit of those taking part in the service. Anyone who was able to read, even if on a very rudimentary level, was given a turn on various Sundays to read a verse from the Bible, a task that was taken on with a great deal of pride. Those who could not read would often memorize a verse they had heard someone speak and would be overjoyed if they were chosen to recite it. Many mistakes would be made but no one seemed to care. The pure hearted love and beaming joy with which it was said well made up for any deficiency in accuracy.

No one could really pinpoint when the service would officially start. The singing of small groups migrated towards the central area and those groups would join together until all were united in song. Prayers and bible verses would be interspersed with the singing, then Bobby or Samson would have an opening prayer. More singing and the official gospel reading, another song and then the message. This was the general format, but many variations of the order were possible and some aspects were often repeated. This Sunday, Bobby started his message with the gospel reading. He read from the fifteenth chapter of the gospel of John.

"This is my commandment, That ye love one another, as I have loved you. Greater love hath no man than this, that a man lay down his life for his friends. Ye are my friends, if ye do whatsoever I command you. Henceforth I call you not servants; for the servant knoweth not what his lord doeth: but I have called you friends; for all things that I have heard of my Father I have made known unto you."

After this reading he began, "Today I will talk to you about friends. Many of you know that Samson and I grew up on this very plantation as best friends. There was a problem with our friendship. Samson was my father's slave and I was his master's son. Whenever Samson would do something for me I could never be sure if he was doing it because he wanted to as a friend or because he had to as a slave.

"We are all servants of God and there is horrible punishment if we are not obedient to his will, but we have a choice. We can obey Him because we love Him and want to please Him as a friend, or we can obey Him out of fear of punishment and serve him as a slave.

"Now I must tell you that I think slavery is wrong. I was facing a dilemma. One day my father will retire and I will inherit this plantation. No one has ever run a cotton plantation in Louisiana without slaves. I was not sure it could be done but I felt it was God's will and therefore He would make a way. Still, I wasn't sure. Perhaps I was making a big mistake. Maybe the southern churches were right and I was in error. However, I was determined that I would seek God's way and do His will.

"Now I know many of you are familiar with my best friend Samson. You must be thinking now, 'what a dunce'. You are aware of Samson's plan. You would think his best friend would know what he was doing. Well, I didn't know. While I was trying to figure out how to run one plantation without slaves, Samson was coming up with a plan to end slavery throughout the south. I have to tell you, my best friend is a genius and I believe he can do it. With the Lord's help we all can do it.

"All of you are my friends. I don't want the hue of our skin to place any difference between us. God does not see our skin but he knows our hearts. Those whose heart is purest rank the highest in the eyes of God. I see before me many pure hearts and for this reason most of you rank above those you are forced to call master on this earth."

As Bobby spoke his parents were listening from the back rows. Mr. Johnson was concerned that these words may lead to an uprising, but Bobby seemed convinced that slavery would end.

"It seems that Bobby has it all figured out," Mrs. Johnson said to her husband.

Chapter Eight
Pre-Approved

Ruthie spent Sunday August 29th, 1824 with her father. He was regaining some strength and was able to sit out on the porch for a short time. His near death experience frightened him and he wanted to make some changes.

"Ruthie, I died and went to Hell the other day. I don't ever want to go back there again. Do you think there is any hope for me?"

"The Bible says God will forgive us if we ask."

"But I really messed up. I never gave a thought to anyone else and I just did whatever I wanted. I don't know if the Lord can forgive me?"

"I'll see if Bobby will come to see you. He knows about those things."

"That little heathen? What could he know?"

"Bobby knows a lot about the Lord."

"Then why was he lookin' to buy Krissy?"

"I thought Krissy was your idea."

"Well I kinda lied to ya."

"I knew Bobby came for Krissy. They've been seeing each other. They probably want to get married."

"I thought Bobby was going to marry you."

"We have no plans."

"You think he'd marry a black girl. Ain't no sense in that. If ya own her you can do whatever you want."

"Bobby's not like that. He'd want to be married first. He wants to do things the Lord's way."

"I know a preacher that has a little on the side with his slaves. Some of the young ones are the splittin' image of that Bible thumper."

"That may be, but Bobby's not like that." Ruthie grew weary of trying to explain. "I will see Bobby when he drops Krissy off and ask him to speak to you. I need to take a little stretch. Will you be alright for a while?"

"If you can help me back to my bed, I will be fine."

Ruthie got her father settled in bed and took a stroll around the plantation. Many summer flowers were blooming and there was fruit on the trees, to which she treated herself as she walked. As the afternoon wore on she watched for the Johnson's carriage to arrive. Her father had given her a reason to speak to Bobby and surely Krissy would not object to her making such a request.

Finally the carriage was in sight and Ruthie moved at a leisurely pace to where she knew Krissy would be dropped off. She didn't want to appear too anxious, but she also did not want to miss Bobby.

Bobby saw Ruthie coming towards the carriage and went to meet her. Krissy slipped away to her quarters.

"Hi, Bobby, where is Krissy?" Ruthie asked.

"I think she went to her quarters," Bobby replied. "She told me you wanted a Bible."

"Yes. God has been dealing with me and I am now a believer. I want to read His word."

"I'm glad to hear that." Bobby presented Ruthie with a deluxe version of the Bible. It was the nicest edition he owned and he was saving it for a special occasion. He could not think of an occasion more special than the present one.

Ruthie accepted the Heavenly Book and looked it over. "This is really nice. It must have been very expensive. I will take very good care of it and return it to you when I have finished reading it."

"This is now your Bible. I am giving it to you to keep. Once you start reading it you won't want to stop and there will be passages you want to read over many times."

"Thank you so much, Bobby, I will treasure it always." Ruthie fought off an urge to give Bobby a hug. Instead she just took his hand as she thanked him, then she recalled the reason she had wanted to see Bobby. "I was wondering if you would do me a big favour."

"I'd be glad to." Bobby smiled and accepted without finding out what the favour was. He was sure he would be delighted to do anything Ruthie would ask.

"Ever since the heart attack, Father has been afraid and asking about God. I told him you knew about those things and I would ask you to speak to him."

"I would be very happy to talk to your father. Is now a good time or would you like me to come back."

"Father has been resting. I think he will be rested enough to see you now. Why don't you go up to the house. Sheila will show you were he is. I want to go and see Krissy." Ruthie was puzzled by Bobby's friendliness and wanted to find out what was happening between him and Krissy. Why had Krissy left Bobby alone with her? Perhaps they had an argument on the way home. Ruthie had to find out.

When Ruthie entered the slave quarters, Krissy was excitedly telling the other slaves about the church service and other events of the day. When she saw Ruthie enter she immediately turned her attention to her friend and smiled as she said, "Hello Ruthie. It is good to see you."

"Hi, Krissy. Can we talk?" The two young ladies stepped

Pre-Approved

outside. "Krissy! What is happening between you and Bobby. Did you guys have a fight or something."

"No! Everything is great between us, in fact it couldn't be better."

"Oh?"

"Ya. We had a talk this morning and we found out we are not in love with each other. Bobby is a really great guy and I like him much more as a friend than as a lover. Fact is he wasn't much good as a boyfriend."

"Why's that?"

"Well, he's got this old flame he can't quite get over. He could never commit himself to anyone else."

"Oh, I wonder who that lucky girl is."

"Duh! Ruthie. Bobby's in love with you. All you need to do is look at him and you can tell. When you said 'hi' to him this morning he went all crazy. Anyone can tell that he loves you."

"You really think so, after the way I treated him. Do you think he still loves me."

"I know he loves you. And I love Samson. That's what we found out when we talked and I have never been happier in my life."

"I thought Samson was ignoring you."

"That's what I thought but the truth is that I was ignoring Samson. He is really busy doing a lot of good things. I spent the whole day with him today. I stayed with him when we talked to the people after the service and sometimes when the men were talking to him, their wives would talk to me. It was so much fun. Samson is like a preacher and I started to feel like a preacher's wife. I know that's what I will be one day. I really like it." Krissy chatted excitedly.

"It sounds like you had a really good time." Ruthie thought about the ordeal her friend had been through the week before and was truly glad for Krissy's present happiness.

"I really did. And I know you can be just as happy if you give Bobby another chance."

"Bobby's been on my mind a lot lately. I think I will talk to him. I have just become a believer in the Lord and I need his help to figure some things out. And one other thing Krissy..."

"What's that?"

"I need to apologize for the way I have treated you in the past."

"Why, you have always been kind to me."

"Yes, I was kind to you as one is kind to a dog. I have never treated you as an equal."

"I'm used to that. I know my place. It is still good that you have been so kind."

"But it's not right. God created us all as equals. It was not right that I treated you as my slave friend. Slavery is not right. From now on I want you as my true friend. I want to do things for you instead of you always doing what I want. First thing I am going to do is to be sure you get your freedom papers. If father won't sign them I will run you up north myself."

Krissy was stunned. Freedom was something every slave dreamt of, but it was always a dream. For such a dream to come true, it seemed like she was living in a fantasy world. She thought of pinching herself but instead she said, "If this is a dream I don't want to wake up."

"It's no dream, Krissy. From now on I want to be your true friend; if you will have me. I don't deserve your friendship after the way I treated you. If I ask you to do something you don't want to do I want you to tell me."

"What about Ella?"

"Do you think I would forget my little sister? Wherever I go she will go, and I will never allow her to be separated from you."

"Thank you so much, Ruthie. You don't know how much of

a relief it is to hear you say that." One of the greatest cruelties of slavery was how the masters would rip children from their mothers without giving it a thought. It was not unusual for a mother to watch her children be auctioned off to a new master, to be shipped to parts unknown, and to never have any contact with them again. "There is one thing I want you to do right now," Krissy added.

"Anything you want my best friend."

"Get to that house and see Bobby before he gets away on you." They both laughed as Ruthie started for the house.

Inside the house, Bobby and Mr. Lancer were having quite a discussion. Bobby assured Mr. Lancer that God would forgive even the worst of sinners and Mr. Lancer assured Bobby that he felt there were no worse sinners than himself. Then Mr. Lancer asked Bobby to forgive him for misjudging him. "I only knew of one reason someone would want to buy a pretty young slave so I thought that's what you wanted her for. But I am still a little confused. If you didn't want her for sex, what did you want her for?"

Bobby replied. "She became my friend and I wanted her to be free."

"You mean you got niggers for friends?"

"Yes I have many black friends. You have already met my best friend, Samson."

"I had heard that Samson was a little sweet on Krissy. So you wanted her to be free for your friend then?"

"No, I just wanted her to be free so she could chose for herself who she wanted to be with."

"So you think them niggers are like regular people."

"I believe God created us all equal and it is wrong to force black people to be slaves. It is also not nice to call them niggers."

"Well Bobby, you have certainly enlightened me. A week

The Alternative

ago I would have called you a lying heathen but with what I've seen this past week I am inclined to agree with you. I just thought of Krissy as an animal I could use for my own pleasure but she turned around and saved my life. I don't quite know how to figure that. It seems she is much more human than me. And you say you want her to be free so she will be free. It seems I should free all my slaves but I'll have to think on that. Don't know how I'd run this plantation without slaves. I'll have Krissy's papers drawn up tomorrow. She can go wherever she wants and she can take her little one with her. She saved my life. It's the least I can do."

"Mr. Lancer," Bobby was beaming. "There is a way to run a plantation without slaves. I don't quite know what it is, but I know someone who has it all figured out. I will have my best friend, Samson, stop by and see you next week. He can explain it all to you."

"You come along with him and don't forget to bring those flowers for my daughter. I don't have much time left and I want to see the wedding before I die."

Just then Ruthie walked in. "What's this I hear about flowers, weddings and dying? What are you guys talking about?"

"Ruthie! Dear! You know I won't be around much longer and you will need a husband to run the plantation. Even if you could run it, you know they won't let a woman own land, so you would need someone to hold the title for you. Now, when Bobby proposes you don't have to come and ask me. I've already pre-approved him so you can accept right away."

"Father! Such talk! You're embarrassing me and Bobby. Let him decide for himself. He's a grown man and doesn't need anyone pushing him into something he may regret. Now stop this talk immediately." Ruthie then turned to Bobby and said, "Roses would be nice."

Bobby didn't know how to take this. If not for his past

experience he would have proposed on the spot. Now he realized he needed to spend some time with Ruthie first. All this was happening much too fast and he needed time to think before making important decisions. He said, "Waldo will be wondering what's become of me. Plus I'd like to be home before it gets dark, so it is best I be on my way." As Bobby headed for the door, Mr. Lancer motioned with his hand that Ruthie should follow. Waldo had brought the carriage to the front of the house. As Bobby was about to get in, Ruthie grabbed his hand and pulled him back to her. She hugged him tightly and kissed him briefly. "Come back real soon and don't forget the roses. I am real sorry about how I treated you. We will talk when you come back." Then she released him and turned him to the carriage. Bobby turned again and tried to say something although he was not sure what he should say but Ruthie simply put a finger to Bobby's lips indicating that no words were necessary. Bobby climbed into the carriage and was surprised when Ruthie followed him in. She planted a big kiss on his lips, jumped back out of the carriage and ran into the house, slamming the door behind her. As Bobby rode away he could see Ruthie watching him from a window.

Bouquet of Roses and Freedom Papers

Bobby's head was spinning. Things were happening much too fast. He could not quite figure Ruthie. He had fallen in love with her and he felt that God had chosen her for him, but then her father had driven him away and he lost contact. He had just about put her out of his mind when she suddenly appeared at the church service on his father's plantation. After having a dream he felt God's guidance to ask Ruthie's father for permission to see her. Permission was granted, but then Ruthie wanted nothing to do with him. Now she obviously wanted him back, but what would happen next? At the moment, it didn't seem to matter. The woman he loved wanted to see him and that was enough.

The Alternative

Bobby was so lost in thought that he was oblivious to the bumpy ride and the sound of the horses as Waldo drove the carriage home. When Waldo stopped the carriage at Bobby's front door he didn't move until Waldo got his attention and informed him he was home. Bobby walked in a stupor to his room and began to read his Bible but found himself staring blankly at the page as he was lost in thought remembering the day's events and dreaming of his next meeting with Ruthie.

When Mauve called Bobby to supper he had recovered somewhat but he still appeared as if he was on another planet. He made his way to the table and sat without saying a word. He simply nodded in response to his parent's greetings.

"Is something wrong Bobby?" Mr. Johnson asked, but the question was only met by a blank stare.

Mrs. Johnson recognized the symptoms at once and said, "Oh no! He's in love again."

"Is that it Bobby?" Mr. Johnson inquired.

Mrs. Johnson was more concerned. "Now Bobby. Don't be getting too carried away. You know how hard you took it when Ruthie dumped you. Krissy might do the same. She may be using you to gain her freedom and once she gets it she will be long gone."

"No, Mom. It is Ruthie." Bobby managed to squeeze out a few words.

"What do you mean?" Sara Johnson voiced the question that both Bobby's parents were thinking.

"She wants me back. Ruthie wants me back," he repeated to be sure he had actually said these words.

"I thought she wanted nothing to do with you," Mr. Johnson interjected.

"Me too," Bobby was afraid he had been caught in a dream. "But either I'm having a very crazy dream or she wants me back."

Pre-Approved

"How can you be so sure. Maybe she is just trying to be more friendly." Bobby's mom voiced this concern.

"No, she told me she wants to see me again and she says to bring roses."

"That sounds serious enough," Mr. Johnson surmised.

"Not only that. When Mr. Lancer suggested that I should soon propose to her she was not against the idea."

"Now that's rushing things a little." Bobby's dad was concerned.

"She dumped you before," Mrs. Johnson added. "You need to be sure she isn't going to change her mind again before you do anything rash."

"Don't worry, Mom. That's why I've been so lost in thought. I have learned to take things one step at a time and to put everything in the hands of God. But I will take her those roses and see where it goes from there."

As they ate their meal they continued to discuss the day Bobby had experienced and how he would go and see Ruthie when Samson went to see Mr. Lancer.

The next morning Bobby went to the field at the crack of dawn and joined the workers there. He found Samson and filled him in on the Sunday conversation with Mr. Lancer.

"That is fantastic!" Samson replied. "This is just the opportunity we need."

"Are you sure it will work?"

"It has to work. Don't you see, Bobby, this is the beginning of the end of slavery. Once your father sees how well the Lancer plantation does, he will be sure to free his slaves, then others will see our success and soon anyone with any economic sense will free their slaves. You and I will be travelling from one plantation to the next to tell them how to do it." Samson predicted the future he had been working towards.

"We will put it in God's hands. If this is His will, we will succeed."

"Do you think God would rather see slavery continue?"

"Of course not. I see what you mean. It is God's will and we must succeed."

That afternoon Bobby worked with the gardener to pick some roses. They were trimmed and arranged to make a large bouquet fit for a queen. Bobby had chosen roses from his parents' garden of the deepest red, the loveliest pink, and the purest white. They were placed in a large vase and Bobby placed the vase in a pail to catch the water that splashed out during the bumpy ride.

In the morning, Samson thought he and Bobby could ride on his wagon but when he saw the bouquet he agreed the carriage would be a better choice.

When they arrived at the Lancer plantation, Bobby carefully took the vase out of the pail and carried his bouquet to the door. Samson tapped on the door then moved back behind Bobby. When Ruthie opened the door all she could see was roses. The bearer of the roses and his companion were hid behind its blooms. Knowing that Bobby must be somewhere, she bid the rose bearer to enter and was completely delighted as she made a spot on a table in the foyer for Bobby to place the vase. "Sheila, Father, Willy. Come and see!" she exclaimed as she admired the bouquet.

Soon the admiring process had been fulfilled and it was time to get down to business. Samson was directed to the kitchen table where he sat down with Mr. Lancer. Ruthie directed Bobby to the parlour. They sat on the sofa and Ruthie immediately turned to Bobby and said.

"Bobby! I really need to apologize for all the time I was ignoring you. I was really upset that you would go to my father and ask to marry me without consulting me first."

"What? I just asked your father for permission to see you. I did that because God gave me a dream that I should do it. When

Pre-Approved

your father came to the store I thought I'd better do it while I had the chance, but I would never ask for permission to marry without your knowledge."

"Oh, Bobby, I knew there must be some explanation. Father got drunk that day and must have gotten things mixed up. But I was also worried about father knowing we were seeing each other. I know he gave permission, but father is so unpredictable. He can say one thing one minute and the next he turns completely around. I was afraid he would drive you away again like he did before. I suppose I thought if I refused to see you it would save both of us the embarrassment."

"Well I do know your father can be embarrassing."

"Yes. His comments on Sunday were something else."

"But you didn't seem to oppose his idea."

"No I didn't. I think father, for once, has the right idea. He just has a really weird way of expressing it."

"So you want me to propose?"

"Bobby!" Ruthie was shocked and embarrassed by this bold inquiry. "Not yet. We need some time to get reacquainted. But if everything goes well I won't be opposed to the idea."

"I am glad. I have put things in the Lord's hands and when He tells me the time is right....." Bobby's sentence drifted off as he didn't quite know how to finish it.

"Well let's get down to the business of getting reacquainted."

As they were talking, a messenger had come with some papers. Now they could hear Mr. Lancer's voice from the kitchen loudly saying, "Good, they are here." He called for Ruthie. She went to see what he wanted and came back with the papers in her hand.

"Come along, Bobby. Father asked me to deliver these and I think you will want to see this."

Ruthie took Bobby to the area were the small children were

being kept and got Ella to come with them as they headed to the field were Krissy was working. Bobby suspected that Ruthie had Krissy's freedom papers but he was curious. "What is it?" he asked.

"You will see soon enough. Now, just come along."

As soon as Krissy was in sight, Ella ran to her calling, "Mommy." Ruthie soon approached with a big smile. She handed Krissy one of the papers. Krissy, not knowing how to read, asked, "What is this?"

"That is a paper that says Ella will forever be free," Ruthie replied, then handing her the other paper she added, "And this is your freedom paper."

"What? So fast! Ruthie you are the best friend ever. You told me on Sunday you would do it and already you have the papers. Krissy wrapped her arms around Ruthie and hugged her tightly. Ella followed her mother's example.

"Now Krissy. I'm not the one responsible. While we were talking on Sunday, Bobby was talking to father. When I came in, father had already decided to set you free. He had the papers drawn up yesterday and they were just now delivered."

Krissy immediately let go of Ruthie and hugged Bobby. "Thank you so much Bobby," then realising what she was doing she added, "Oh! I'm sorry Ruthie."

"That's quite alright Krissy. Bobby is now my man and my best friend can hug my man anytime she wants to."

"It wasn't my doing," Bobby tried to explain. "Mr. Lancer decided quite on his own that he wanted to free you. He said it was the least he could do after you saved his life."

Krissy suddenly had a sullen look on her face and Bobby was surprised at the reaction. Ruthie explained.

"Bobby, Krissy didn't really intend to save father's live. In fact she had more reason to want him dead than most. But it was God who used her actions to save my father." Then she turned to Krissy, "Don't worry. Your secret is safe with Bobby." Back to Bobby. "If anyone knew that, Bobby, you know they would have her lynched." Again Ruthie addressed her best friend. "See, God made it all come out okay. You're free now and you can do what you want. Samson's at the house. You can come now and see him if you like." The four friends went jubilantly to the house.

A New Man

"Are you sure it will work?" Mr. Lancer was questioning Samson when the happy foursome entered. "Nobody in the south has ever run a plantation without slaves." He then turned his attention to those entering the room. "Krissy, it is good to see you. You know you will always have a place here. You have been one of our best workers. Of course you are free now and can go where you want, but you are welcome to stay and, if you go, you are welcome to come back any time." Mr. Lancer then pulled a handful of money from his pocket. "Here, take this. It is not near what I owe you but it will help you get settled if you should decide to leave."

"Now I have another announcement." Mr. Lancer was too excited to let anyone else say a word. "Krissy is the first but the Lancer plantation will not be using slave labour any more. Samson has explained to me how it will work and I will be doing the paperwork to free all the slaves under my control."

"Now, Mr. Lancer," Samson interjected, "There may be some bumps along the way, but I know God is on our side, so we will succeed."

"Please call me Fred." Mr. Lancer stated. "You, Samson, are the greatest gentleman and the smartest businessman I ever met." For one who had not considered "niggers" to be human, this was a startling confession. In the past, Mr. Lancer had been anything but predictable, but anyone who knew him could never have predicted he would pay such a compliment to a person of colour, but ever since his near death experience, Mr. Lancer had become a new man, different in every way from the horrid excuse for a human he had been. "Your experiment is in the hands of the God you have such faith in. I pray you will teach me that faith. I am certainly not deserving of any benefit, but for my daughter's sake, I hope I will have something to leave her and her husband when I depart from this earth. Now, Bobby, I see you brought the flowers. Please don't take too much time in taking the next step. I don't have much time left and I would like to see my daughter married."

Mr. Lancer was in a euphoric mood and his happiness had given him the most strength he had since his heart attack, but now he was becoming weak and needed help to get back to his bed. As he made his way he asked Bobby to call on the lawyer in town and ask him to come out to the plantation so that legal papers could be drawn up. Mr. Lancer was far too weak to make a trip into town.

Freedom had come to Krissy and her child so quickly that she was not sure what to do. She wanted to discuss her future plans with Samson. Bobby and Ruthie took Ella to the parlour to give them some privacy at the kitchen table.

"Samson, now that I am free, I suppose I need a job. Do you think the Johnson's would hire me?" Krissy asked her friend. "Mr. Lancer gave me this." She showed Samson the money. "I don't know how long that would keep Ella and me."

Samson counted the money. "Fifty dollars," he announced. "That would get you a place to stay and food for a few months. But it is dangerous out there. There are many that would rob you and steal your papers. You could find yourself sold back into slavery if you are not careful."

"What should I do? I can't read and I don't know how to count money. Where will I go?"

"Mr. Lancer said you are welcome to stay."

"I think I would rather go with you. You don't know what

that man has done to me."

"I can imagine, but it sure appears he has changed."

"I don't trust him."

"The Bible tells us we need to forgive."

"If you knew what he did to me you would not ask me to forgive him and you wouldn't forgive him either."

"Now Krissy. I have been a slave and I know what happens to young girls. I can see by your daughter's eyes who her father is. I know it is hard to forgive such behaviour, but the Bible says we must. Forgiveness isn't to help those who hurt us. We need to forgive so we can go on with our own lives."

"I was only thirteen when he did that to me and got me pregnant. But that's not all. You don't know what had happened the day he had the heart attack."

"I know you didn't intend to save his live." Samson whispered so no one else would hear. "I can only guess what must have happened. I know it must have been horrible for you. It is not safe to talk about it here, but you can talk to me about it if you want. You don't have to. I pretty well have figured out what happened. It happens to young slave girls all the time. That is why we must take steps to end slavery. Now, I can't force you to forgive Mr. Lancer and I won't blame you if you can't do it, but you must try for your own sake and for the sake of all the young girls that will suffer the same fate unless we do something about it. Mr. Lancer has given us an opportunity to show the south that a plantation can be profitable without slaves. We need to make that happen or it is all for nothing and what happened to you will continue to happen to others. God has given me the plan and I need you to help."

Krissy remained in silent thought for several moments, then she said, "Okay. What do you want me to do?"

"Stay here and continue to work as though nothing has changed. Don't say anything about being free until Mr. Lancer has the papers for everyone. I don't want to get their hopes up.

The Alternative

Mr. Lancer may not follow through on his promise," Samson cautioned Krissy. "Now I need to get home before dark. I will be coming back the day after tomorrow and will be spending some time here during the transition and probably stay through the harvest." They hugged and said goodbye.

Krissy suddenly remembered her money and the papers. "Here, Samson, keep these for me. I'll just keep one dollar and you keep the rest of the money and the freedom papers for me." Krissy took a bill out of the pile and handed the rest to Samson.

"That's a ten dollar bill. That one is worth quite a bit." Samson informed Krissy with a smile.

"Oh Samson. I can't figure this out. Take this one too."

Samson took the ten and extracted a one dollar bill from the stack. "Here is a one dollar bill. I will keep the rest safe for you. Just let me know when you need more."

They then went to the parlour. "Mommy's going back to work," Krissy told Ella. She gave Samson another hug and left. Bobby said his goodbyes to Ruthie and went with Samson to the carriage. Ruthie chose to spend the rest of the day with her now free little sister.

Chapter Nine

Becoming Free in Slave Territory

When Krissy got back to the field, the gossip was flying. Someone had seen the papers presented and overheard the words, "You are free."

"What are you doing back here?" Evangeline asked. "Ain't you free now?"

Rudy said, "If they freed me I'd be long gone by now. How come you's still here?"

"Samson wants me to stay," Krissy said politely. "Please don't treat me any different."

Just then Rose came on the scene. "So you thinks you's better'n us now. You throws yerself at a white boy an' he buys yer freedom."

Krissy realized that they thought Bobby was responsible, but things could be worse if they knew the truth. She also remembered Samson's warning not to say anything. She couldn't control what they thought so she just said, "Leave me alone, I got work to do."

Leave her alone they did. "Damn if I'll work with a free nigger," Rose said as she stomped off to work in another part of the field. The others echoed her sentiments and moved off leaving Krissy to work alone.

That night in the slave quarters things got even worse for Krissy. "Ain't you too good for us now. Why's you stayin' here?" one would shout as another exclaimed, "Ya Miss Uppity. You's white now. You's should stay in the big house."

Cassie was watching and suddenly felt the need to go to Krissy's aid. "Look you guys. Krissy's one of us. At least give her a chance to explain." Then she turned to Krissy. "Did they really give you your freedom papers?"

"There are some things in the works," Krissy replied, "but I'm not at liberty to talk about them now. You will all find out in a couple of days."

"Not at liberty," Rudy mocked. "Now you's even talkin' like 'em white bastards. You's may be black on the outside but you's as white as any on the inside."

"That's enough, Rudy." Cassie put a stop to his insults. "Krissy did nothing to harm you. You are just jealous." Then she looked at Krissy. "We are all jealous. Nothin' anyone wants more'n be'n free."

"Oh, Cassie, just be patient. You remember Samson talking about his plan. In a few days you will hear more."

"Suppose'n you's gonna set us free now. Well if you's gonna set us free I's just as soon be a slave." Rudy was indignant.

"You don't mean that Rudy," Cassie was quick to reprimand. "Samson did say if we stuck to his plan we'd all be free one day."

"He's just say'n that so we'd work without gettin' whipped."

"So I s'pose you prefer gettin' whipped."

"Naw, I jest went along wit' it so I won't git whipped, but we's never gonna be free." Rudy began to have second thoughts about badgering young Krissy, so he and the others backed down. Even if the system was a fake they certainly had a better life than before Samson came along. Now, no one was sure Krissy was really free. If she was, then why was she still here? Krissy wasn't telling them anything.

Rose approached. "Krissy. I'm sorry about the way I treated

you in the field. Cassie's right. We heard you's free and we's just jealous. If you go back to the field tomorrow I'll work with you."

The next day was Wednesday, and true to her word, Rose worked alongside Krissy all day. She was there when Ruthie came out to visit her friend. Ruthie urged Krissy to come out of the field and relax, but Krissy said, "There's a lot of work to be done. I'm needed here."

"Well if you won't come away, I'll just have to work with you. Show me what to do."

Rosie fetched a spare hoe for Ruthie. She and Krissy showed her the art of hoeing cotton. When Ruthie broke a branch on a cotton plant, Krissy joked, "You'll get twenty lashes for that."

"Really," said Ruthie. "Is that what they used to do to you guys?"

"Much worse than that." Rosie saw a chance to have a sympathetic ear. "We was always so nervous and always lookin' out for the overseer. We ended up makin' lots of mistakes. Hardly a day went by we didn't git whipped for somethin'. That's why we's happier now and we gits a lot more done in a shorter time." After a pause Rosie could no longer keep her curiosity in check. "Ruthie, 'is it true we's gonna be free."

"You will definitely be free some day. One day Bobby and I will take over and Bobby doesn't believe in owning slaves." Ruthie said slyly. "Be patient. Things may happen sooner than you think." Just then Ruthie broke another branch. "I better give up and leave this to you experts before I ruin the whole field." Ruthie put the hoe away and went back to the big house.

That day they were done their work early and headed back to the slave quarters with daylight to spare. The old system would never allow this, so there was no incentive to work quickly since none would be allowed to quit until it was too dark to see. In fact, if one accomplished too much, they would be expected to repeat it every day, so one soon learned to appear busy, especially when the overseer was watching, but only do enough to prevent being whipped.

As they made their way out of the field the news of Rosie's conversation with Ruthie spread like wildfire. The story was exaggerated with each telling and soon it was being repeated that they may be gaining their freedom that very night. They were joyous as they talked among themselves. What would they do when they got their freedom? Some said they would look for their children that had been sold away from them. Others talked of fathers and mothers they never knew. No one talked of staying to keep the plantation going.

When they headed back to the field on Thursday, September 2nd, 1824, it seemed their talk of freedom the night before had been a dream. Everyone was busy working when they saw Samson approach. Work was immediately stopped as they all rushed toward the one they were sure was coming with good news.

Samson, seeing that he had everyone's attention, spoke cautiously. He wasn't sure if Krissy may have let the news out prematurely or if the Lancer slaves may have gained the knowledge in some other way. "Since I have your attention I may as well tell you now that I'll be coming back to help with the harvest."

No one was interested in hearing about the harvest. "Is we gonna be free?" someone shouted, then everyone joined in. Samson raised his hands to quiet the crowd.

"There are no guarantees at the moment, but Mr. Lancer is working on some legal matters and there is a chance you will have your freedom papers before the harvest, however the harvest will still need to go ahead." Samson tried to calm the crowd. "Now this is very important. With freedom comes responsibility. You will still have to work to earn a living and there will be work for everyone right here. This is the work you know. If you go elsewhere...."

"I'm not stickin' around to give that mean old bastard any satisfaction," someone shouted cutting Samson off in mid sentence. Other's shouted similar sentiments until Samson attempted to regain control.

"If we want this to work we have to work together," Samson shouted over the noise of the crowd. He soon saw that this approach was useless. "I want the cooks to go and prepare a big feast." Samson yelled as loud as he could. Some heard the word "feast" and urged others to be quiet to hear what Samson was saying. Samson waited for the quiet. Soon there was a hush such that a pin dropping could have been heard.

Krissy came to stand by Samson's side. "I didn't tell them anything," she explained.

Samson turned to the crowd and spoke distinctly. "It is time to start the harvest. The weeds left in the field will do no harm at this point. Today we will take the rest of the day off to celebrate. However, there is one thing I need in return. I want to talk to everyone of you individually. If anyone has whiskey hidden away some place, keep it hidden. It is not a day to get drunk. We all have some serious decisions to make and I want you to have a clear head when I speak with you. Now, anyone who is going to cook or set up tables, go now. I will talk to you later. Everyone else can start to tidy up and put the tools away. You can start getting things ready for harvest while the cooking is being done. I will talk to as many as I can now. If you have family, I want to see the family together. Otherwise, one at a time." Samson picked out an elderly couple and took them aside. He told them that Mr. Lancer was looking into the possibility of setting them free. He did not ask for any commitment but he explained what freedom meant and the responsibilities that went with it. He explained his greater plan to bring freedom to all slaves in the south and how that plan required success on this plantation. He got through to some.

Some were indifferent and some argued that his plan would never work and that they would get as far away as they could if they were set free. Samson tried to appeal to the better circumstances they had enjoyed since the experiment began. Some asked about pay and when Samson suggested they may have to work for a period without pay until the system began to work properly, they objected saying they would still be slaves but they would be expected to be voluntary slaves. As the day wore on, Samson took the time to address any concerns and told them the south could be transformed if they would cooperate.

The feasting and relaxed atmosphere had a calming effect on some and they agreed that their best chance to maintain freedom was to stay and work. Others strongly opposed this idea. The majority were undecided. It would be Monday September sixth when Mr. Lancer would have the papers ready. By that time, most knew what they would do.

No Price Too High

Samson was having second thoughts. He had assumed the Johnson plantation would be the first free plantation, but a near death experience had changed Mr. Lancer to the point where a cruel slave master had decided to set his slaves free. Mr. Johnson had been a kind master and most of his slaves would stay under the same circumstances. Although Mr. Lancer's slaves were glad they would be free, they hadn't forgotten the cruel treatment of their master. They knew about his heart attack and many regarded his actions as an attempt to buy his way into Heaven. Most doubted that such an evil man could make it past the Pearly Gates. Many thought he should pay the price for what he had done and the torment of eternity in Hell was the price he needed to pay.

Samson spent much time in prayer, yet he was uneasy in this transition. If it failed it would appear as though a religious fanatic had taken advantage of a dying man. He needed time.

With the cotton harvest starting it was not the right time to make major changes. If a significant number of slaves left there would not be enough help to get the job done. Even if workers could be hired to take the place of those who left, they may be unwilling to work with the free blacks that remained. He went to Mr. Lancer to suggest an alteration of the plan.

"Fred, I think it may be best if you wait until after the harvest to give out the freedom papers."

"Well, Samson, I don't know if the Lord will give me that much time. You said He would make everything work out."

"But I fear many will leave when they get their freedom papers."

"If that happens we will have to deal with it. The cotton harvest will do me no good if I'm in Hell."

"But you could end up losing the plantation."

"Where I'm going I don't need a plantation? Although I would like to pass it down to Ruthie and Bobby, they will do fine without it. Mr. Johnson has a bigger plantation that Bobby will inherit one day. You told me this is God's will. If the plantation is the price I have to pay to do God's will then that is what I'll pay. I have been a very sinful man and I am very grateful for the Lord's forgiveness. There is no price I wouldn't pay."

Sometimes the faith of a new believer can be stronger than even the most faithful long time believer. Samson always had complete faith in God, and he still did, but with the stakes so high he wanted to be sure that this was God's will. He could not see that God would want slavery to continue, but was his plan the one the Heavenly Father would use to end slavery? When Samson thought of the great evil committed against God's people he wondered if the Creator would demand more retribution for such a great evil. Maybe death, destruction and misery were necessary to pay back the debt for such horrible deeds. Perhaps God would bring down Hell on Earth and it would take a devastating war to amend for such a crime. Although there were kind masters as well as cruel, the whole system of slavery was unjust and all were suffering from this injustice. Perhaps men needed more persuasion than economic advantage to change their minds about this evil system that the south took for granted.

The plan Samson had come up with was starting to unfold. He had prayed and asked God for guidance each step of the way. Now it had picked up a little steam and Samson was not able to slow it down. The Lancer slaves would be freed on September 6th, 1824, just as the cotton harvest was beginning.

Fred Lancer's slaves had gone to the field that morning as usual. There was much grumbling among the ranks as some were starting to doubt that the rumors of freedom were true. Some were talking of running. Few had incentive to work and the harvest was progressing slowly.

About ten in the morning Mr. Lancer was dressed in his best suit. He asked for Willy to assist him to the carriage and they rode into town. An hour later they returned carrying a bag filled with about fifty envelopes. Each envelope bore the name of a slave and contained freedom papers and seven dollars.

A supply wagon arrived with lots of food. It was quickly unloaded and immediately made ready on serving tables in the yard. Fresh bread, delicious cakes, fruits, vegetables and many ready to eat items were placed on the tables to accompany the large pots of stew that Sheila already had hanging over fire pits in the yard. Promptly at noon, the slaves were called to come and gather around the big house.

Mr. Lancer's voice was weak due to his illness. He sat on the porch with a table in front of him and the bag with the envelopes by his side. He spoke to Willy and Willy got the crowd's attention repeating what Mr. Lancer asked him to say. "There will be no more work today. It is a day to relax and celebrate. There is good food for everyone. Mr. Lancer wishes

The Alternative

to speak to each one of you today. When you hear your name called, please come to the porch. While you are waiting, help yourselves to the food and relax." After that, Mr. Lancer took an envelope from the bag and told Willy the name on it. Mr. Lancer greeted each slave as they came forward. He apologized for the way he had treated them and handed each one an envelope saying that it contained freedom papers and some money which was a small token of his appreciation. He told all that they were now free but he hoped that they would continue to work for him. He said that he hoped he would be able to pay more in the future and that he would help them in any way he could regardless of what they decided to do.

There was joy and nervousness as each slave heard the speech and received the envelope. All were happy to be free, but since they had never experienced freedom, they didn't know what to expect. A few took their first moments of freedom to release pent up anger at this cruel master that they despised. Some would spit on the ground by their former master's feet. Some would tell him this was too little too late and that he would go to Hell for what he had done. Others would express their gratitude but most were speechless, not knowing what to say. All were happy to be free. Some were also happy that they were leaving, and as soon as they had their fill of the food, there was an exodus as many packed their few belongings and walked away.

Regardless of their reactions, Mr. Lancer felt a sense of relief as he freed each slave. As happy as they were, Mr. Lancer was more joyful. Once he had given the last of the freedom papers out, he felt as though a great burden had been lifted from his shoulders. He had been a slave to the system of slavery all his life and now, finally, by freeing his slaves, he himself had become free.

Bobby had anticipated that his uncle's store would be busier than usual and went to help out. Many of the newly freed slaves went there to see what their money could buy. Bobby and his uncle treated them fairly, but those who ventured elsewhere found a different experience. Many merchants and bar tenders were glad to take advantage of those who had never possessed money before and had no idea of its worth. Some got drunk and when they sobered up they found themselves in a slave pen with no money and no freedom papers. Having no place else to go, most who were able eventually went back to the Lancer plantation to spend the night.

The next morning less than half of the newly freed workers returned to work. Some ventured out to seek employment elsewhere. Those who were readily hired on neighbouring plantations had mixed results. Many obtained employment at low wages and once they were reintroduced to a driver with a whip, they soon realized that they were better off at the Lancer plantation and returned to their home plantation. Others were offered full pay but when pay day came they were informed that the charges for food and lodging were more than what they had earned. They had been required to turn their freedom papers over to their employers and would not get them back until the debt was settled. They were told they must work harder and do with less food in order to get ahead; however, each week when their wages were announced, they never had earned quite enough to cancel the debt. When they tried to leave they were detained and told they must pay back their debt before they left. They soon learned that they had been tricked back into slavery. Although a few successfully escaped and made their way back to the Lancer plantation, one was caught and whipped to death for trying. The rest had to face the fact that they were again slaves.

A small group decided to get out of slave territory. A few made it to the Mississippi river and spent their money for a passage on a boat sailing north. Two of them, while separated from the group met with slave catchers. When they produced their papers to prove they were free, the slave catchers simply destroyed those papers and took them as prisoners to the closest slave pen to be sold. Slave catchers could earn a good living by collecting reward money for runaways, but a black person with no freedom papers and no owner would earn them much more. Blacks had no rights in a court of law so, unless a white person could be found to testify on the black person's behalf, the law would allow those slave catchers to sell their stolen goods.

Each day that week, a few more left the Lancer plantation, but many who had left on previous days came back. Samson gave daily pep talks on the importance of making this plantation profitable so other plantations would free their slaves. The workers that remained worked wholeheartedly doing their best to make up for the shortage of help. By the end of the week, fifteen of the original fifty workers were either unwilling or unable to come back.

Although the harvest got off to a rough start, when the work force settled down it was found that thirty-five dedicated workers could do the work of fifty slaves. However, due to the illness of Mr. Lancer, the harvest had been started late. The late start and early labour problems meant they were still behind in their work.

Bobby was aware of the struggle and had immediately volunteered his services. He did not want this great experiment to fail and he worked as long and hard as any of the other workers. Ruthie also joined Krissy in the field. Krissy, being the best cotton picker on the plantation, was able to train Ruthie to do an adequate job. No one kept track of the weight of the cotton picked by each worker, but Samson kept track of daily totals. There was no punishing or even acknowledging of slower workers. Thus each worker was left to help all others to obtain the best results as a team. Those who were not so good at picking would carry the cotton, bring supplies and provide water for the pickers. How different this was from the days when an overseer would whip anyone who wasn't picking. The slavery system required each slave's production to be weighed separately. There was a minimum production quota required for all workers and each slave would have a quota based on his or her abilities. Those failing to bring in their quota were whipped. If they brought in more than their quota, the amount was adjusted and they would be required to produce the new amount from that point on. Thus slaves were just as fearful of bringing in too much as they were of falling short of their quota.

Now, instead of individuals being concerned with getting just enough done to avoid punishment, they became a team aiming for the best overall production. Each day, as the daily total was announced, a cheer could be heard when the workers congratulated each other on a job well done.

Sundays were well deserved days of rest for the plantation workers. They worked very hard from dawn to dusk for six days of the week and they needed a day of rest to recuperate.

By the end of the first picking, four more workers found their way back to the Lancer plantation after finding they could not do better elsewhere. Mr. Johnson, being aware of the difficulties his son was dealing with volunteered to send a couple of his slaves to help out. Soon they were back on schedule and the extra help returned home. The Lancer work force now had thirty-nine of the original fifty workers working on the harvest and, not only were they keeping up with the work, they found they could now start taking more leisure time and still get all the work done. Another bonus was that they were producing more cotton than previous years. It appears that, being more conscientious of their work, less cotton was getting wasted in the field. Also, they finished well before sunset each day and no one had to work in the dark.

At first, Mr. Lancer paid fifty cents a day to every worker while also providing food and lodging. Later, a new deal was negotiated were they would receive one dollar a day, the going rate for labour, but they would buy their own food. This allowed the workers to chose what they wanted to eat and they gained experience in making financial decisions. Bobby would often take their orders and purchase the food for them at his uncle's store. Most enjoyed the benefits of having their meals prepared for them, so cooks were hired and each worker contributed toward the cost of this service. As they became more accustomed to the new method, they had more free time which often was used to go into town. They were soon able to purchase treats for themselves and luxury items for their lodgings. The gourds and shells they used were soon replaced with proper dishes and the wooden planks they slept on were gradually covered with mattresses. The cooks soon had proper pots and pans for cooking.

Experience taught them that Robert Taylor would treat them fairly, so it was his store they would most often patronize. Other businesses did not want blacks coming into their stores, but when they saw Robert's store flourishing, attitudes began to change. It was also a fact that the former slaves soon learned the value of money and how to count change, so it became more difficult to deceive them. Soon Hamburg was bustling with activity as shopkeepers would cater to their new clientele by painting pictures of their goods on signs so an illiterate customer would know what was available.

Cotton picking usually progressed from late August until January, each field being picked four times over. After all the cotton had been sent to market, the profits for the year were determined. Mr. Lancer held back enough to cover expenses for the next year and put the rest into Samson's hands to be divided among the workers who had earned it. The profits had been slightly lower than previous years due to paying wages and the other disruptions, but there was a small amount available for each worker. It was also explained that profit sharing would be done every year and the more the plantation earned, the more each worker would receive.

After consulting with Bobby and Ruthie, Mr. Lancer turned the management of the entire plantation over to Samson. Thus Samson was able to experiment with crop rotation, and fertilizers without restriction. After the last picking of cotton, the corn was brought in. Corn was again planted in February while cotton planting started in March so work was pretty steady throughout the year. The workers of the Lancer plantation were given tasks they had never done before. Some were bringing in soil samples for Samson to analyze. Some were looking for bugs and larva, reporting their location and density. Weeds were identified and the conditions around each species were noted. Samson developed a science of farming that aided him to maximize production and profit.

Chapter Ten
Wedding Plans

Ruthie was amazed at the transformation Bobby and Samson were making on the plantation. As the workers became more accustomed to the new method, the schedule became less hectic and the two lovers had a chance to socialize, however watching each other work gave them excellent opportunities to learn each other's values. Ruthie's admiration for her man grew and she anxiously awaited his proposal. It was January of 1825 when they announced their wedding plans to all.

Krissy was spending much time with Samson. She took a great interest in his experiments and soon learned how to analyse and compile data. To do this she needed to learn to read and write. She was an excellent student and learned fast. When she and Samson learned of Bobby and Ruthie's plans, Krissy turned to Samson and said, "This is what I want to do for the rest of my life. I enjoy working with you, Samson, and I want always to work by your side."

Samson, being of logical mind, immediately saw the merit in what Krissy was saying. He realised how beneficial Krissy's brilliant mind was to him and thought of sending her off to college. "You are also very valuable to me, Krissy, and you would be more valuable with an education, so I think that, once you improve your reading and writing, you should go to school."

This was not quite the response Krissy had expected, but she was eager to learn, so she replied, "Of course, Samson. If me going to school would help you I would be most willing to get an education."

"There is just one other thing I would like you to do."

"What's that?"

"I would like you to marry me so we can share a room when I go to school with you. There are a couple courses I would still like to take." Samson spoke in a matter of fact tone as though he was completing a business deal.

"Yes, yes, yes." Krissy threw her arms around him. "I will, Samson, I want to spend the rest of my days with you." She spoke excitedly. By now she knew Samson's personality and realized she would have to be excited enough for both of them.

Bobby and Ruthie had been out for an evening stroll when they heard Krissy's shrieks of delight coming from the shed. They went to investigate and saw Krissy jumping around in excitement as Samson was calmly comparing soil samples.

"What are you so excited about?" Ruthie asked her best friend.

"Samson just asked me to marry him."

Bobby and Ruthie both looked at Samson to see his reaction. Perhaps Krissy had misunderstood his intention. He was showing no sign of emotion. When he looked up and saw their inquisitive looks Samson simply said, "It's true."

Now Ruthie joined in the jubilation. "That's wonderful, Krissy. You're my best friend and Samson is Bobby's best friend. We should make it a double wedding. What do you think?"

"Yes, that would be wonderful," Krissy replied immediately. "What do you think, Samson?"

Samson thought carefully as though he were considering a new piece of data. "I think that's a good idea." He said with an expressionless face.

Although Bobby knew Samson better than the others he was not sure Samson was understanding the implications of the conversation. "Samson," he said, excitedly. "You are getting married. Aren't you excited about that?"

Samson looked at his friend and finally cracked a smile. "Of course I am. I guess I'm just not as good at showing it as others are." Then to Krissy he said, "Krissy, I love you more than you can ever know. I know that God has put you in my life and together we can accomplish what he has purposed for us. I know that God has many wonderful things in store for us. Things more wonderful than we can now imagine."

In this way Samson made his commitment known. Ruthie and Krissy went off discussing wedding plans. Bobby and Samson heard them talking about matching wedding dresses as they left the shed.

"It looks like the girls are going to have everything planned," Bobby said.

"Yep. It looks like all we have to do is show up," Samson replied.

It turns out that they needed a little more commitment than just showing up. Soon Samson and Bobby found themselves being fitted for tuxedos. There were questions to be answered as to the location of the ceremony and who to invite. Where would they live once they were married. Then the big question came. Who would officiate the service. Black preachers were not recognized as having authority to solemnize a wedding, but that didn't usually matter as blacks had no legal standing and a marriage between blacks did not need to be recognized by the government or the church. A white preacher was not likely to agree to marry a black couple as it would be seen as completely unnecessary. Blacks were regarded more as livestock than human, so a white preacher would just as soon marry two dogs as to marry a black couple.

Both couples chose Saturday May 21st as the wedding day. Preparations continued as plans were made, but no pastor was chosen. Samson was very involved in maximizing profits on the Lancer plantation. Spring planting would be finished before the wedding. Bobby and Ruthie chose a little nook on the Johnson plantation to build a house. Soon construction began and Bobby supervised the carpenters on a daily basis.

Opposition from Southern Preachers

The church services continued on the Johnson Plantation and a smaller group began meeting at the Lancer's. This did not go unnoticed by the mainstream pro-slavery churches. Most assumed the Lancer plantation would collapse when the slaves were freed. Now they became alarmed. "If the blacks could become free those niggers might take over and whites would be forced to serve them. How unchristian such an arrangement would be. These evil agents of Satan need to be stopped. They are preaching equality of the races. How can good white Christians tolerate such a thing?"

No more venomous were the teachings of these preachers than the words coming from the pulpit of Reverend Ichabod Kempler. He had been the spiritual guide of Bobby Johnson and wanted to make it clear that he did not approve of the young man's ideals. He warned the slave owners to keep their slaves away from the influence of the evil Bobby and his "nigger" friend. "Samson has used African black magic on the unsuspecting Bobby Johnson," he would say. "Surely he has bewitched this young man and they will teach all the slaves how to bewitch their masters. Look what they did to poor Mr. Lancer as he lay on his death bed. Now, when this once godly man dies, he will go to the pit of Hell. We must protect ourselves of such evil."

As slave owners prevented their chattels from attending, numbers began to fall but Bobby learned that secret meetings were being held on neighboring plantations. Those who attended Bobby's services would speak to small groups on their home plantations. The message of unity was still reaching its intended audience, but something else was happening. More and more white people were coming to hear Bobby's message. Some out of curiosity. Some to try and shut him down. And some because they felt the preaching of Reverend Kempler did not make sense.

Thus Bobby had a challenge. He and Samson would pray about the situation. They had two strong allies in Krissy and Ruthie who prayed with them and stuck by their sides through good and bad.

Often hecklers would arise at a Sunday service but after raving like lunatics for a few moments, another of the audience would say, "Shut up. I want to hear what he has to say." Thus Bobby and Samson seldom had to directly face their attackers. When they did, they would calmly listen to the accusation and reply that everyone has a right to his or her opinion. "Yes," Bobby replied to one such attacker who was angrily affirming the inferiority of the blacks. "It seems that most of the churches in the south agree with you and you are free to attend their services." Bobby spoke calmly without accusation. "I am just investigating another possibility. I believe that each of us is responsible for his own belief in God and therefore I don't want to take a man's word for it. I will search the scriptures and pray to God for the correct answer. Would you like to pray with me and ask God to reveal to both of us the truth of the matter?"

It was very seldom that the attacker would want to pray, but when they did they left much more calmly than they came. Some would try to take control of the prayer and use the accusing poisonous words they heard from their preacher, but when Bobby didn't react they would soon give up. The onlookers in these situations soon recognized which party was speaking evil hateful words and which was exhibiting the patient love of God, so these attacks did more to convince the undecided than any words that Bobby or Samson could speak. It would be untrue to say that these attacks had no effect on Bobby. They caused him to stay up late and pray many a night, but that had the effect of making him stronger and wiser. He avoided controversial topics when preaching to a white audience and found many righteous topics they could agree on. Soon Bobby saw his congregation grow again. The slave owners relaxed their restriction on their servants and many of them would also attend. Bobby inherited the belief that kindness yielded better results than the whip from his father and his Christian belief reaffirmed that. This message was often preached when white people were present and they found it was true when they put it into practice. As a result the outdoor gathering at the Johnson's and Lancer's grew larger while other churches in the area, such as those under Reverend Kempler's guidance, saw a drastic decline in attendance.

When Reverend Kempler found his congregation dwindling while Bobby's was growing, he prayed for Gods guidance on how to stop this great evil. One night he had a dream. He dreamt that the children of Israel were following Moses out of Egypt. He awoke trembling, but he could not understand the meaning of this dream or why it made him tremble. Almost every night, after he prayed, he would have the same dream with minor variances. Sometimes, he would see Aaron with Moses. The next night, he would see Aaron as a black man. Then he would dream that the Jews were all black. It seemed that God was trying to show him a parallel between the slaves in America and the slaves in Egypt. Ichabod shuddered. Was he wrong about the black people and God was about to lead them to freedom. He prayed fervently for God to give him an answer and again he had the dream. This time he noticed that Moses and Aaron were really Bobby and Samson and it was the blacks of African descent that were being led to freedom. Then he saw a small trembling Jewish boy. "What should I do? Where should I go?" the youngster cried out. A voice said, "He will tell you what to do. Do whatever he says." He watched as the child went to Bobby, then he realized the boy was a younger version of himself.

Reverend Kempler could not sleep the rest of the night. Surely God was not telling him to go to Bobby for answers. But night after night he would be awakened when the voice in his dreams said he should do whatever Bobby told him to do. It must be some kind of test. Perhaps he was being bewitched by some African magic. He kept praying and the message in his dreams kept getting stronger.

Finding a Minister for the Wedding

In March of 1825, Samson, Krissy, Ruthie and Bobby were sitting in the Johnson parlour discussing wedding plans. Samson had faith that a pastor would be found who would agree to the double marriage, however it was looking more and more doubtful that this could be done in Louisiana. They thought of bringing a pastor down from the north or going north for the wedding, but no agreement could be reached.

"We need to pray together for an answer," Samson stated. He had no doubt about an answer coming from God. "If we all pray in agreement of what we want God will surely answer us."

"I would like to find a local preacher who will agree to conduct both ceremonies together." Bobby weighed in his vote.

"With our reputation it would be difficult to find a local preacher that will marry us," Ruthie surmised. "To find someone that will agree to marry Samson and Krissy in the same ceremony seems impossible."

"It may be impossible for us," Samson added, "but with God all things are possible. If that is what we all want we should ask God to intervene for us."

"I think that would be ideal," Krissy said, "but if it is not God's will we need to come up with another plan."

Samson and Bobby looked at each other. Suddenly both smiled simultaneously. The best friends had been involved in many such discussions and each new what the other was thinking. God had spoken to Bobby's heart when he first met Ruthie telling him she was the one for him. As the relationship went through bumps and turns he doubted that this was really God's desire, but it all had been a test. As a result his relationship with Ruthie was much stronger than it would have been if they had gotten married without any problems. "You are right Samson," Bobby stated in reply to Samson's thoughts. He put his arm around Ruthie and pulled her close to himself. "Sometimes God puts us through tests to be sure we are worthy to receive His blessings. Once it is all over we realize how it has made us stronger."

"Then, let's pray," Samson said as he lead the group in a prayer of faith. Each in turn added his or her thoughts as they talked to their God about their wedding plans. They asked for God's blessings and pleaded that He would send a preacher of His choice to officiate the marriages of both couples in one ceremony. They were so deep in prayer that they didn't hear the approach of a mule and wagon.

When they finished Ruthie said, "That's it then. We do not have to worry. God will send us a preacher soon." When she heard the tap on the door it reminded her of the time her father brought her breakfast. She knew it was their preacher even before Bobby could answer the door.

It is true that Reverend Ichabod Kempler preferred to travel with his trusty mule. Mules can be unpredictable and stubborn, but the preacher always had good luck with his animal. Ichabod had tried to put his dream out of his mind, but when he was passing by the Johnson's that day in March, his beast decided on its own to proceed up the laneway. The good reverend decided he could no longer avoid this confrontation.

Bobby was surprised when he opened the door. "Reverend Kempler," he greeted the pastor of his youth by name. "What brings you here today?" Bobby feared this reverend had not come for a friendly mission. He was fully aware of the reverend's attacks on the work he and Samson were doing. For

The Alternative

the moment, the thoughts of their prayer they had flown from his mind, but even if he had thought of it he could never have imagined that this knock on the door was the answer so soon.

Ruthie, however, had the benefit of experience. In fact her very conversion to Christian belief had been the result of such a miraculous answer to prayer. She knew why the good reverend had come and greeted him excitedly. "Reverend Kempler. Do come in and sit. We were just discussing our wedding plans. Come, have a seat right here." She whisked the reverend to a chair and pulled in another for herself.

Bobby stared in disbelief at his fiancée. This surely was not the answer to their prayer, but Ruthie seemed to be assuming it was. Not to worry. He would soon find out what Ichabod's mission was. Before Ruthie could embarrass the group with her assumptions, he sat down facing the reverend. "What can we do for you today Reverend Kempler?"

"Wedding plans." The words echoed in the reverends mind, but he said, "I'm not sure why I'm here, but I had a dream that I was supposed to talk to you." Ruthie dropped the empty cup she was still holding in her hand. She remembered questioning her father about the breakfast and all he could say is, "something told me I should do it."

"Look, I wasn't even planning to come here today, but my mule had other ideas, so I'm here. In my dream, God told me you would tell me what to do. I don't understand why, but I'm supposed to do whatever you tell me," Kempler continued.

Now, if Bobby had something in his hand, he would have surely dropped it. "Not Reverend Kempler," he thought in a silent prayer. "God, this must be a joke. You can't mean you want this minister to conduct a double ceremony with a black couple. If you pull this off I will know You can accomplish anything." Bobby finished the thoughts he was conveying to his Heavenly Father and stared at Reverend Kempler in disbelief. The others all pulled their chairs closer to the pastor. They were

Wedding Plans

witnessing a miracle and didn't want to miss a thing.

"Well," Kempler was visibly agitated. "Tell me what you want me to do."

Bobby could not form a word. Samson urged him. "Yes, Bobby. Tell the reverend what he should do."

This was all too much for the girls. The look on Bobby's face. The agitation of the clergyman. The matter of fact tone of Samson. The shock of having a prayer answered so fast. They burst out laughing. It was contagious and even Samson could not stop laughing when he noticed the expression on his friend's face.

"What is so funny?" Kempler asked as he, too, was catching the laughter bug.

Bobby finally found words and said, "You would have had to be here before you came in the door to understand. Now, Reverend Kempler. Let me get this straight. You want me to tell you what you should do."

"I'm not sure I would put it that way, but I had a dream where a voice told me to do whatever you told me to do." Kempler was starting to doubt that this voice was really from God so he made a slight change in the interpretation of his dream.

"Are you going to tell him or should I?" Ruthie was getting impatient.

"Ruthie and I are getting married," Bobby began, but he was not at all sure Ichabod was the man to officiate.

"And we want you to conduct the ceremony." Ruthie finished the sentence for Bobby when she saw him struggling.

"No, no, no," Reverend Kempler groaned. "Anything else. You must have heard about the things I've said about you. I will never be able to face my congregation again if I conduct your wedding now. There must be something else I can do. How about I just promise not to run down your church anymore?

Wouldn't that be enough? You are going to completely ruin me if you insist on this."

Ruthie looked at Bobby and saw him wavering, so she took over. "Reverend Kempler. Bobby has told me so much about you and we would both be greatly honoured if you would do us this service. Besides, just before you came in we were praying that God would send a minister for our wedding. God sent you so none of us really have a choice. Personally I am thoroughly delighted with God's choice and I am sure Bobby is too." She looked to Bobby. "Well, say something Bobby. Aren't you happy with God's choice?"

"Well, I... I mean I..." Bobby struggled to find words that would not be a lie but would also not sound offensive. "But I.... Maybe I should..." As he struggled his thoughts became clearer and it was as though he had received a revelation. "Of course I am delighted." He looked to the ceiling. "Thank you God." His brain suddenly processed the events of the day as he looked at Reverend Kempler and said, "You are absolutely perfect for the job." Looking up he said, "God, You are so Glorious and so Wise." Back to Kempler. "You are the perfect and most logical choice and you must do it. It is God's Will."

Reverend Kempler was getting caught up in the spirit of faith. He looked up and said, "Okay, God, I will do it, but that is all. Please don't ask me to humble myself more than this. When this is over take me away from here so I won't have to face the people. Better yet, take me from this earth." Kempler preferred death to having to admit to a multitude that he was wrong. But God works in mysterious ways and He wasn't done with the reverend yet.

"So what will it be? Just a small gathering with family and a few friends I suppose?" Kempler said wistfully.

"We were thinking of something a little grander than that," Bobby stated.

"Well how many guests are you expecting." The reverend

was hoping none of his congregation would be included.

"First of all it's to be a double wedding. Our best friends, Krissy and Samson, will be getting married at the same time." Ruthie indicated the two friends in the room so there could be no doubt as to who she meant.

"You mean I... you...they..." Kempler tried to make sense of it as two smiling black faces looked at him. As black as they were, Kempler turned a shade of white never before seen. As he considered the implication he suddenly said, "No way, I will die first." He headed for the door and made a speedy exit slamming the door behind him.

"Well, we tried," Bobby said after a few moments. "I suppose God will send another."

"Don't be too quick to write Kempler off." Ruthie interjected. She was looking out the window and the others followed her gaze.

Kempler was out in front doing everything in his power to get his mule to move. His faithful steed was not going anywhere. He tried shaking the reins, he hollered, he bribed it with a carrot but got no reaction until he kicked it. At that the beast sat down. Kempler tried pushing and pulling but could not get his animal back on its feet. There is only one thing that can be more stubborn than a mule once it decides not to cooperate, and that is a mule operating by the will of God. Finally, he gave up and stormed back to the house. Ruthie opened the door as he approached. "Okay I'll do it." He shouted in the door loud enough that the mule could hear. He stormed back to his wagon, got on the seat and shook the reins. The mule immediately stood and began pulling his master home.

Chapter Eleven
The Wedding

After freeing his slaves, Mr. Lancer finally felt free himself. He hadn't realized how much he had been enslaved by the slavery system. Previously being forced by the system into thinking of his help as livestock, he now discovered a whole new humanity in the workers. As a slave owner, he had been the enemy of his slaves. He now enjoyed the friendship he had with his help. Now that they were free, they were hesitant to form a friendship with one who had treated them so cruelly, and Mr. Lancer understood their reluctance. This only made him work harder at proving he had become a new man. Gradually his workers realised the sincerity of his efforts to right his wrongs and some of them bonded with him in a spirit of friendship that was unquestionable.

By the time the spring planting was done in 1825, there were few who would make a disapproving remark about Fred Lancer. If someone were to voice an objection or doubt the sincerity of the man, he would be sure to be met by disapproving stares, and someone would always come to the defense of the man they worked for. If a passerby should ask who their master was they would reply that they had no master. They were free and they worked for their friend, Mr. Lancer. Indeed they worked harder for this friend then any had done for the man with the whip. Productivity and the quality of work improved to the highest standards possible. The work was completed faster and they had more free time then they ever had before. Many used that time to sit and talk with their new friend.

Under Samson's direction, less acreage was planted in cotton and several new crops were introduced. Samson investigated which crops would have a market and continued experimenting with crop rotation to find the best rotation for all crops. He also introduced poultry and livestock to the plantation to provide dairy, eggs and meat for the workers as well as for market. All manure and by products were recycled and used as fertilizer for the fields. His plan was to rotate pasture fields with the crops so animal feces would fertilize the crops during following years. Thus each year was destined to increase profitability on the Lancer plantation as the operation got more organized and the land recovered from supporting only cotton and corn for so many years.

May of 1825 was an extremely busy time for both the Lancers and the Johnsons. Samson took on the responsibility of organizing the labour on both plantations. Saturday May twenty-first was fast approaching and Samson planned to take some time off to be with his new bride. Thus lead hands were appointed to look after various aspects of the work. When someone would come to Samson with a problem, he would refer them back to the lead hand. If the lead hand couldn't solve the problem, he would be asked what he thought he should do. If it seemed it would work he was told to go ahead and do it. Thus the workers were trained to work out problems among themselves and to think for themselves.

Reverend Ichabod Kempler became a blessing to Bobby and Samson. Just as the apostle Paul saw the light and became a promoter of the word of God, Reverend Kempler saw the errors of his ways and became a powerful agent spreading the news of a new slave free system. Kempler no longer tried to control his mule when it took him off his intended path. He was sure that God was in control of his animal. When he found himself on a strange plantation he would rise to promote the cause he'd grown to love. This often led to him being chased by dogs, threatened with guns or otherwise thrown off the property. However no abuse was too great for Ichabod to endure if it meant making up for the wrong he had committed in the past. Interestingly, the ones that met him with the greatest resistance were often the first ones to free their slaves once it was proven to be more economical than the system of slavery. However we are getting ahead of ourselves. We have a wedding to deal with now.

Reverend Kempler became very cooperative once he saw the wisdom of the way Bobby was teaching. His dreams had shown him a parallel to the Hebrew slaves in ancient Egypt and the American slaves of his day. He soon saw that freedom from slavery was the Will of God and he was happy to be involved in a wedding involving the promoters of a new system that would one day end slavery. He began to read the Bible with a new understanding. He threw out the interpretations taught to him by the mentors of his youth and investigated the reality of the scripture through prayer which gave him an understanding inspired by God.

When Ichabod Kempler became acquainted with Krissy and Samson he realized their humanity. He had always thought of the African Americans as livestock and the idea of conducting a wedding ceremony for animals was beneath the dignity of a pastor, but now seeing these two very intelligent humans, he realized their behaviour and moral standards were above those of most of the white people he knew. It became a great honour for him to conduct such a history making ceremony, the first double wedding ceremony involving a black couple and a white couple that he had ever heard of. When he heard criticism from others he was quick to defend the rights of his new found friends.

Wedding preparations helped Ruthie to get to know her mother's brothers, their wives and children. More importantly, it gave Uncle Jack, Aunt Sue, Uncle George and Aunt Frieda a chance to get to know their niece. Ruthie met her cousins for

The Wedding

the first time and they were all included in the wedding plans.

Gossip of the upcoming wedding was spreading rapidly throughout the area. Everyone seemed to have an opinion and few were positive. There was talk of a protest, but most saw this as an experiment that was sure to fail and not worth the effort. If someone wanted to share their wedding day with a couple of farm animals, why would that be of concern to others? Maybe when their children got married they would want to see their horses get hitched the same day. However silly it seemed, what was the harm?

The Lancer plantation was also a subject for gossip. A religious fanatic had convinced a dying man to give up his slaves. As sad as that was they knew he had no heir to pass the plantation on to anyway and perhaps, when it failed, young Bobby would give up his notion that a plantation could be profitable without slaves. How could anyone in their right mind believe that they could pay their help and still make a profit? Slave labour was available and the cost of buying a slave would be offset later when excess breeding would produce a surplus that could be sold. There was no logical reason to believe that slave labour was not necessary on a cotton plantation.

Uncle Jack would struggle over the fact that his niece had chosen to share the most important day of her life with former slaves. He had been frustrated when, at fourteen years old, Ruthie considered a farm animal to be her best friend, but now she was eighteen and getting married. Surely she must see the error of her childish ways by now. Uncle Jack was reluctant to have his family involved in such a ceremony, but he was finally getting a chance to spend some time with his departed sister's daughter, so he went along with the plans. In the process he got to know Krissy and Samson and wondered if his opinion about "niggers" may have been wrong.

May twenty-first arrived and Reverend Kempler's church was filled to capacity. In the past he would have been dismayed at the number of blacks in attendance, but this day he was overjoyed. Ruthie and Bobby didn't have many white friends, but the help of both the Lancer and Johnson plantations were invited. The only whites in the crowd were the families of the white couple.

Krissy and Ruthie had matching wedding dresses and, with white gloves and a veil in place, it was difficult to know who was who. Bobby and Samson watched from the front as the wedding party marched in and the two Brides came down the aisle side by side. The wedding vows were said with each of the men making their promises and then the two women replying with their vows. Then the final pronouncement that both couples were now man and wife was uttered by Reverend Kempler.

The two happy couples rode off together to spend their honeymoons in parts unknown although it is rumored that they had found a little hideaway on the shores of Lake Providence about 170 miles to the north.

With their weddings behind them, the happy foursome had much to do. They needed to end slavery on time to stop a devastating war. That would not be an easy task but it was one they knew they must accomplish. The alternative was much too horrible to imagine.

Chapter Twelve
Progress

Bobby and Ruthie moved into the new house that had been built for them on the Johnson Plantation. Ruthie gave her room at the Lancer plantation to Krissy and Samson. Mr. Lancer offered them a couple of adjoining rooms so they could make a little apartment for themselves. There was much visiting back and forth and Bobby learned more about the plan that Samson had initiated to end slavery.

"So you believe that you can convince all plantation owners that paying free workers will earn them more profit than using slave labour?" Bobby queried Samson.

"Not all at once, but when more and more plantations start using paid labour and at the same time show greater profits, eventually they will get the idea," his friend replied.

"If they have to pay their labourers, how will that earn them more profit?"

"The quality of the work will make a difference. It is all about respect. When one has respect for the workers that earn the profit, they will naturally want to work harder and smarter than before. One of the big problems in slavery was the lack of respect and the treatment of slaves as dumb animals. No one thought the slaves might have some ideas of their own on how to do things more efficiently. By working with the help and discovering with them better ways to get the work done and using their brains to develop tools, you will soon find that less than half the labour force is needed to run the plantation."

"But even if they have to pay only half the number of workers, wouldn't that cost more than the slave rations they now provide."

"By tapping into the mental power of the workers, new ways will be found. I am now working on ways to get higher yields by experimenting with crop rotation, fertilizers, pest control and weed control. I am only one person and already we are seeing a difference. If every worker was working together on this we could soon see dramatic improvement in crop yields. As new crops are introduced, less acreage will be in cotton, but I believe we will be able to produce just as much cotton on less land. The profit from the other crops will be a bonus."

"If that works I can see how we can convince the other plantations, but they will need to see big improvements. Right now the Lancer Plantation is a subject of curiosity. No one seems to think it will even survive let alone prove more profitable."

"Bobby; It was you who told me that you felt God was telling you slavery is wrong. We can't approach this by thinking 'if this works.' It has to work and we need to make it work. Soon will be the time for the second harvest since Fred Lancer freed his slaves. Last year there were some problems. This year it must go perfectly. We are being watched as through a microscope. Once we show more revenue flowing, we need to approach your father. He has a better relation with his help than Mr. Lancer did, so the transition should be much easier. But just look around on the Lancer plantation now. You wouldn't believe it was the same place. Everyone is happy. Everyone gets along. The workers love Mr. Lancer and are quick to defend his honour. The work is done quickly and thoroughly. Under slavery this was a place of gloom. Now it seems the sun shines brightly every day."

Even Krissy, who had suffered so much at the hands of her master, now saw a changed man and forgave Mr. Lancer for the wrongs he had done her. She worked hard in the fields through the day but, while in the big house, there is nothing she would not do for the man who became her friend. She brought him tea every night and she and Samson had breakfast with him every morning.

Mr. Lancer had lived to see his daughter married. He died July 15th, 1825 and didn't live to see the harvest that year. He left a few surprises in his will. He specified that the plantation be shared equally between his four children and their spouses. He named Otis, Ruthie, Willie and Ella as his heirs. The problem was that no one knew Otis.

He specified that Samson and Krissy would administer Ella's portion until she became of age and got married. He suggested that management should be left up to Samson unless the heirs decided on someone else and that half the income each year should be split into four equal amounts to be distributed to each of the heirs. The other half of the income was to be divided among the workers in a fair and equitable manner according to how much each had contributed to earning the wealth. That is, one who laboured all year would receive a greater portion of the profit than a seasonal worker who only helped out at specific times.

There was sadness on the Lancer Plantation as the workers mourned the loss of their friend, but everyone was at peace. They knew the day of his demise was inevitable as they watched his health dwindle, but the last days of Mr. Lancer were days of joy. Although he had given his servants freedom, it could not match the freedom that this act gave to himself.

No one worked on the Lancer plantation the day of the funeral and Hamburg had not seen such a large funeral. Reverend Kempler gladly agreed to conduct the service and eulogies poured out from many of his friends of a darker complexion. His relatives had endured a wedding where there were more Black faces than white, but the funeral service was attended by every hand who had worked for him and many came from neighbouring plantations. Many who couldn't get passes risked severe punishment to sneak away for the funeral. Indeed, the neighbouring plantations soon gave up trying to get any work out of their slaves that day. Never had the little town seen such an outpouring of love to a white man from the African descendants.

After the funeral, things began to return to normal but slaves began to express discontent. They knew the workers at the Lancer plantation were free. They got paid and worked under pleasant conditions. The plantation owners saw how freedom had affected the workers and how they were getting more done than those in slavery did. They reasoned that, if freedom could get more work out of a worker, than more whipping would entice the same level of work from their slaves. As conditions got better at the Lancer plantation, they became much worse in many other places.

As the slaves grumbled their owners grumbled more. The delicate system of slavery had been upset. They wanted nothing more than to see the plantation that started all this shut down. They talked of causing mischief and destroying property. There was even talk that Samson should be lynched. But no one wanted to be the first to inflict more grief on a grieving family, so they let it slide. Besides, no one believed that an industry that was slave driven could exist without slaves, so they believed the Lancer experiment would fail. Gradually the plantation using paid workers became a bit of a curiosity but was largely ignored.

The Johnson slaves had more to complain about. They had been promised freedom and had believed they would be the first to be free, but now another plantation was free and they were still slaves. Bobby and Samson urged them to be patient. "When Mr. Johnson sees how well the Lancer plantation does, he will set you free," they informed the loyal workers.

"But what if the Lancer plantation does not do so well?" they asked. Not even the slaves were sure a slave free system would work. For generations they had been conditioned to think their role as slaves was one necessary to the economy. Some were so accustomed to being treated like animals that they began to see themselves as such. Many saw the white man as superior and having greater intelligence, so they doubted if they could make it without masters to tell them what they should do. Samson and Bobby had their work cut out for them. Not only did they need to convince the slave owners to give up their slaves, but it appeared that, in some cases, they had to convince the slaves to give up their masters.

The cotton harvest went very well at the Lancer's and they had breaks after each picking before the cotton was ready for the next picking. Many of the workers volunteered to help out at the Johnson plantation. Some got hired for temporary work on plantations that were falling behind.

Between cotton pickings, they had their other crops to harvest. Under Samson's supervision, all crops did well. Each year, new crops were introduced and they had much fresh produce for themselves and lots to sell. The workers at the Lancer plantation began to eat better than most white people and the produce was in high demand. Although profits after that second harvest were not as high as Samson and Bobby had hoped, they were at least as high as they had been during the slavery years, so they could safely say that they had made enough extra to pay the wages.

As the profits were divided according to what Mr. Lancer stipulated in his will, there was a little for everyone. Samson made sure that enough capital was kept back to cover operating expenses for the next year. Willy was not yet sixteen years old, so Samson and Krissy helped him to invest his share allowing him part of it to do with as he pleased. Ella's portion was invested in a trust account and Ruthie's portion was turned over to her and Bobby. But they were not sure what to do with the portion allotted to Otis. Ruthie had not heard of such a person, but she thought he may come back to the plantation one day, so she suggested his portion be invested for a few years. If no one came forward to claim it, it would be divided among the other heirs in the future. Everyone felt this was fair and so it was done.

One day, Samson, Krissy and Ella were invited to dinner at the Johnson plantation. The talk around the table was about the successes they were realizing. Mr. Johnson himself acknowledged that a slave free system could work. He said, "It is too early to tell for sure. It may have just been luck this year, but I think you are on to something."

"Dad! You know I can never own slaves. If I am to take over this plantation, I will free all the slaves. I am sure they will stay on and work for us," Bobby commented.

"I am not quite ready to turn it over yet, but I think we will start doing things a little differently. I believe you are right that the slaves should get some reward for earning a profit so I will share some of the profit with them this year. I won't be quite as generous as you guys, but I will allot a third of the profit for the workers."

"That will be quite a benefit," Samson weighed in. "Once your help realizes that the more profit they earn for the plantation, the more they will earn themselves, they are sure to work more efficiently. They will work harder and be more conscientious of waste. You will see an improvement right away."

"But why not go all the way and give them their freedom?" Bobby inquired. "If you're going to pay them anyway it makes sense to set them free."

"Well it may seem that way, but I want to be sure they stay around," Mr. Johnson replied. "Besides, if they got money and are treated well, what is the big deal about being free?"

"The big deal is having respect," Samson began making his point. "When one human being owns another human being he cannot respect him. The owner and the one owned can never be on equal terms. It is natural to feel superior to one you consider your property. Thus, the system will not work unless every slave becomes free."

"Samson, you are a very exceptional negro," Mr. Johnson said. "But you can't believe that every black person is equal to whites across the board. There is an inherent inferiority among your people and they need the white race to guide them. How far do you think they would get without a white man to run the plantations for them?"

"It seems that Samson is doing alright," Bobby interjected. "He does everything here except own the land, and he manages Lancer's plantation quite well. He has even sold the crops and managed the money there. If the law allowed him to be a land owner, I believe he would do quite well."

"As I said there are exceptions," Mr. Johnson mused. "Samson got an education and he has done well, but most negroes are ignorant and can't even count their money."

"That is just the point, Mr. Johnson," Samson let it sink in for a moment. "Education." He paused again for effect. "Why are the white folks so afraid of the blacks getting an education? It is clear that they know they would have no advantage over us if we were afforded the same rights. It is very important that everyone is given the opportunity to get an education, otherwise half the brainpower of the world will not be tapped. So long as the whites see the blacks as ignorant they will remain ignorant themselves. Once everyone gets an education you will see advances in civilization that you never dreamed of before. One will be able to climb into a machine and it will whisk them to distant parts in a fraction of the time it takes now. One will be able to speak into an apparatus and be heard many miles away. Many things will happen that we cannot even dream of today, but to do this we need to employ the minds of people and not just their bodies."

"You may be right Samson."

"I am very appreciative of the opportunities I have had. You took a risk in allowing me an education, but I should not be among the privileged few."

"I will give that some thought," Mr. Johnson said. "But now I believe dessert is being served."

It is more difficult for one who has been accustomed to certain standards all his life to make changes in his later years. Mr. Johnson had known nothing but the system of slavery since he was a child. Now, with his son recently married, he would soon be a grandfather. It was very difficult for him to see another way. However, he was willing to try, which was more than most the slave-owners of his generation.

Another Free Plantation

Mr. Johnson thought long and hard on what Samson had said. He recognized in Samson the abilities of a white man but never thought that this could be true of others of his race. If Samson was right and blacks were just as capable, a huge injustice had been done. If it were true that a black man was incapable, then why were there laws to prevent him from learning? No such law was in place for horses or dogs.

Samson had talked about a new society emerging when everyone was given equal rights to an education. If this was true, lack of educational opportunities was not only hurting the black race, but all of society was suffering from this injustice. Mr. Johnson became troubled and irritable. Although he doubted the standards he had grown up with, his natural instinct was to defend them. If anyone questioned his right to own slaves he would retaliate by saying that there has always been a master class and a serving class. It was recorded in the Bible and it was a fact of life that we must accept.

Bobby and Samson had to steer clear of Mr. Johnson for a while. Every time they met, he would say something else in support of owning slaves. The young men were about ready to give up, thinking that they had lost the battle when, in the summer of 1826, they were summoned to Mr. Johnson's office. He had boxes full of papers when they arrived.

"You boys were right," he announced when they entered. "It took me a while to see it, but I can see now how slavery has hurt us all. I have here the freedom papers for every slave on the plantation. I was going to hand them out, but I don't feel I am deserving of that honour, so, Bobby, I am officially retiring and the operation of the plantation is now in your hands. I did not want you to be burdened by being a slave owner for one minute, so there are no slaves to pass down to you, but I leave it to you to tell them about their freedom. If you need my help for anything, let me know. I will stay close by in the house, but this office is now yours, so I leave it to you."

Bobby was speechless and Mr. Johnson left the office before he could collect his thoughts. He now officially owned his father's plantations and the slaves were free. The system Samson had put in place was working wonderfully and the plantation practically ran itself, but what of the finances? His father had always looked after financial matters.

That night when the workers came from the fields, they were informed they were not to work the next day, but that they should gather in the area were the church services were held.

Bobby and Ruthie joined his parents for supper that night and Bobby expressed his surprise and thanks to his father at the table. He asked for some help learning the finances and his father said he would be glad to spend as much time as necessary going over the books with him. "Have you handed out the freedom papers?" he asked.

"Not yet. I've given everyone the day off tomorrow and we will do it then."

Early the next morning, the employees of Bobby Johnson gathered to hear what their boss had to say. Many had guessed such an announcement that would warrant a day off work must mean their freedom, and so it was with much anticipation that they gathered. Many were visibly nervous and paced about as they awaited Bobby Johnson. Finally he arrived.

"My father has passed this plantation on to me as of yesterday," Bobby began.

"When will you set us free, Bobby?" Manfred asked.

"You are already free. My father got your freedom papers before he retired. That is why I've called you here today. I will commence handing out the papers right away. Please come forward when your name is called."

As the names were called, the first few took the papers timidly, not sure what they should do with them, but Gregory said, "I don't want them. I ain't known nothin' but bein' a slave. I don't know any other life. You keep those papers and I will go on as I always have."

"Well, certainly, Gregory, we will keep this in the office for you and you can get it whenever you want, but let it be known that you are no longer a slave. That doesn't mean that you have to leave or that anything has to change. You can keep on as you were, but now you have the choice. You can stay if you want or go if you want."

"I don't want to go anyplace. I heard about what happened to some of Lancer's boys when they left his plantation. They got their papers stole and ended up back in slavery. I don't want to end up worse off than I am. I'm stayin' right here. You don't have to pay me nothin'. Just give me some food and a place to sleep. I'll keep right on workin' for ya."

After that, many were afraid of losing the papers and asked Bobby to keep them. Some wanted to take them and hold them for a while, but soon realized they would be safer in Bobby's office, so they gave them back to him for safe keeping.

One day, Reverend Kempler stopped by to see Bobby. He warned Bobby about the grumbling among the neighbours. A second and larger plantation was now slave free and it began to appear as though change was inevitable. Change never comes without resistance and slave owners were complaining that their chattels were becoming discontent due to this irresponsible behaviour of Bobby Johnson. They also knew Samson was the main force behind it and rumors were rampant that Samson would be lynched. Bobby and Samson decided to take a low profile for a while. They didn't flaunt their success and soon there was relative calm.

Although Mr. Lancer had left his plantation to his children, none of them were legally entitled to own land, so Bobby held the land for them. Bobby's father also transferred the deed of the Johnson plantation to him and he became the legal owner of both properties. These plantations, operating without slaves, were a curiosity. There was much speculation on their chances of survival and none of the neighbours would predict they would experience greater success than a slave driven operation.

Learning that others had gained freedom caused some slaves to express discontent. After a few whippings, they soon reverted to the old standard of saying they were content no matter how dishonest that statement was.

Bobby and Samson worked hard to work out difficulties on the plantations under Bobby's control. Operations became smoother and more profitable every year. As promised, Samson took Krissy north to get an education. Bobby escorted them so there would be no trouble and then returned to manage his properties.

Mr. Johnson educated his son well on how to find the best markets and get the best prices for the crops. This resulted in higher profits again, and paying attention to the quality of the crops, Johnson and Lancer cotton became much sought after. As workers became more efficient, Bobby reduced their working hours and when there was still difficulty finding enough work to keep them busy, more land was bought and the operation was expanded.

When Krissy and Samson returned, they secretly conducted schools for the workers and their children. Everyone knew this was breaking the law, so they were all sworn to secrecy. Since the law could prosecute a land owner who allowed this activity, they didn't officially tell Bobby of it.

Bobby never flaunted his success but the affluence of his workers was harder to hide. Talk was that Bobby Johnson, although a bit of a fanatic, was very smart. Often someone would comment, "He makes more money than us while he pays his help. Just think of how much better he would do if he would use slaves. That crazy man could be a millionaire if he had any sense."

Eleven years after Bobby took over and used only paid labour, some plantation owners came from the Marksville area to find out how Bobby was doing it. They wanted to know how Bobby was making such a profit and were willing to pay handsomely for that information. Bobby called Samson into the office. "These men want to know how we manage to do so well," he told Samson.

"Have you told them what they must do?" Samson asked.

"No, you are the originator of the plan. I will leave that to you."

William Ford did not seem to stir but Edwin Epps was not about to be taught by a 'nigger.' "We heard you was crazy," Epps said. "But if you think we's gonna believe an ignorant nigger came up with your plan you're crazier than we thought."

"Well, it so happens that Samson did come up with the plan and the whole plan revolves around having respect for those who work for you," Bobby said nonchalantly.

"We just want to know how you manage to produce more cotton and get a higher quality," Ford was much more refined than his friend. "We're not planning to set any slaves free, but we wanted to see how your system works so we can use some parts of it. We will pay well if you can show us how it will work."

"Mr. Ford," Samson addressed him politely. "As Bobby said, the key is respect and you cannot respect someone you hold as a slave. The system will not work if you don't free your workers."

"But I heard you have developed new tools and use new methods. Why can't we do that using slave labour?" Ford inquired patiently.

"I have developed no tools," Bobby informed him. "The tools and new methods were all developed by the workers. Samson has developed many and has experimented with ways to get better yields. I have little understanding of what Samson does, but I know it works. If Samson was a slave we would have none of this."

Epps became more irritated by this last pronouncement. "If a nigger can be induced to do this by a promise of freedom, I have a whip that will convince my niggers faster. Come on Ford. Let's get outta here. These goons ain't gonna tell us nothin'."

The meeting seemed to prove fruitless, but strangers do not come to Hamburg unnoticed and the local plantation owners wanted to know what they were after. When they stopped in town for a coffee a man asked them about their visit with Bobby Johnson. "The man's crazy," Epps replied. "Says you gotta free yer niggers to make money."

That man, Mr. Kearney, became the next plantation owner to free his slaves. He was watching Bobby Johnson close enough to know that his system worked and decided that, if it was getting interest from further away, it should be worth trying. During the transition, Bobby and Samson spent much time with Mr. Kearney. They brought experienced help from home to teach the system. Mr. Kearney sent some of his help to the Johnson plantation to observe firsthand how they operated. They were trained in the art of making tools and taught how to use them. The biggest challenge was to teach them to think for themselves.

Kearney had grown nothing but cotton for many years. He saw his yields dwindle year after year. He was considering giving up his plantation and moving to fresh soil when he decided to give Bobby and Samson's method a try. He didn't really want to move, but his soil was spent. Samson explained that crop rotation could fix that and fertilizers would help. They suggested no cotton the next year and after that, no more than a third of the land in cotton, being rotated to a different third every three years.

Samson already had the knowledge of what crops would do well after cotton had used up the soil. He also knew which crops would leave behind the nutrients the cotton plants needed. So Kearney did very well on his substitute crops the first year and within a few years he grew almost as much cotton on a third of his land as he had on all the land before the new system. He was very happy with the results but one thing he hadn't anticipated. He suddenly felt free. "Strange," he thought. "I set my slaves free but it feels like they have set me free." Yes, Mr. Kearney was now free. Free to try new things. Free to think for himself. Free to learn from his workers. Never before had he ever felt such freedom.

In the summer of 1841, Bobby and Samson would join their friend, William Lloyd Garrison, in a grand anti-slavery convention that was held in Nantucket. As there friend was the main organizer they had little chance to talk to him. They talked to a few about their idea for a free south but were not given a chance to address the crowd. "We are raising money to help slaves reach freedom. If we start rumours that the South could be free it may hurt donations." Thus those who controlled the convention did not give them an opportunity to voice their plan.

Fredrick Douglass was also at that convention. He had a more sympathetic ear. "I would love to hear how that works out for you. It would be great if I could go home to where I'm known and live as a free man. I hope you succeed." It would be many years before Bobby and Samson would again see Fredrick Douglass in the office of the president of the USA.

Chapter Thirteen
1845 Crop Destruction

Bobby had a dream on May 23rd, 1844. In it he saw the world made new with many wondrous inventions. There was no slavery and machines were doing most of the work. When he told Samson about it, Samson said he felt that something was going to change soon. Religious unrest seemed to be spreading all over the world. Many groups were expecting the eminent return of Christ. Some even sold all they had and some went to the Holy Land to await His arrival.

Bobby read from Matthew, Chapter twenty-four. "But know this, that if the goodman of the house had known in what watch the thief would come, he would have watched, and would not have suffered his house to be broken up. Therefore be ye also ready: for in such an hour as ye think not the Son of man cometh."

"It seems that no one knows when the Lord will come," Bobby said. "When He comes, He should find us doing the work He has for us to do."

"By the time one sees the signs of a thief, he has already been there and done his damage," Samson observed. "Perhaps the Lord is already on the earth. In the Book of Revelation it says, 'Remember therefore how thou hast received and heard, and hold fast, and repent. If therefore thou shalt not watch, I will come on thee as a thief, and thou shalt not know what hour I will come upon thee.'"

"It would be good if He found the world free of slavery,"

Bobby added. "We've been at this for a while and so far there are only three plantations without slaves, and we control two of them."

"Don't be disheartened. I feel something big will happen this year and everyone will know the new system works."

"Something needs to happen soon. Even though our workers are free, they can't really go anywhere. If they were carrying their freedom papers, someone would steal them and force them back into slavery. We need to get the laws changed."

"That will happen, my friend." Samson replied thoughtfully. "First they must see the economic advantage."

Towards the end of 1844 Samson made some other observations that alarmed him. "Bobby, there is going to be a bad infestation of caterpillars next year. The conditions all point to that and I am already seeing an increase in the numbers of butterflies. I hope we will be able to save the cotton crop."

"Do you think it will be that bad, Samson. I have seen years were caterpillars have done a lot of damage, but it would take a lot of them to completely destroy the cotton plants."

"If they get on them early enough they can devour the whole plant before it has a chance to grow," Samson replied. We need to ward them off as long as we can. There are some plants that repel them. If we can keep the butterflies away so they don't lay eggs on them when they first emerge, we may be able to save the crop."

Samson let his concerns be known and an older gentleman, Elwood, remembered hearing some stories passed down from Africa. "There is a weed that grows in these parts that is similar to one in Africa. When you burn that weed, the smoke will kill the butterflies and caterpillars that eat plants. I've seen quite a bit of it growing near the swamp."

Samson gathered up some of those weeds and dried them. When he noticed a large number of butterflies in one of the fields, he placed the weeds so wind would blow the smoke over

The Alternative

the field when he set it on fire. The experiment proved a success. After the smoke had cleared he checked the field and found thousands of dead butterflies. He checked under the cotton plants and found many dead caterpillars that had fallen.

As expected, the caterpillars arrived early in 1845. Samson had the natural repellents planted among the cotton and around the perimeter of the cotton fields and that was having some effect, but April already showed signs of damage to the newly emerged cotton plants, so the smoking process was used to kill off the insects. This knowledge had been shared among the three plantations that were slave free, but others were not interested in speculations about caterpillars. The growers noticed the early damage, but cotton would recover once it had a chance to grow, and it would take a lot of caterpillars to destroy mature plants. They had survived other years when the damage was bad, but no one anticipated the total destruction that happened in 1845. That is, no one except Samson. Even his workers thought he was going overboard on his efforts to defeat this enemy, but when they saw the only cotton left standing was in the fields that Samson protected, they were glad they had taken the extra effort.

It is a well-known fact in the agricultural industry that commodity prices are affected by supply and demand. When everyone has a good crop, prices can drop so low that the producers barely break even. However, if one has a good crop while others have low yields he stands to make a good profit. If all other crops are wiped out and a producer has the only crop left standing, buyers will compete aggressively to get a piece of that crop.

In Louisiana the only cotton not totally destroyed by caterpillars during the 1845 growing season came from three plantations that used paid labour. In this way the whole state learned about these slave free operations. Everyone in the whole country wanted to know how they avoided the damage others had suffered. They sought out Bobby Johnson to find out how he knew the caterpillars were coming and how he protected his crop against them. Of course Bobby had to refer them to Samson because such observations and methods were beyond Bobby's understanding.

"Those who work directly with the plants have a better chance at understanding what makes them grow and what their natural enemies are," Samson would tell them. "You need to encourage them to think for themselves and they will learn what to do for your crops."

"None of our niggers said anything about the caterpillars until it was too late. You mean they could have saved our cotton."

"No, your 'niggers' would never be able to do it, but a respected employee may have been able to do some good."

"If the niggers knew how to save the crop they should have done it. We will whip that knowledge out of them so it won't happen again."

"You don't seem to understand," Samson continued. "When you employ a slave you only employ his body. You don't allow him to think. If he has an idea that may improve production, he would be punished for putting it into action. You are the brains and he must do what he is told and do it the way he is told to do it. You cannot expect such an animal to make any meaningful discoveries. But when you treat your employees as people and honour their intelligence, then they can begin to learn how to do things better. That is no guarantee that they would have discovered the caterpillars on time or found a way to prevent their damage, but at least they would have had a chance to discover it. I knew last year that this was going to be a bad year for caterpillars, but when I tried to tell you, everyone thought I was over reacting. Now, I could have been wrong and my efforts could have been for nothing. If I was a slave I would have surely been punished for that, so you see a slave could do absolutely nothing to help the situation.

But being free, I am free to make mistakes and free to learn from them. This is how I've learned to read nature and predict certain things. I never knew that the caterpillar infestation would be this bad, but I knew it would not be good. That is why I took steps to protect the crop. My knowledge alone would not have done it. I found a man who had some knowledge passed down from our African ancestors that saved the crop, thus it was a team effort. You may have had someone on your own plantation that had this knowledge, but he would have been subject to a whipping if he had come forward with it.

"Now if anyone wants to try our methods," Samson made his pitch, "we can send a team out to train your workers, but that will only work if you treat them as equals. You must give them their freedom first. Then we will begin to train them to think. You will notice a change of attitude almost immediately and in a few years you will earn more profits than ever before. You must share those profits with your workers. That is the only way it will work."

Slaves were purchased for one purpose only, and that was to work. If a horse was not needed it could rest in its stall. Dogs used for hunting or chasing runaway slaves could often be seen sleeping when they were not needed. But to have an idle slave was unthinkable. With no cotton to tend there was not enough work to keep the slaves busy. Many owners hired their slaves out to sugar plantations further south. Some were willing to offer Bobby Johnson free use of their slaves. That way the slaves could learn the new, more efficient methods and surely Mr. Johnson would not object.

"Certainly we would be glad to train your workers, but we never use slaves, so you would have to obtain free papers for them first." Bobby set this one condition.

"How will we know they will come back and work for us?"

"You won't know that, but the training will do no good if you don't set them free."

The plantation owners did not know how to run a plantation without slaves, so Bobby suggested, "Perhaps you would like to come and see for yourselves how we do things. Then, if you like, we can send teams out to train your workers next year."

The caterpillar infestation of 1845 gave the slave free system a lot of publicity and there was great interest in the three plantations. Bobby received many request to talk about the new system. He and Samson had many opportunities to spread the news as the slave free plantations received many visitors.

It is difficult to change after two hundred years of doing things the same way, so, despite all the interest, only three plantations were willing to free their slaves in 1846. There was enough doubt cast on the slavery system that no one in Louisiana bought a slave that year. In 1847 the number of slave free operations again doubled as six more were added to the list and many plantations were using some paid labour.

By 1848 attitudes had changed in Louisiana. The state withdrew the restriction on education and the African Americans were allowed to attend schools. Slave owners still had the right to refuse to let their slaves be educated and the white schools would not accept black students. Krissy, and others she had trained, could teach openly and a school building was soon constructed on the Lancer plantation. Krissy also assisted Bobby and Ruthie to set up a school at the Johnson plantation. Krissy was as talented at teaching as Samson was in agriculture, and it became obvious that her students were getting a superior education. The plantation owners soon expressed interest in sending their children to the new schools. As the schools became integrated those desiring the best for their children were willing to pay high tuition. The quality of education in the white only schools deteriorated as enrolment dropped and teachers left. Children of prejudiced whites found that they had missed out on a great opportunity.

For a while, outside help was hired to meet the demand, but soon there were enough local teachers who were much better at teaching in an integrated system. As students graduated, some would go to teachers' college in the north and return to teach in the ever growing number of schools.

With blacks being educated, paid labour spread rapidly throughout Louisiana and there was talk of making slavery illegal. Samson knew that the mutual respect between worker and management would be lost if owners were forced to give up their chattels. As this was an important part of his new system, it was necessary to get as many owners as possible to willingly free their slaves. It was, however, recognized that the worst offenders would never voluntarily give up slavery, but until a majority could be found to make it illegal, education seemed to be the best method of informing plantation owners of a better way. Bobby and Samson were kept busy travelling to various plantations to introduce the new methods.

With many plantations in Louisiana becoming free, travel within that state became much easier for the former slaves. Many who had just received their freedom would travel to find lost relatives, many times obtaining work closer to where their loved ones lived.

With growing popularity, there was also growing opposition. The opposition, although coming from a minority, was vocal and violent, and many who wanted to try the new method were hesitant to do so because of fear of retaliation. However attitudes did change, and many allowed their slaves much freedom even if they did not officially emancipate them.

Chapter Fourteen

Otis

In 1849 the new system crossed state lines and Mississippi had its first free plantation. There was a man about forty-seven years of age who was bought when he was about two years old. He found, through sales records, that he was sold from Hamburg, Louisiana by a Fred Lancer, in 1804. He came to Hamburg to find if he had any relatives left living. He stopped into a store and made his inquiry.

"Fred Lancer passed away many years ago," Robert Taylor was there to answer his questions. "My nephew married his daughter. They may be able to find some information." Mr. Taylor drew him a map of how to get to the Johnson plantation.

Mr. Johnson was in the big house and directed the traveler to Bobby's house. As he approached the door, Ruthie saw him and came out to the porch. "Hello," she said.

"Hi. My name is Otis and I was sold from Fred Lancer's plantation in 1804. I am trying to find out if I have any relatives in this area."

At first Ruthie took no particular notice, but the name Otis should have some meaning. She remembered her father's will. He left everything to his four children. They had set up a bank account to deposit the share of the lost brother who no one seemed to know, now what was his name? Yes it was Otis. "Otis?" she inquired as she stared into his eyes.

"Yes that is the name I've always gone by and I believe it was given me by my mother. According to the records, she went by the name, Mammy."

All the children of Mr. Lancer had inherited his eyes. Ruthie stared into the eyes of Otis and she saw her father. "Yes," she said. "Come in. You have found your family. I am your sister."

Otis was surprised by this announcement, and Ruthie was a little confused. 1804 was the year before she was born. She knew that her father had children from his slaves after her mother had died, but Otis was older than her. However, the mystery was solved and, for the first time in her life she was meeting her older brother. "When Bobby comes in, we can go over to the other plantation and you can meet your brother and other sister. You said Mammy was your mother? We can see her as well. We are a bit of a mixed up family as it seems none of us have the same mother."

"So you know my mother then?"

"Oh yes. She raised me until I was three. Then Sheila, who is your brother's mother, took over. My mother died when I was born, so Mammy and Sheila were the only mothers I knew."

"What can you tell me about my father?"

"He became a changed man shortly before he died. He was the first slave owner to free his slaves. He had lived a very miserable life, but he died a happy man."

"So this is where it all started. My owner in Mississippi heard about this new system and he is the first in that state to free his slaves. Bobby Johnson is the subject of much talk, both among the slaves and the owners. His theories are often discussed and many plantations no longer use a whip. They have found that kindness is much more productive. Master Black realised that, in order to be truly kind, he could not own his workers, so he gave all of us freedom papers. He even helped me find out where I was born. He warned me I might not like what I found. He said one of the reasons he bought me was that Master Lancer was treating me very badly. He said Missus

Lancer seemed to have something against me and couldn't stand the sight of me. She was most happy to have me sold."

"I suppose I can understand why. I know my father had children with his slaves after my mother died, but I always thought that he was faithful to her while she was alive. I am quite surprised that he had a child with one of his slaves before I was born."

"Are you sure I am his child?"

"He named Otis as one of his children in his will. That is the first I knew anything about you."

"But perhaps it is another Otis he was referring to."

"No. It is you for sure. One trait my father passes down to all his children are his eyes."

"That's why you were staring at me when I first came."

"Yes, you definitely have my father's eyes and that is the only proof I need to prove that you are my brother."

"You said I was in his will."

"Yes you were. He left you an equal share and we have been putting your share of the profits aside for you. I don't want to put anything in the way of us enjoying our family reunion and money sometimes complicates things, so we will talk about that later, but rest assured, you are not a poor man."

They continued to talk until Bobby came home. Ruthie jumped up at the sound of him at the door. "Bobby, I want you to meet my brother Otis."

Bobby looked at the stranger and back to his wife. "Are you sure, Ruthie." Bobby was concerned that someone may have heard about the inheritance and was after the money by pretending to be Ruthie's lost brother.

"Look into his eyes." Ruthie used the same conclusive proof that Sheila had used so many years before to convince her that Willie was her brother. She had recognized those same eyes in her sister, Ella, and today a stranger had arrived bearing her father's eyes. "You can't tell me that you don't see father in those eyes."

Bobby studied the stranger for a while. He wasn't as quick to see it as Ruthie was, but she had known her father better. "He does bear a resemblance to Willie." Bobby said finally.

"Yes, and speaking of Willie, we need to take Otis over to the other plantation to meet his other sister and brother. I was hoping you would be home sooner so we could go tonight, but since it is getting late, why don't we eat and relax tonight and go over first thing in the morning."

Otis had come from Mississippi by foot while wearing slave's clothing. He was not used to the comfortable treatment he received as a guest of his white sister. Ruthie made up the guest room for her brother and, for the first time in his life, he slept in a comfortable bed. He was given a basin of water to wash up and some clean bed clothes to wear that night. He was about the same size as Bobby who picked out some clothes for his guest to wear the next day.

Mammy Recounts the Birth of Otis

In 1849, Bobby and Ruthie had been married twenty-four years. They had three children. The oldest, John, was twenty-two years old. Harry was nineteen and Jenny was fifteen. The children spent as much time at the Lancer plantation, visiting their cousins, as they did with their parents. When Otis arrived they were all spending the night at various houses at the other plantation.

Krissy's oldest daughter, Ella, who was also a half sister of Ruthie, would be thirty years old in 1849. She had dated a few of the white boys from Hamburg who, many times, thought they could take advantage of her inheritance. They knew she owned a share of the plantation and many saw her only as an ignorant nigger. However, Willy looked out for her and would investigate. When Hank told Willie that niggers weren't welcome, Ella very quickly broke off with him. She settled on Oliver and married him in 1841. By 1849 they had three children, Thomas (seven), David (five) and Anna (two). They lived in the big house were Ella looked after the elderly that could no longer work in the field.

Krissy and Samson also brought four more children into the world. When Otis arrived Jimmy was twenty-three years old, Martha was twenty, Harvey was sixteen and Christine was twelve. Samson had a house built on the plantation for his family.

In 1831, Willy married Karen who was a worker on the Johnson plantation. By 1849 they had five children. Billy was sixteen, Mary was thirteen, Sam was eleven, Edward was eight and Sally was five. They lived in a house Willy had built close to Samson's house.

All these children considered themselves as one big family, and the parents of one child would act as the parents of all. They enjoyed a great deal of freedom but were well disciplined. They were all well schooled and also began to work on the plantations at an early age. The colour of their skin made no difference in their social standing and they all had utmost respect for each other's parents. An order given by any one of them was the same as if one's own parents had given the instruction, and it was carried out immediately.

When Bobby and Ruthie arrived with their special guest, Karen was doing some housecleaning with the help of Jenny. Sam, Edward, Thomas, and David were playing in the yard. Jenny spotted the Johnson carriage and ran to meet her mom. Karen followed and met them by the big house. They soon got Ella's attention and Otis was introduced. The young boys who were playing in the yard were dispatched to round up Samson, Krissy, Willy, and Oliver who were working in the fields. It was summer and when Krissy had no school children to teach she liked to spend her time working in the cotton fields so she would not lose her talent. Of course, the children working with her were often corrected on their diction or asked to count the bags of cotton in each row and add them together.

Along with his family and in-laws, the nieces and nephews also flocked into the big house and Otis was introduced to them. Mammy, now retired, was resting in one of the rooms and she was brought to the parlour. When she was introduced to Otis he said. "Momma, it is so good to finally meet you."

"Hold on a minute, young man," Mammy replied. "I'm not your momma. I may have given you a start in your life but I didn't birth you."

"The records show you as my mother," Otis stated bluntly.

"That may be true, but the records are wrong." Mammy suddenly began to look very sad and tears came to her eyes. "I'm not sure you want to hear the truth of it, but your momma died the day you were born."

There was a sudden silence in the room as everyone gathered around to hear what Mammy had to say. Many of the elders who were present in the big house crowded into the room and all stood or sat in silent anticipation of what was soon to be disclosed.

"Oh how I prayed I would never have to remember that day, but I could never completely forget it," Mammy continued in a sorrowful voice. "Your Mamma," she addressed Otis, "was a young child named Trudy. She was much too young and much too small to be having a baby, and it was more than the poor girl could take. She died that day in agonizing pain. No one could do anything for her. She screamed until she had no energy left to scream and then she laid there moaning and bleeding. Finally the grim reaper gave her the peace she deserved.

"Massa Lancer would often go after the little girls and he used to make them do the most disgusting things. If they pleased him he would give them candy and if they didn't he would whip them. Trudy got very good at pleasing the Massa. She would often brag about all the candy she got.

"Usually he had enough restraint that he wouldn't go into them, but the night he did that to Trudy he had been drinking more than usual. We heard screaming coming from the shed and we thought he must be whipping her. But Hiram sensed that something was wrong and he picked up an ax saying he would kill the bastard. By the time he got to the shed, Trudy was staggering out naked and in a bloody mess. She collapsed on the lawn and Hiram picked her up and rushed her to me. She almost died that night and I often wish I had let it be so, but I worked to save her life that night, and that only led to more suffering for the poor girl. One would not think that a human being could have done such a thing as what was done to that dear girl. It had to be a monster from the pit of hell that left her is such a condition.

"Massa never touched her again after that night, but that may have been because she ran and hid every time he came around. Eventually it became evident that she was pregnant and the pregnancy was brutal. She suffered more and more as she got closer to term. I don't think she ever understood what was happening to her. She was much too young to understand.

"I think he was too embarrassed to put a child's name on the records as the mother. When I found out he used my name, I told him he had no business doing that. He gave me a severe whipping and told me he would put whatever name he pleased on the record.

"I was nursing my own child when you were born, Otis. You were about one year old when the missus got curious how I could have two children so close together. I set her straight and got another whippin' for tellin' the truth. But after that, she told Massa to get rid of that child or she would leave. Finally she went to stay with her brother, George, saying she wouldn't be back until the child was gone. Massa sold you pretty quick to the first buyer that would take you.

"Missus came back the day that Mr. Black picked you up and she was glad to see you go. Some of us heard her yelling at

Massa that if he ever touched a nigger child again, she would leave him for good. Nelly heard her and could do a pretty good imitation of how she sounded that night. They soon made up and Massa was on his best behaviour for a while. We soon learned that Missus was pregnant. She died when Ruthie was born and I again weaned one of my own children so I could nurse one for Massa Lancer.

"We were afraid Massa would go back to bothering the children after Missus died. He started drinking more than he had before. He would often come out to our quarters at night when he was drunk and, if we seen him lookin' at the little ones, Nelly would do her imitation of Missus screaming at him. We would hear him saying, 'I'm sorry Jeanette. I'll shape up. I won't do it again.' That way we kept him away from the children and he left them alone until the day he got Krissy pregnant. He still got after the young ladies but he was usually too drunk to do much. He got Sheila pregnant a few years after Ruthie was born. It was about ten years after that when Krissy was thirteen years old that he got her pregnant. At least she was old enough to handle the pregnancy and we still have her with us today.

"I hoped I would never have to talk about this. That is the whole story. There is nothing left to tell, so please don't ever ask me to tell it again. Now you know the truth. It may have been better if you never heard it."

After that Mammy took her cane and hobbled back to her room. There was a stunned silence and no one dared speak in the room where this announcement was made. Gradually the crowd dispersed and you could hear murmuring outside the house and in adjoining rooms. The children were instructed to go back to what they were doing before Otis arrived and the adults retired to Willy's house to discuss the future.

Once inside, Bobby was the first to speak. "Ruthie, I am so sorry you had to hear that. When I married you, I became part of your family and I share in your pain and your shame. I think

Mammy was right, that we should never speak of this again. But we must be wise enough to know that Fred Lancer was not unique. So long as slavery exists these same things will happen to others. Mammy has been free for more than twenty years and she finally felt free enough to tell us the truth. Slaves and even free blacks that make such accusations against whites often find themselves hanging from a tree before the day is done. It took a lot of courage for Mammy to tell us the truth. Now we must have courage to act on it and end slavery."

Otis had something he wanted to say, but forty-seven years of slavery had taught him that a black man did not speak in front of a white man unless first being spoken to. Willy noticed his discomfort and said. "Otis, my dear brother. I am sorry you had to hear our family's dirty secrets, but I would like to welcome you. I am glad to finally make your acquaintance. The only indication we had that you existed is when father named you in his will. No one ever talked about you and none of us knew anything about you. The fact that he put your name in his will shows how he changed at the end of his life. For most of his life he was a cruel, bitter, and selfish man, but for the last ten months he became happy, kind, and generous. The system of slavery taught him that black people were just objects to be used for his amusement. In the end, he recognised that this was wrong and he finally treated me as his son rather than as his slave. He finally became a father to me, and as horrible as he was in the past, he became a good father. If it weren't for the system of slavery, he may have been a good person all his life. I wish you could have known him during his last days. Although I feel shame at what my father was, I am very proud of what he became."

Ruthie was in tears. "You are so right my dear brother. When I heard Mammy talking, I started to think about the times I wanted to kill my father and was starting to regret that I hadn't done it. I remembered all the pain he put us through. When I heard what he did to your mother, Otis, I could not see how God could ever have forgiven him. I thought of his last while on earth as a feeble attempt to buy his way into heaven, but I was sure he was burning in eternal Hell as we heard Mammy speak. But brother Willy, I believe you are right. His conversion at the end of his life was genuine. He did become a changed man. That does not make up for the horrible things he did in the past, but he did what he could to make up for it. It may very well be the system of slavery that made him as he was. I grew up with my best friend Krissy, but it wasn't until after I met Bobby that I recognized her as an equal. When I was a child, it was great having a best friend who was a slave and had to do anything I wanted her to do. Perhaps I was just like my father and who knows what I may have done if I had continued as a slave owner. Bobby saved me from all of that and my life has been so much better since he became a part of it."

"Otis," Ruthie continued. "I would like to join my brother, Willy, in welcoming you to our family. This must be quite a shock for you. I never knew anything about you and, although I knew my father had done many terrible things, I was shocked by these facts. I always thought my mom and dad were happy together and I thought it was mom's death that made my father so bitter, but you were born while momma was alive. Why don't you tell us a little about yourself?"

Otis had now been asked to speak and he was glad for the opportunity to unload his thoughts. "My master, Mr. Black, was a very kind man. When I told him I wanted to find my family, he told me I may not like what I find. He said that, one of the reasons he bought me was because of the cruel treatment I was getting. He usually didn't buy children preferring to acquire slaves that were ready to work." Otis paused for a moment to collect his thoughts, then continued.

"It was quite a shock finding out how I came into this world and I am not quite sure what to make of it. Unfortunately it is not that surprising. I have heard other similar stories in the past, but never when white people were present.

"This is all very new for me. A few days ago I was a slave in Mississippi. Last night was the first time I ever slept in a bed. It felt very strange to me. And these clothes that Bobby lent me. Why I look like a regular man. I just don't know what to make of it all. And this house. I can't believe this house belongs to my brother. This don't look like no black man's house. Even the big house back in Mississippi is not as fancy as this."

"Brother Otis," Willy addressed his sibling. "If you think this house is nice, you can build a finer one than this. Samson has been putting your share of the profits in a bank account for you for the last twenty-four years. You will have that with interest to spend on what you like."

"Yes, Otis," Samson added. "We will go over your finances tomorrow. Bobby and I can help you with them. Money carries with it responsibility and it is pretty easy to lose it, so I would advise you to seek proper advice before making any deals with anyone."

"I'm not sure if this is a good time to bring this up but I found the story told by Mammy to be very disturbing." Bobby began to speak uneasily. "I know we should be celebrating a family reunion and it should be a happy time." Bobby paused to collect his thoughts, then continued, "We have made some changes in Louisiana and we have been sitting around thinking how wonderful we are that we managed to end slavery in our little corner of the earth, but slavery is still out there and as we are sitting here enjoying our happy time together, a little girl is being abused by her master and no one can do anything about it because the law sees her as his property and he can do anything he likes with her."

"We have done quite a bit," Ruthie said in support of her husband's efforts. "There are a lot of people who have better lives because you took the initiative."

"That is just it," Bobby retorted. "I have not done enough and I never have done enough. When I was a teenager, God spoke to me and told me slavery was wrong. I knew I could never be a slave owner and experienced a great deal of anxiety trying to figure out how I could run a plantation without slaves. Meanwhile, my best friend, Samson, was coming up with the plan to end slavery. My vision was short sighted. It was Samson who started this whole thing. And now we have had a great deal of success running our plantations without slaves and we have shown the world that, not only is it possible, but it is more profitable. Again, I didn't see that. It was Samson who had the vision to show this to the world. It is because of him that I learned that, not only slave owning was not necessary, but that it was actually holding back the economy. We have enjoyed twenty-five years of this freedom. When Fred Lancer freed his slaves he himself became free. He was as much enslaved by the system of slavery as the slaves he owned. Now we have our little plantations and a handful around us that have broken away and become free of the slavery system, but it is not enough."

"Relax, Bobby." Willy tried to calm the situation. "It will take time to change the system. As you have said, we have shown the world that it is possible. It will take time for the world to catch on, but eventually everyone will see."

"That is just what I was thinking, but I was thinking wrong. It is not just what happened to Trudy. We were robbed of the presence of our brother, Otis, for many years. How many more families must be broken up? How many little girls must be tortured? And what are we doing? We are sitting around patting ourselves on the back saying we started something good. Maybe we have the time, but there are thousands of children out there that do not.

"Now I have heard some rumors that indicate that we better act fast before it's too late." Bobby continued. "There is an abolition movement in the north that is helping slaves to escape from slavery. The slave owners are not taking it lightly and they want their property returned. They are threatening to pull out of the union if the north does not do more to return the runaway slaves and punish those who help them. We already have a tide of proslavery activist to fight against. If we don't act now, the opposition will get worse and we may find ourselves in the middle of a war."

"Bobby," Otis began to address his brother-in-law. "I have just become a free man and haven't even had time to enjoy my freedom, but if what you say is true, count me in. I will do whatever I can to end slavery. You say I have money. Let me use it to end slavery."

"That's very generous of you, Otis," Bobby replied, "but perhaps you should find out how much money you have before you give it away. Anyway, I have taken up enough of your time. Today we are celebrating the homecoming of a long lost brother. Let us celebrate today. Tomorrow we will try to figure out what we should do next."

The celebrations continued the rest of the day and into the evening. Everyone in the room took their turn to welcome Otis and he was given a tour of the plantation that he co-owned. He was very impressed with the worker's accommodations. Some had used their money to build their own cabins and a little village of homes had sprung up on the plantation. The old slave quarters had been torn down and a rooming house for unmarried workers was constructed with separate areas for the male and female workers. The big house had been converted into an old age home with the exception of an apartment occupied by Ella and her family. Ella had studied health care and was a great asset to the elderly retired workers that had rooms in the same building.

When Otis saw some workers analysing soil samples he asked what they were doing. "We are developing a science of farming," Samson told him. "Many of our workers have university degrees and we continue to study and develop farming strategies. By knowing what is in the soil, we can predict what crops will do best and learn what fertilizers will help. We also sell the information to agricultural companies that use it to develop new products. The tools and technologies we use here are the most advanced in the country."

Otis learned that, with their success, they periodically expanded their operation and new land was acquired. Whenever the partners agreed to buy more land they would each put an equal share towards its cost, and yes, an equal share was taken from the account set aside for Otis, so he was a full partner in all they had.

Everyone wanted a chance to play host to Otis, but Willy won the first round. They all had the evening meal together. Willy had the honour of giving his brother a room for the night.

Chapter Fifteen

Saving a Nation

Bobby and Ruthie gathered up their children and rode home. John drove the carriage and Harry sat with him on the driver's seat. Jenny rode in the carriage with her parents. Bobby held Ruthie close to himself as Jenny looked on.

"That was quite the speech you gave," Ruthie said to her husband.

"I just don't think we are doing enough," Bobby replied.

"Momma, did grandpa really do those things that Mammy said he did?" Jenny posed the question.

Ruthie looked to her husband for support. Her child had heard the ugly truth. How could she explain it?

"Jenny, darling," her father made the reply. "Grandpa was a victim of the slavery system. He did just what many other slave owners are still doing. It usually doesn't get talked about and we seldom hear the truth. Don't tell anyone what you heard today. Mammy could be in a lot of danger if word got out that she spoke about it."

"Did grandpa Johnson do those things too?"

"No darling. My father was different that most slave owners. There are not many that would do what Grandpa Lancer did either, but the law allowed them to do it. It may not happen that often but it should not happen at all."

"Grandpa Lancer must have been a very evil man."

"He did some horrible things, but he didn't know any better.

When he owned slaves he considered them as animals. Most slave owners only see their property as livestock like horses or pigs. Grandpa Johnson was kind to all his animals, but Grandpa Lancer thought you had to be mean to animals to make them work. When he did that to Trudy, he didn't think of her as a person. Even Willy and Ella were just animals to him before he changed, but you see he recognized them all as his children in the end. Even Otis was left an equal share in his will. Most slave owners would think he was crazy. They would see it as the same as leaving an inheritance to horses or dogs. He really changed when he learned that black people were humans and he began treating them with much respect. Now we must teach every slave owner the same thing. Once they see their workers as human beings, they will no longer want to keep them as slaves."

Bobby did what he could to comfort his daughter and his wife. He also needed comforting and found some in his own words as he spoke to his daughter. Yet he could not sit around and let such things happen to others. Samson was the one who had the vision to end slavery. He would go back the next day and have a meeting with Samson. There must be something they could do.

That night, before they went to bed, Ruthie had some mother/daughter time with Jenny and Bobby took the opportunity to talk with his two sons. "I am very proud of how you boys turned out," he said. "You had a very different life than me. I grew up with slaves for friends. I'm glad you never had to know what it was like being a slave master's son. Now don't get me wrong. My father treated me good and he was, and still is, a kind and generous man. However he was burdened by being a slave owner until he saw that it was wrong to treat black people as animals."

"Yes father," John replied. "Grandpa often tells us about that. He says it was you that showed him how slave owning was wrong. He said he gave you quite a hard time about it and wouldn't accept it for a long time. But he also said that, once the slaves were free, he felt as though a great burden had been lifted from him. He always tells us to listen to you and do what you tell us."

"Well, son, after what I heard tonight I feel I must make a renewed effort to end slavery. You boys know about as much as I do about this plantation. I may have to do some travelling. Do you think you can handle things here for a while?"

"I am willing to do anything to help," Harry replied. "I didn't realize that these things are still happening and I don't want to see another child get hurt. I will do whatever I can to put an end to the slavery system. If keeping the plantation running while you travel is what you want me to do then I'll do it."

"You know this plantation practically runs itself," John observed. "I don't think we will both be needed here. I can look after things and you can take Harry with you if you want."

"Oh yes, father." Harry was excited by the prospect. "Let me help you. I can help you design posters and advertisements for the newspapers. Please let me help."

"Ok," Bobby said to his sons. "Let's sleep on it. We have a big day ahead of us tomorrow. If everyone feels the same way in the morning we will make our plans." They said their goodnights and went to their rooms. Bobby was getting ready for bed when Ruthie entered the room. "How's Jenny?" he inquired.

"She's taking it kind of hard, but what you told her has helped quite a bit. Actually it helped me as well."

"At least we now know who Otis is and how he came to be. It must have been hard for him to hear about his mother like that. What bugs me is that someone is probably doing the same thing to some poor innocent child tonight. We need to work on getting the laws changed to protect the innocent ones."

"Bobby! I am so glad I married you. If you hadn't come

along, who knows how I would have turned out. Although I hated the things my father did, I wasn't much different. Krissy was my best friend, but I treated her like a favorite pet. It scares me to think of what I might have done if you hadn't come into my life."

"Ruthie, darling! I could not have made it without you. Not only are you beautiful, but you are smart. I could not have done half of what I have without you. And now I am going to need your support more than ever. I just have to try to bring an end to slavery. If I don't succeed I feel like there will be a great disaster in this country."

That summer night in 1849, two lovers talked about saving a nation. Would the USA go to war with itself and cause more destruction of lives and property than any outside force could ever inflict? It is strange to think that two ordinary people could make decisions that would alter the fate of a nation. That night they talked about plans to end slavery, a system that was so vile and evil that it had the power to split a nation and cause a devastating war. Yet what kind of effect could two lovers, sharing pillow talk, have on the fate of a nation? Perhaps the love they shared would be strong enough to keep the nation together. Yes, these were two ordinary people, but they were about to do extraordinary deeds. Already they had changed the community they lived in. Now they were about to change the whole country.

Making Plans

John was up early and checked on the status of the work of the plantation, then came into the house for breakfast. Right after breakfast, Harry saddled his father's horse and then his own. As they prepared to leave Ruthie said, "I'll be praying for you."

"Me too," Jenny said.

Bobby and Harry rode off to see Samson on the Lancer

Plantation.

When they arrived, Samson was in his office going over the books with Otis. "I never knew there was so much money in the world," Otis said.

"Twenty-four years of your share of the profits has added up to quite a sizable sum," Samson stated.

"I don't even know how to sign my name," Otis said. "Perhaps you can keep managing it for me until I learn to read and write."

Just then Bobby walked in. "Hello guys," he said. "So you're going to get an education, Otis. That is an excellent idea. We managed to get the laws changed so at least it is now legal to educate blacks in Louisiana. Krissy has been a good teacher and your sister Ella can help you as well. I think you will do okay."

"What brings you here today?" Samson inquired. "I suppose you want to get started on your plan to end slavery."

"Yes I would like to," Bobby observed. "But it seems the plan has come from you. I don't know if you can explain it to this thick skull of mine, but I have to do something. So tell me what I should do."

"I don't rightly know," Samson replied. "My plan was to start a profitable plantation without slave labour, and we've done that. I thought the idea would catch on and everyone would want to try it. I suppose we got to get the word out."

Harry had a few ideas of his own. He took a large piece of paper and drew out in big letters. "Do you want to double your profits?" Then in smaller letters. "Find out how."

"This is how we can start," he informed the others. "You told me the profits of your plantations doubled within a few years of starting your system. If we put up posters and hand out invitations to a meeting for this purpose, I think people will come. Then we can explain how it works."

"I think you're on to something Harry." Bobby was beaming at the contribution his son had made. "Now all we got to do is decide where to start."

"You can count me in," said Otis, "and I think a good place to start is by talking to my old master in Mississippi. He just heard about your system and decided to free his slaves, but he really has no idea how to make it work. If he fails, it will be a big setback. We need to get him started. Plus I told him I would come back after I found my family. I would appreciate the escort. I heard about slave catchers that will steal free papers and sell free black men back into slavery. I would feel safer travelling with a white man."

"You are right, Otis," Samson said. "We cannot afford to have any failures at this point. It is already difficult to get slave owners to free their slaves. If one fails, it will be almost impossible to get anyone else to try."

They began to make their plans. The next day was Sunday July, twenty-second and they had church to think about. Bobby was leading services on the Johnson plantation and Samson looked after things on the Lancer plantation. There were many other capable souls that could take over a service at either location. There was no official minister but the gatherings were always filled with the Holy Spirit and everyone felt spiritually recharged after attending. "I will find someone to take our church service tomorrow and we will join you. It will be our first Sunday with Otis and the family should all worship together," Bobby stated his intentions.

Bobby rose early that Sunday to get the carriage ready. He let his wife sleep in while he made flapjacks for the family breakfast. Once they had eaten they got in the carriage and rode off. As usual, John and Harry took the driver's seat and would take turns handling the reins.

When Otis attended his first church service on the Lancer plantation, they had been happening each Sunday for twenty-five years. Over that time discussion had been made about building a proper church building, but the congregation seemed to prefer the outdoor atmosphere. A shelter had been constructed that would protect them from rain during the wet times and keep the sun off their heads during hot days. But it was open on four sides with the exception of a small backdrop behind the preacher platform which helped to project the voice out to the crowd. Benches had been constructed and most times everyone had a place to sit, but often the crowd would overflow the shelter and the seating capacity. On those days some would sit on the side of a little hill outside the shelter.

The July twenty-second service was overflowing. Many had heard the long lost heir of the Lancer plantation had come home. Many wanted to meet him. Some wanted to help him spend his money, but all wanted to welcome him. The front benches were quickly reserved for the family and there was much excitement throughout the crowd as each one vied for a better position. As usual, there was impromptu singing as the crowd gathered and eventually the song leader would announce songs for the congregation to sing together. The songs were interspersed with prayer and praise. Samson then read a few verses from the Bible. Next came the time for announcements, and Samson had many.

"Bobby and Ruthie Johnson are here today with their family to welcome Ruthie's brother, Otis, to our community. I would also like to extend an official welcome to Otis on behalf of this congregation. Welcome Otis. Would you like to say a few words?"

Otis joined Samson on the stage. He turned to the crowd and said, "A few days ago I was still a slave. I have never seen anything like this gathering before in my whole life. Over the last few days I have had many new experiences. I have, at last, met my family. First, my sister Ruthie who brought me here the very next day to meet my brother Willy and my sister Ella. I have also met their wonderful families." Otis hung his head down in bewilderment as he said, "I didn't know it was possible for a black man to live in such luxury. I also didn't know I had a white sister who doesn't see me as any different from her white friends and family. She recognized me as her brother right away and welcomed me with open arms. My master, back in Mississippi has been kind to me. He gave me my freedom and I feel I must go back and help him for awhile, but, if God is willing, I will be back to settle here." Many cheers arose as Otis went back to his seat.

Willy stood up and said, "As the brother I have already welcomed Otis to my home. I now, on behalf of myself and my sisters, would like to welcome him to our community."

Samson continued his announcements. "Since Bobby is with us today, it is only fitting that he deliver the message. Bobby, would you now come and share with us what the Lord has laid on your heart?"

Bobby stood and read from his Bible. "This passage is from the gospel of John, Chapter eight starting at verse thirty-four. 'Jesus answered them, Verily, verily, I say unto you, Whosoever committeth sin is the servant of sin. And the servant abideth not in the house for ever: but the Son abideth ever. If the Son therefore shall make you free, ye shall be free indeed.'

"Prior to this Jesus said, 'And ye shall know the truth, and the truth shall make you free.'

"Otis is my brother-in-law but I consider him a true brother. When I married Ruthie twenty-four years ago, her family became my family, and although I did not know Otis at the time—none of us did—he became my brother. My brother has suffered in slavery for many years. Shortly after I married Ruthie, her father passed away and left his plantation to his four children. He named Otis as one of the heirs. Until a few days ago we did not know who he was and for twenty-four years he was a plantation owner living as a slave, not knowing that he was part owner of this property." Bobby looked toward Otis.

"Brother, Otis, I am sure this is all overwhelming for you."

Turning to the crowd Bobby continued. "Less than a week ago, Master Black gave Otis his freedom. I know some of you here today are still slaves but many have enjoyed freedom for more than twenty years. Some of you younger people never knew what it was like to be a slave. But Jesus told us in the Bible that, if we sin, we are a slave to sin. This is the sad truth. Many of us don't even know we are still slaves. I didn't know. I have been a slave to my sin for these many years. God had a purpose for me. I neglected to serve him as I should. We did a little, but a lot was expected. We freed our own slaves. Thankfully my father freed our slaves before I ever became a slave owner. I owned one slave for a few hours and it felt so horrible that I couldn't get his freedom papers fast enough. That is how my best friend, Samson, became free.

"The word got out that a plantation can be run without slaves and a handful of plantations in this area have freed their slaves. Otis has now brought the news that one plantation in Mississippi is slave free. I have been relaxing and raising my family, feeling pretty smug with myself, thinking how wonderful I have been, but meanwhile, my brother, Otis, was in bondage. Thankfully he was owned by a kind master, but many masters are not kind. Many hundreds of thousands, perhaps even millions of human beings in the south are still slaves, and what am I doing about it. I am sitting around thinking how great I am that I have convinced a handful of slave owners to free a few slaves in this area.

"And how free are you? Can you travel to visit friends and family? Some have tried and had their freedom papers stolen and were forced back into slavery. Is this freedom?" Bobby paused to allow the congregation time to reflect.

"I have sinned and come short of my duty. This country has one set of laws for blacks and one for whites. The law protects the rights of the white people while taking all rights away from the blacks. The law gives a white man the right to own another human being and gives him the right to do with his property anything he wants to do. If someone buys a fancy vase and smashes it, people will say he is crazy, but no one denies his right to do it. If someone buys a 'nigger' and kills him or tortures him the law takes the same stance. The property owner has all the rights, the property has none. God showed me a long time ago that it was wrong to own another human being. In my short-sightedness, I thought only about how I would survive without slaves. I thought nothing of the other slaves that are held as property. My father was a kind slave owner and if I had become a slave owner I would have been kind, but there are horrible things happening anywhere that slavery exists. Little girls are being raped by their masters, and the law says it is okay. Sometimes he causes them injury and they will suffer for the rest of their lives. Sometimes they die, yet the law says it is okay. It is their property. They can do as they please with the chattels they own.

"Today marks a new day. Today I have been awakened. Today I stand up and say, 'I will not tolerate this in the country I live in.' Today I will begin to march forth and proclaim freedom for all. Freedom from slavery. Freedom from sin. I will labour and strive to end slavery while I yet live, or I will die trying. But, when my Lord asks what I did, I cannot tell Him I did nothing.

"The key to ending slavery, is having profitable plantations were slavery isn't used. Samson and I may be traveling for a while and we are depending on the workers of this plantation to keep it profitable. In this way, you can help to end slavery. In this way, you can eventually live in a country where you are equal and respected citizens. As we prepare to travel, we will be praying for success. Please keep us and our efforts in your prayers as we go. The Lord has shown me that, if we are not successful, this country will suffer great destruction. We must succeed for the sake of all."

Bobby turned the service back to Samson who led the

The Alternative

congregation in prayer. Everyone knew that God was on the side of good and were assured that there would be success.

Over the years the social part of the service had become a big feast. As the participants became more affluent, the quality and variety of the food served became greater. Today, many had brought delectable treats and a huge meal had been prepared for all.

Not every black person who came was free. Many slaves would get passes so they could attend the Sunday service and many slave owners would also attend. Attitudes had changed over the years and the slave owners no longer felt threatened by these services. Many were considering the new system and contemplating freeing their own slaves. It took Bobby's sermon to push some of these over the edge and there were five plantation owners, who still owned slaves, present that day who came to Bobby and thanked him for his message, informing him that they would immediately start proceedings to free their slaves. They also offered Bobby money for his travelling expenses.

A mule and a wagon were spotted coming up the long laneway. Rev. Ichabod Kempler had developed a habit of allowing his mule to take him wherever it would go after Sunday service at his church and he was not at all surprised to find himself approaching the Lancer plantation. He had heard about the arrival of Otis and suspected many of his own parishioners had come to the Lancer church service. He also wanted to meet Otis and have a chance to fellowship with his friends. When his parishioners apologized for abandoning him, he replied, "If I wasn't the minister, I would have skipped my service and come here myself." He made inquiries and was informed of the inspired talk that Bobby had given. When he approached he said, "Hello Bobby. I heard you gave a rip roaring and inspired message today."

"Yes Rev. Kempler. We are taking a new direction and are, more actively, working towards a slave free south. We already had many confirmations that we are doing the right thing. I believe that three or four plantation owners have approached us today to say they will free their slaves."

"It was five, Bobby," Ruthie interrupted.

"That's right. I can't keep up. The Lord is working wondrous miracles. He is changing the hearts of the south as we speak. I don't doubt that the south will be slave free very soon."

"That is a mighty high ambition, Bobby. Slavery has been in the south for more than two hundred years. I don't think it is possible that attitudes will change overnight." Ichabod expressed his opinion.

"With us it is impossible. But with the Lord all things are possible. I remember a time when you preached nothing but pro-slavery. The Lord did a fine job with you."

"You are right as usual, Bobby. It took God and a dumb mule to get me turned around. I don't even try to control my animal anymore. I let God guide it so it takes me where He wants me to go. Brought me here today."

There was much rejoicing that Sunday afternoon, and festivities went into the evening. When it was time for Ruthie and Bobby to go home, they invited Otis along.

"Ella is teaching me how to write my name and how to read books. I think I will stay here and learn as much as I can before I go back to Mississippi." Otis declined the invitation. Jenny also decided to stay with Ella and help with the teaching. Bobby and Ruthie returned to the Johnson plantation with their two sons.

It Could Get Dangerous

First thing Monday morning, Harry rode into town and bought paints and poster paper at Uncle Robert's Store. He went right to work making posters, leaving a space at the bottom to put a location and time for the talk. He showed his

The Alternative

work to his father. "These are great," Bobby said.

"I can add in the location and time at the bottom when we set up the meetings," Harry explained.

"But you've put so much work into these. It will be a shame to use them only once. When we give talks we will get some hand bills printed and attach one on the bottom of the posters. That way all we need to do is attach a new hand bill each time we use them."

Just then, John came in. "Wow, Harry. You have done a fantastic job. I am glad you are going with Dad. You are really helping the cause."

> **Plantation Owners And other business owners**
> Would you like to learn how to
> **Double your yearly income**
> Bobby Johnson and Samson Johnson of Hamburg, Louisiana will show you how.

"What's this I hear about my son and grandson running off to Mississippi?" The older Mr. Johnson and his wife made their appearance.

"A few years ago we would have thought you were crazy," Sara Johnson added. "It could get dangerous out there. You be careful; and don't go starting any fights with the locals."

"Don't worry, mother. God will protect us. I wouldn't be taking Harry with me if I thought there would be real danger." Bobby tried to sound confidant, but he knew trouble could arise very quickly. He was willing to sacrifice his own life, if necessary, but he was having second thoughts about having Harry come along. Yet his son wanted to serve the Lord in this way. How could he say "no?"

Over the next few days, Bobby spent a lot of time praying in his study room. The plan to end slavery was a grand one, but he was not sure if it would work. There was limited success in their area but the newspapers of the south were full of ads offering rewards for the return of runaways. Many times, owners did not care if their property was returned dead or alive and sometimes they offered more money for proof that their slave was dead. Slave catchers loved the dead or alive ads as all they needed to do is bring proof of death to claim the reward. This was much easier than trying to return a reluctant slave to his master. The slaves knew the torture they would be subject to when returned and many times would prefer death, so there is nothing they wouldn't do to try to escape.

To Bobby, it made no sense. Why offer a reward to have a slave killed? The dead body of that slave is not going to profit the owner. Yet they wanted to teach a lesson to other slaves who were thinking about escape. If the prospect of running could be seen as much worse than staying, perhaps they wouldn't run. But ask any slave owner if his slaves were content and he would assure you they were and that none of them had any desire to run away. Ask any slave if he was content and you will also get an affirmative answer. The punishment for being discontent was severe, so it was much safer for a slave to say he was content. Yet many would run if given a chance.

Education was another indication of the incongruent nature of slavery laws. Slaves were regarded as animals that were incapable of human intelligence. Yet there were laws to prevent one from educating a slave. No such laws existed for any animal in the south. The fact that there was such laws indicated that the lawmakers knew it was possible to teach a slave and that they were intelligent human beings. Yet the slave owners blinded themselves to the obvious truth and therefore blinded themselves to the potential of a remarkable people. Keeping them in a state of ignorance prevented them from contributing to society and as a result the whole society suffered.

Bobby saw the injustice. He knew his black companions were as intelligent as himself and he found his best friend, Samson, to exceed himself in intelligence. As he thought of his friend's accomplishments and how he had transformed the plantations he had worked on, inventing new tools, developing new farming methods, experimenting with crops and livestock, Bobby was overcome with admiration. If he had been satisfied with the status quo, he would have become Samson's owner and would have suppressed this potential.

Agricultural technology was getting noticed. Samson had sold several of his ideas to farm implement manufacturers and his inventions were available in the retail market. Agricultural supply companies were buying his research results to aid in developing fertilizers and seeds that would produce healthier plants and produce higher yields. Crop rotation was being taught to farmers all over the world and analysing soil samples to determine which crops would do best was becoming more common. This new technology was being accepted all over the world, but in the southern USA, it met more resistance. The new technology would make the slaves' lives easier and most slave owners had no desire to do that. Some realized that, by using these new tools, they wouldn't need as many slaves, but number of slaves had become a status symbol. If someone found that, by using new tools, he could have fifty slaves do the same work that one hundred were doing, he would want nothing to do with it. He already owned a hundred slaves and to reduce that number would reduce his standing in the community.

The slavery system had so blinded the slave owners that they could not see their own best advantage. This new system, initiated by Samson, could make life easier for all, but the slave owners could not see such possibilities. Bobby lamented and poured his heart out to God, pleading for answers. He had second thoughts as to the wisdom of the plan he was about to embark on. Had he not done enough? Slavery had ended on his plantation and several others. Would it not be better to let time do the healing? Surely the rest of the south would eventually see these advantages and voluntarily become slave free. Had

Bobby Johnson not done his part? Surely the fate of the south was not his responsibility. He was about ready to give up when he remembered Trudy and Krissy. These ones were children when they were bred by their master. The indignities and torture they had suffered in the hands of slavery was inexcusable. Bobby knew their stories were not unique. The property rights of the slave owner assured that their property had no rights. Anyone who interfered with those rights was seen as a thief trying to steal valuable property.

Bobby's thoughts turned to another friend he had met many years ago. William Lloyd Garrison had started an abolition movement and was doing his part to free slaves. Garrison preached about the evils of slavery and advocated for immediate emancipation, but many abolitionists thought the problem could be solved by smuggling slaves to free states and Canada. He, and other abolitionist, were being met with anger from the south who thought the north was not doing enough to return their property. As Bobby followed the news, it seemed it was about to explode into violence. No attempts were being made to reconcile the opposing opinions and the divisions were becoming more pronounced. Bobby was sure there would be a devastating war if this continued. Bobby was motivated by this sense of urgency as he plotted to find a way for the south to voluntarily give up slavery. In doing so he risked being seen as an enemy of the south. He had to make it clear that he was not attempting to steal the slaves or to lure them away, but was promoting a new way of life were black and white could live together in harmony. He was proposing a system of cooperation rather than competition. Slavery was the ultimate example of competition. You had winners and losers. The slave owners won and the slaves lost, but as a result the society, as a whole, lost. Much more could be gained by working together, allowing everyone to contribute.

Bobby had learned a lot in the twenty-five years since the plantations he worked with had freed their slaves. He had paved the way and made it easier for those who followed, but he had been unable to do more than make a dent in the attitudes of the south. Although he had learned much about the advantages of having a respected work force, he had also learned much about the impossibility of changing the attitudes of most slave owners. He would cry out to his maker, "Oh God, how can I succeed in this task you have given me. You have shown me that slave owning is against Your will, but how can I make the blind to see unless You first restore their sight. Lord, You see that the people are unaware of their best advantage and even if slave owning was made illegal, they would only find other ways to exploit the people they employ. I know, Lord, that we can accomplish much more through cooperation, but most refuse to see that idea. Lord, show me what you want me to do."

Ruthie had heard Bobby's voice in his study and went to check on him. As she approached the door, she realized he was praying and waited until he was again silent. She then quietly tapped on the door. Bobby invited her in.

"I was concerned," Ruthie explained. "You have been spending a lot of time in here and I heard you calling out to the Lord."

"Yes, Ruthie. I am having second thoughts. I'm not so sure I should be taking Harry with me. It could get dangerous."

"But you have always said that God will protect us."

"Yes. I have been praying to determine if this is really the Lord's will. I know He will make a way if this is what He wants us to do, but it seems so impossible. We could be risking our lives for nothing. We may be unable to change anything."

"It sounds like you need to have a talk with your Uncle and with Samson. Why don't you pay Uncle Robert a visit and I will send the kids to invite Samson and Krissy for supper tonight?"

Ruthie's advice seemed sound so Bobby set out for Hamburg.

Chapter Sixteen
Mississippi

Bobby returned from Hamburg early and was able to help his wife prepare a meal for their guests. "What did Uncle Robert say?" Ruthie inquired as they worked.

"He thinks I should be sure about what I'm doing before I go," Bobby replied. He agrees that it could be dangerous and urged me to be cautious. Uncle Robert will never tell me what I should or shouldn't do, but it seems that he thinks I should stay at home."

"It is a lot for one person to try to do," Ruthie sympathized with her husband. "I don't think God wants you to end slavery all on your own."

"There has been quite a bit of support in our area," Bobby mused. "And it seems we have at least one friend in Mississippi."

"So you will go then."

"I'll hear what Samson has to say about it first, but I think we should at least go to see Mr. Black in Mississippi."

They heard a carriage approach and went out to greet Samson and Krissy. The friends greeted each other in the manner that best friends often do and went into the house. Krissy helped Ruthie with the finishing touches of the meal, adding a contribution she had brought. Samson and Bobby sat in the parlour.

"Are you excited about going to Mississippi?" Samson inquired.

"That is what I want to talk about, Samson. I have been doing a lot of praying and I am not sure on how to proceed. I want to get your opinion."

"Prayer is a good place to start, then do whatever the Lord lays on your heart."

"That's just it. My heart is not sure. You always seem to know exactly what the Lord wants us to do, but I am always second guessing myself and wondering if it really is the Lord's will."

"Yes! You often do that, but you are usually right from the beginning."

"It is certainly not easy. I guess the Lord wants me to be sure so He puts me through a lot of tests, but in the end it is always worth it."

"When you take one step at a time, you get through it okay."

"Yes," Bobby observed. "I suppose that is good advice. Perhaps we should just concentrate on the trip to Mississippi and then see what the Lord wants us to do next."

"The trip could prove dangerous, especially for Otis and myself. If the patrollers want to think that you own us, I wouldn't suggest trying to set them straight. It will likely be safer for us all if they think we are your slaves."

"I never even thought about that. I suppose this will be much more dangerous for you. Are you sure you want to go through with it?"

"As dangerous as it is for me—just think about Trudy. Being a slave is dangerous for every slave out there. Even the free blacks will never be safe until the system of slavery ends. Yes, it will be dangerous, but not as dangerous as it would be if we did nothing."

"As usual, you are right, Samson. I can always count on you to make sense of things. Ever since I heard about Trudy, I can't get her off my mind. I wonder how many little girls are being tortured by their masters right now? How many will die a horrible death because of what slavery is doing to them? You are right Samson. We must do something right away."

"It sounds like you two are making progress." Ruthie entered the room to let the men know that supper was ready. "Come let's eat and you can talk more during our meal."

As they ate, the friends reminisced and talked of future plans. Their children were old enough to keep things going on the plantations and they talked of travel and where they might go. They anticipated problems and prayed that God would keep them safe.

"When do you think we should leave?" Samson inquired.

"That will depend on when Otis is ready." Bobby thought carefully. "I feel a real sense of urgency and feel like we should already be gone, but I should say goodbye to my congregation on Sunday. It would be good if we can get an early start on Monday." So they set the date of departure to Monday July 30, 1849 provided Otis was in agreement.

On Saturday, Otis arrived at the Johnson Plantation with a new wagon and horse he had purchased. Willy had taken him shopping and he had also picked up some clothes and provisions for the trip. Otis looked quite the gentleman in his new attire.

He was introduced to Bobby's congregation on Sunday and after the service the social time turned into a going away party for the travellers. Ruthie had gone home early to pack for the trip and when Otis and Bobby came in, they were surprised that she had also packed a suitcase for herself.

"This trip will be much too dangerous for a woman," Bobby tried to explain.

"Do you think I'm not tough enough?" Ruthie said turning her face to make the scar on her cheek more visible to her husband. "You are the one that had it easy. You might need some help if you run into trouble."

Bobby was wise enough to know that anything he could think of to change his wife's resolve would only make her more determined to go. Otis was alarmed. "Do you know what ruffians would do to a woman traveling in these parts?"

"I'll have my brother, son, husband and God to protect me. There is just as much danger if I stay home without my husband's protection."

Monday morning they left early and went to Uncle Robert's store to pick up more supplies. Bobby had hooked up a team of horses to the family carriage and Otis had his horse and wagon. Samson met them at the store. Krissy had come along to see her husband off and Willy drove their carriage for them. Samson's luggage was transferred to the wagon and, after their goodbyes, Willy took Krissy home while the rest headed for Macomb, Mississippi. They estimated the distance to be about 130 miles and planned to camp one night along the way.

As they started out the second day, Harry had a little too much coffee at breakfast and they were forced to take a rest stop. Samson and Otis were riding ahead in the wagon and hadn't noticed the carriage stop. Suddenly three men on horseback burst out in front of them. They were a rough looking bunch looking to pick up extra cash by catching runaways.

When they had forced the wagon to stop, the leader said, "Who do you boys belong to?"

"We are free men," Otis said, producing his emancipation paper.

It is doubtful that any of this gang was able to read but they pretended to scrutinize the paper. "This don't mean nothin'," their leader said as he tore up the paper and threw it away.

"If they don't belong to nobody we can sell them at the market," one of the companions stated boldly. "And we should be able to get a pretty penny for this horse and wagon as well."

"This horse and wagon belong to me and I am a free man," Otis yelled frantically.

The Alternative

"Where's your papers, nigger. 'Taint no such thing as free niggers in these parts. You probable stole that horse and wagon, and look at those fancy threads. Did you kill a white man to get those?"

Samson spotted the carriage approaching. "Otis, you must stop joking with these fine gentlemen. Can't you see they are serious?" he said to his companion, then turning to the ruffians, "Here comes our master now. We thought he was right behind us."

Harry stopped the carriage a safe distance away and cocked his pistol. Bobby got out to see what was going on.

"Are these here yer boys?" one of the ruffians inquired.

"They must have gotten ahead of us somehow." Bobby was careful not to tell a lie while allowing them to believe what they assumed to be true.

"We thought they was runaways," one of the hoodlums replied. "Sorry to have inconvenienced you." Just then Ruthie stepped out of the carriage. "Hey, they gots a woman wit dem."

"Yah, looks like we's gonna have some fun."

Otis and Samson took advantage of the distraction and, by the time these would be attackers turned around, they had rifles pointed at them.

"Hey, no niggers gonna shoot us. They'd hunt you down and lynch you for sure."

Bobby and Harry now had their handguns pointed at the intruders. "Not if I were to say I did it protecting my goods and family from ruffians. Who do you think they will believe?"

"Okay, don't shoot, we's leavin,." They turned their horses and galloped away as quickly as they could.

Otis was highly agitated by the whole incident. It was his first confrontation as a free man and he was irritated that his freedom was so easily discounted. "Why didn't you back me up?" he said to Bobby. "I thought you were a friend. You let those hoodlums believe I was your property."

"He was saving your life," Samson interjected sternly. "You will do well to be more careful and have respect for your friends when they bail you out."

Ruthie was shaking. "I should have stayed in the carriage."

"Well, no harm done," Bobby took charge. "But I don't trust those guys. They probably think we have money and may come back with reinforcements. I think we should change routes. Do you know another way, Otis?"

"When I was coming to Hamburg, I took some back roads. If we go back about a mile, I think we can cross a creek and get to the other road."

"Okay, let's do it." Bobby directed the drivers. He got Otis to lead the way as they retraced their route to a fork in the road and took the other direction. They travelled all day and thought they may be lost but eventually came upon a settlement. They found it was called Brookhaven and they were twenty-six miles north of McComb. They rented some rooms at the local inn. Again Samson and Otis were assumed to be slaves and, when Samson played the part, Otis soon followed his example. Once inside their comfortable rooms they again acted like the good friends they were.

In the morning, Bobby made inquiries and soon found someone who could direct them to Mr. Black's Plantation. "What do you want with that crazy old coot," Mr. Smith said. "He freed all his niggers. Most of them scattered and I caught me one. Took me a day or two to convince him he weren't free, but he's as good a worker as any of them now."

"One of them came to my plantation and I wanted to talk to Mr. Black about his plans," Bobby chose his words carefully so as not to expose his true purpose in unfriendly company.

"There's no need for that. He don't want him. If you caught him you can keep him, sell him or do whatever you want with him. If someone turns a dog loose and don't want him he

The Alternative

belongs to whoever catches him."

"Well, I just want to hear it from his own mouth." Bobby needed directions. "Could you tell me how to get to his place."

"Yeh! About twenty miles south, there's an old trail. Rundown abandoned shack on the corner. Turn west and go about five miles. The road's a little rough and you may have to move a few fallen trees to get through with your carriage, but you will save about fifteen miles. Otherwise you would have to go clear to McComb, go west five miles and come back north five miles."

"Thank you Mr. Smith," Bobby said politely. "We are much obliged."

They set out in a southerly direction and found the abandoned shack. The trail was obscured but they could make out a clearing with a horse trail. "Do you know this trail, Otis?" Bobby inquired.

"I think I have walked it a time or two, but never tried to get a wagon or carriage through."

"Well it will take us two hours longer going the other way, but it could take more than two hours to clear trees." Bobby calculated the advantages. "I think we should go around."

"Problem is that most everyone in McComb knows who I am." Otis was concerned. "You heard what Mr. Smith said. Mr. Black's freed slaves are fair game for anyone who finds them. I think we should avoid McComb."

Bobby had the logical solution. "You and Samson can ride inside the carriage with Ruthie. Harry will drive your wagon and I will drive the carriage. We will go right through McComb without stopping."

With that plan they proceeded and therefore never found out about the friends of Mr. Smith who thought they could pick up a couple of free "niggers" that could easily be lifted from some strangers that would be trying to get through the old trail.

Mississippi

Once they had entered McComb and turned right, Otis was in familiar territory. He had travelled the road often with Master Black and knew the turnoff to the Black plantation very well. He still needed to keep out of sight as Black's neighbours would be likely to recognize him, however, he managed to point the road out to Bobby. When they were a mile from the plantation Bobby stopped the carriage. "Otis, you should drive your own wagon home and arrive in style. Harry can take over here."

Otis rode ahead and Harry followed with the carriage. When Mr. Black saw them approaching, he did not recognize the driver. Strangely, Otis had been afraid of being recognized by neighbors and townspeople, but his previous owner did not know who he was until he said, "Hello."

"Otis, is that you?" I thought a dignitary was coming to see me. Where did you get those fine clothes, and that horse and wagon?"

"I bought them in Louisiana," Otis replied.

"Did you rob a bank or something?" Black was puzzled. "You didn't leave here with enough money to make such fine purchases.

"Turns out my father left me an inheritance."

"I guess you're not coming back to work then?" Black inquired.

"I told you I would come back to help you and I am a man of my word. However, with my inheritance, whatever you could pay me wouldn't mean much, so I will work for you for free."

"You don't have to do that. I set you free. You don't have to come back if you don't want to."

"Well, Massa Black. It turns out that my family in Louisiana are the first ones to set their slaves free and they all want to make sure you make it okay. Let me introduce you. This here is my sister, Ruthie, and her husband, Bobby, and the young lad driving the team is their son, Harry. Samson is the brains behind the free plantations and he married my other sister's mother. I also have a brother, Willy, back at the Lancer plantation."

Now Mr. Black was really confused, "You mean your family is white?"

"We all have the same father but there are four different mothers," Ruthie explained. My mother died when I was born. Father had three other children from his slaves. He set all his slaves free shortly before he died and he left the plantation to all four of us. Bobby holds the title for us as Louisiana law does not allow any of us to be the legal owner of land, but it is operated as though we own it together, so not only is Otis my beloved brother, he is also one of my business partners." Ruthie put her arms around Otis to show her affection for him.

"We all heard about you freeing your slaves and we have been operating our plantations slave free for about twenty-five years now," Bobby began to explain the purpose of their trip, "so we thought we might be able to share our knowledge with you and get your profits up."

"I don't expect to make as much as I did," Black replied, "But I am hoping to make enough to pay salaries. Right now it is a real struggle and I'm just trying to hang on."

"We will show you how to make more money than you did when you had slaves."

"Is that possible? How can I pay my help and still earn more profit? Right now I'm struggling just to find people willing to work for me."

"What happened to the ones that were working for you?"

"You mean my slaves?" Black was more puzzled. "I set them free, and I'm not so sure that was a good idea. Many of them are worse off now and some have been forced back into slavery on other plantations. There is still a few around town but they have to hide from slave catchers and they can't get work."

"You need workers, why don't you hire them."

"I just assumed they would want to go elsewhere. Otis was very close to me and he said he would come back, but none of the others indicated they wanted to work for me."

Samson joined the conversation. "Their options should have been explained to them before they were set free. They obviously know the work on your plantation better than any other work, so most would likely have stayed if they knew they could."

As they talked, a lone traveller was walking up the laneway. He was ragged and obviously suffering from hunger. "Massa Black," he called out. "I beg you please take me back. You don't have to pay me nothing. Just give me back my old bed and some food. I will work for you same as before."

Such perfect timing had to be the work of God. "Do you think any of the others would come back?" Black inquired.

"Why yes, Massa. Most everybody wants to come back. Just say the word and I'll go fetch them."

With their first problem solved, Mr. Black invited everyone into the big house for lunch. His returned worker, Clovis, was most grateful for the meal and was ready to set out at once to fetch the others, but Black was afraid of him being captured. Plus, Clovis informed them, many were near collapsing from lack of food. It was decided to send out a wagon for them. Black got his wagon hitched and Otis proudly volunteered his own. His and Samson's supplies were quickly stowed away to make room. They headed into town with both wagons. Bobby rode with Otis for added protection, but with Mr. Black ahead of him, he was not worried. Clovis rode with Mr. Black to show him the way to the hideout. When they got close, the wagons were stopped and Clovis proceeded alone on foot so the former slaves would not be frightened. He went to the encampment and explained what was happening. Once the plan was established, water and corn cakes were brought in to feed the famished. Then they picked up their few belongings and got on the wagons. There was joy as they rode back to Master Black's plantation. They had been exiled from their homes and had suffered a horrible ordeal, but they were going home. They knew not if the conditions would be any better than when they left, but they had enough of freedom and were ready to go back to slavery.

Problems on Black's Plantation

Because of their ordeal. Mr. Black's former slaves were terrified of freedom. They begged Mr. Black to never set them free again and pledged their allegiance to him, saying that they wanted nothing except to be his faithful slaves for the rest of their lives. Thursday morning, they anxiously went to work. Samson formulated a plan to train them in the new methods, but he had to go back to the way he did things before the Lancer and Johnson plantations were free. Mr. Black's workers saw themselves as his slaves and were terrified by even a suggestion that they were not. It would take time to for them to heal and learn what freedom really was.

The travellers told Mr. Black about their plan to end slavery. "Most of my neighbours thought I was crazy to free my slaves," Black told them. "The way I messed up, they will be more convinced."

"We do need to get things fixed here first," Samson added to the conversation. "Perhaps we can talk to a few of your friends and let them know what we are doing. I think I should stay for a while to get things running smoothly. But I am missing my wife. Bobby, if you could take your family home with a few of Black's workers, they could experience what it is like to work on a free plantation and learn our methods. Then you could bring back an equal number, with Krissy, to help teach the new methods here. We could stay a few months, then you can bring Mr. Black's workers back and we could have some meetings down here to show what we have done."

The next evening, Mr. and Mrs. Black arranged to have a few neighbours over to meet their new friends from Louisiana. Mrs. Black was concerned about the seating arrangement, not being sure that her friends would agree to sitting at the same table as black men. "That's okay, Mrs. Black," Samson said. "I can eat with the workers. I don't need to join you."

"Nonsense," said Ruthie. "I want my brother sitting with me and Bobby should have his best friend beside him." So the table plan was made. The head table was set up with Harry at the left with his uncle Otis beside him, then Ruthie, Bobby, Samson, Mr. Black, Mrs, Black and their son, Ronny taking the right end seat.

Four families were coming with their older children so two other tables were set. Mr. and Mrs. Reid had only one small child who had been left with a baby sitter. When the guests were seated, the visitors were introduced and the meal was served. Many thought it strange that "niggers" were sitting at the head table, but the Blacks were a weird family and if even if they had wanted their dog to sit with them, what business was that of their quests?

After the meal, Bobby talked about how he and his wife were running two plantations in Louisiana with no slaves. He explained that the slave free plantations were the most profitable in the state, then he introduced Samson as the genius that made it all happen.

When Samson began to speak there was a shocked hush in the room. They listened to him out of curiosity. They could not imagine what a "nigger" would have to say to a group of people and had never before witnessed such a spectacle. They were sure he would be an embarrassment and expected he would have nothing intelligent to say. To watch him speak was more like someone showing them a dog that could do a new trick.

They were expecting to laugh and, as Samson spoke, a few chuckles started going around the room. Samson explained how even a small amount of money was much more incentive for the black man to work than a whip could ever be, and how the workers could concentrate on what they were doing much better when they were not in constant fear.

Then Ruthie took her turn. She began to explain how her father was so much happier after he freed his slaves and how he felt as though he had freed himself. This was too much for Mr. Reid. He stood up and stated that he was not going to listen to a woman tell him how to run his plantation. This does not sound so stupid until you get a picture of who Mr. Reid was. He was a timid little man with a stocky burly wife. Mrs. Reid decided that Mrs. Johnson was well worth listening to and told her husband, "Shut up and listen. She just may have something intelligent to say." After that Ruthie continued without further interruption.

After the formal speeches, the guest got up and socialized. All the wives and daughters took time to greet Ruthie and told her how brave they thought she was. "Perhaps not as brave as Mr. Reid." She laughed and they all laughed with her, except for Mrs. Reid who failed to find the humor in it.

The ladies thought that being slave free was worth a try. Ruthie continued to tell them of the seemingly miraculous transformation of her father when he freed his slaves.

"That sounds like my husband," Mrs. Horst said when Ruthie described her father before his conversion. "Seems like whenever he's in a bad mood he takes it out on the slaves. He gives one or two a good whipping and comes back in a worse mood than he was. And the slave children, I'm embarrassed to say how many bear his resemblance."

Bobby was not having so much luck with the men. "Novel idea, but it will never work. Plus I enjoy owning slaves," said Mr. Horst. "It relaxes me."

Most of the men agreed. There were too many advantages

to slave owning, and even if they could make a little more money by freeing them, which they found doubtful, there was the social status that slave owning gave them, and the feeling of power. Mr. Reid added, "They gotta do whatever I tells them and they can't talk back to me. Don't think I could get by without slaves."

Samson was ignored as "niggers didn't belong in a social gathering other than as servants." Some were curious if he could do any other tricks. "Can you get him to roll over and play dead?" Mr. Miller inquired.

After the gathering, the Blacks and the Johnsons sat down to discuss the results. Bobby was discouraged as he felt he didn't influence anyone.

"Perhaps you should let you wife do the talking for you," Mrs. Black stated bluntly. "The ladies sure seemed to rally around Ruthie."

"Yes, I got a lot of positive feedback from the ladies," Ruthie explained. "Perhaps we have to get to the men through their wives. I think they could put the pressure on."

"Well, I thought my husband was crazy until I heard you explain it, Ruthie," Mrs. Black stated. "I didn't think we could get by without slaves, but the way you guys explain it, it makes sense. And when you talked about the freedom your father felt when he freed his slaves, well I saw the same thing in my husband. I thought he was going to ruin us financially, but when I saw how much happier he was, I thought that, at least, we would go down happy. Now if you guys can keep us alive and we can stay this happy, I'm all for it. I don't care if we get rich or not. So long as we can survive, I'm happy."

With mixed feelings, they turned in for the night. Ruthie and Bobby shared much pillow talk as they went to sleep. Bobby knew that their plan was important to save the world from misery, but was the encouraging pillow talk from his wife enough to give him the strength to go on?

Chapter Seventeen
Arson

Saturday morning Samson and Bobby discussed the finer points of their plans. They asked Mr. Black if they could hold a church service on his plantation the next day. The idea was immediately approved. Samson and Bobby both worked in the fields with the workers. At first they were afraid of Bobby, thinking that Mr. Black had hired a new overseer, but Bobby soon put them at ease. They had never seen an overseer doing slave's work and Bobby worked as hard as any of them. Following his example, they all put a little more effort into what they were doing.

Otis had discovered that his new clothes did not serve him very well in the field, but his old slave clothing was very uncomfortable. On Sunday, he dressed up for the church service and invited his co-workers to join him. "We don't have any church clothes," they would tell him.

"That's okay. We will have an outdoor service right here. You don't need church clothes." But many were uncomfortable to show up in their slave threads. Finally Otis switched back to his old garment and tried again to invite his co-workers. Now many of them accepted.

When Otis told Bobby and Samson about the problem he had, they also decided to come to church in their work clothes. After the singing of a few spirituals, Bobby and Samson took turns reading from the Bible and explaining how all mankind were equal in God's sight.

After the service Bobby and Samson tried to socialize with Black's workers. The former slaves knew they were friends of Otis but were still distrusting. They also found that Otis had become a new person and did not know what to make of it. They talked about taking a few workers to Louisiana but found the workers reluctant to consider this plan. Clovis said, "None of us want to go. We want to stay here and serve Mr. Black. Nobody wants to be free. If Mr. Black orders us to go, we will go, but we would prefer to stay right here."

Monday morning, they prepared to leave. The carriage could seat up to six on the inside and up to three could sit on the driver's seat on the outside. Four of the most promising workers were selected and were persuaded to go. Clovis was among them. He had shown initiative when he returned to Black's plantation for help. It was felt that he would make a good leader.

Earlier that day, Otis had asked Mr. Black to accompany him to town. He also asked Harry to come along to help him in his task. He found a store that sold comfortable work clothing and ordered enough for all his fellow workers. He brought the four sets that were on hand home with him for the workers that were leaving. The others would have new comfortable clothes when the order came in. Otis did not want to continue wearing his old slave clothing, but he also did not want to be dressed better than those he worked with, so he bought clothing for all. Harry had come along to help him make out a bank draft to pay for his purchase. The clothier questioned accepting the draft and said it would have to clear the bank before he released any of the clothing, but Mr. Black promised to be responsible for the four sets taken.

The travelers did not want to spend an extra night camping along the way, so they decided to leave early Tuesday morning. This also gave the four that would be leaving a chance to say goodbye to friends and family. By morning, two others asked if they could join, and Mr. Black readily agreed. Otis was concerned that he did not have their gift of clothing available, but Bobby assured him that the workers would be well provided for when they reached Hamburg.

Bobby, Ruthie and Harry rode on the outside so their darker skinned companions could be securely hidden inside the carriage. They found a secluded spot to set up camp when it started to get dark. They then continued the next day and reached Hamburg in safety. Stopping at Uncle Robert's store they picked up the extra two sets of clothing.

"Hello Bobby," Uncle Robert greeted his nephew, but his tone was grave. "How was your trip?"

"We are a little anxious to get home, but everything went well," Bobby replied, but sensing that Uncle Robert wasn't being his usual jovial self, he asked, "Is something wrong?"

"I'm afraid there have been some problems," Uncle Robert said sadly. "Some raiders disguised themselves and rode onto the Lancer plantation and burnt down the big house. Everyone got out okay, but the house was destroyed."

"Is Jenny alright?" Bobby was concerned for his daughter who was staying with her Aunt Ella in the big house.

"Yes. No one was hurt except for one of the raiders. When Willy's dog, Sparky, tried to chase them off, one of them kicked at him and he bit into his leg and hung onto for a good two minutes."

There were a few customers in the store during this conversation. One of them quickly left. Ruthie came in to see what the holdup was. "Why was that guy in such a hurry to leave?" she inquired. "He was walking with quite a limp."

"Did you get a look at his face?" Bobby asked excitedly. "Someone burned down your father's house and he was likely involved."

"I know who he is," Uncle Robert spilled the beans. "That was Peter Kroft. He doesn't come in here often, but when he does he is trouble. He always insists on being served ahead of any black customers. When I refuse he rants about us being no good nigger lovers that should be driven out of town."

"Way to go Sparky!" Bobby said excitedly. "That is why he was limping. Sparky bit his leg."

With their purchases in hand, they left for the Lancer plantation to deliver the workers. Bobby was in a hurry. They found Ella and her family had to move in with her mother and the elders who occupied the big house were spread around wherever there was room. They saw the damage to the big house. There was nothing left but ashes and a few charred timbers. Ella and the other inhabitants had lost all their possessions. Bobby wanted to get to the magistrate to file a complaint against Peter Kroft as soon as he could, so he left Harry to explain about the workers. He, Ruthie and Jenny headed back to town, where Bobby made his complaint against Peter Kroft. The magistrate asked "How can you be sure it was him? We have already investigated and they were all wearing disguises. Oliver was out in the field and he was to only white man present, so even if someone else recognized anybody, the courts won't accept the word of a black man. How will you prove it was him?"

"You just issue the arrest warrant and we will worry about the rest." Bobby said.

The magistrate said that Peter was already a suspect but without proof they could do nothing. He warned Bobby that, if he could not produce reasonable proof, he may be charged with making a false complaint. But Bobby stuck to his resolve and said he wanted the culprit arrested.

"We will let you know when a court date is set. It will likely be within a week. I believe the judge is in town on Monday."

The Trial of Peter Kroft

Bobby had a meeting with Willy, Ella and Ruthie about plans to replace the burnt dwelling. Willy had some practice when building his own home and was already coming up with a design that would more adequately fulfill their needs. Willy proposed a building with comfortable rooms for the senior residents and perhaps a separate dwelling for Ella's family. All thought this was good, but Ella wanted her residence attached to the main building so it would be easy for the senior residents to call her when she was needed. Willy continued to draw up the plans with those considerations and felt construction could begin within a week.

Samson had asked Bobby to return to Black's plantation with Krissy and six volunteers from the Lancer plantation to help train Black's workers. With the arrest of Peter Kroft, Bobby was required to testify in court, so the trip back to Mississippi had to be delayed. Krissy wrote a letter to her husband explaining the developments and the reason for the delay.

Monday August 13 arrived. Peter Kroft limped into court and entered a plea of not guilty. The judge asked why he was limping. He said he had been hunting coyotes. When he checked one that he had shot, he found it wasn't dead and it bit him. Two friends had been hunting with him and they could testify to his whereabouts when the Lancer building was burnt. He said he was sorry that the house had been burnt but that the Johnsons should expect trouble if they were going to continue to upset the system that had worked in the south for over two hundred years. He predicted that, if they didn't stop what they were doing, every building on both the Lancer and Johnson plantations would be burnt down.

The prosecution called Oliver Stanton to the stand and, when he was sworn in, he testified that he had seen three men arrive on horseback carrying torches. He had been working in the fields but, immediately, he and the other workers ran to the house. By the time they got there, the horsemen had fled and the house was burning. They formed a fire brigade and put out the fire that was blocking the back door. They managed to get the residents out, but the house was burning in two other locations and they couldn't save it.

"Did you see or recognize any of the horsemen?"

"I only saw them from a distance. They were gone by the time I reached the house."

"Were any white men present besides yourself?"

"No."

Next the prosecution called John Robert Johnson to the stand.

"You filed a complaint against Mr. Kroft for burning your father-in-law's house. What makes you think Kroft is guilty."

"I noticed he had a limp," Bobby replied.

"He testified that he had been bit by a coyote."

"I believe he was bit by Willy Lancer's dog, Sparky."

"Can you prove that?"

"No sir, but if you call Sparky to the stand, he can identify the guilty person."

"How will he do that?"

"Well, Sparky is a very friendly dog, unless someone kicks him. When he gets the scent of the person that kicked him, he will attack for sure."

"Is Sparky here today?"

"Yes. Some friends are holding him just outside the courthouse."

"Objection," the defence lawyer spoke. "A dog cannot testify in a court of law."

The judge thumbed through his law book. "Says here anyone of African descent or anyone born in slavery cannot testify against a white man. Even spells out that someone born of a slave mother cannot testify whether or not he is a slave. Was this dog of African descent or born of a slave mother?"

"No, your honour," Bobby replied. "He was not."

"Well I don't see anything here which says a dog can't testify, so I will allow it."

Sparky was brought to the stand and sworn in. "Do you swear to tell the truth?"

"Woof," Sparky replied.

"That means yes," Bobby translated.

"Can you identify the man that kicked you last Monday afternoon?" the prosecution lawyer asked.

"Woof, woof, woof."

"That means, if I can get his scent I can identify him."

"Well let's have a line up," The Judge suggested. "The defence lawyer may choose who he wants in the line up with his client."

After conferring with his client the lawyer choose four men from those present in the courtroom.

"Does the prosecution have any objections to these choices?"

"No, your Honour."

"Would you like to add anyone?"

"No, your Honour."

The four men were spread across the front of the courtroom and the accused was added to them, being placed second from the right. Bobby led Sparky out of the witness box, holding tightly to his leash. "The leash is only to protect the guilty. Sparky would never harm anyone who didn't try to harm him or a member of the family," Bobby explained.

Starting from the left side, Sparky went up to each one, wagging his tail and sniffing at their boots. As he approached Peter Kroft, he began to growl and tucked his tail between his legs. Bobby held the leash tightly to prevent Sparky from lunging at the culprit.

"Get that beast away from me," Kroft cried out while

kicking at him with his good foot. Sparky grabbed on to Kroft's leg and hung on. Bobby had to pull Sparky back.

"Let go Sparky! Now that's a good dog." Identification done, Sparky went back to wagging his tail. He even went to the last man in the line up, wagging his tail and sniffing at him. There was laughter in the court room.

"You seen it," Peter Kroft hollered. "That beast bit me again. He should be put down. He's a menace to society."

"So he bit you before?" the Judge picked up on Kroft's mistake.

"Yeh," Peter tried to cover up and was thinking wildly, searching for an excuse. "When we were on our way home from hunting coyotes that thing ran out on the road and bit me."

"So you were bit by a coyote and by Sparky that day?" The judge inquired. "I thought you weren't hunting anywhere close to the Lancer place."

"We took a detour on the way home. Maybe I was wrong. Maybe it was another dog at another plantation that bit me." With no time to plan his lies, Peter Kroft was digging himself in deeper.

"Doc Smyth. Could you examine our victim and determine the extent of his injuries?" the Judge ordered.

Doc Smyth examined both wounds and reported. "They are deep but not severe. One thing is certain though. The bite marks are identical. They were both made by the same animal. I see no sign of a third bite."

"Okay, I was there." Kroft was frantic. "But I didn't burn the place down. Jimmy Coutts and George Cutridge did it. I went along because I thought we were only going to scare the niggers a little. I didn't know they were going to burn the house."

"You lying bastard," George Cutridge was in the back of the court room. "You know the whole thing was your idea.

Jimmy and I were trying to stop you."

"Your Honour," the prosecution Lawyer addressed the judge. "I believe we can sort this out by calling Oliver Stanton back to the stand. Now that we know the three suspects it should be easy to determine who did what."

Oliver re-entered the witness box.

"You previously testified that you saw three horsemen with torches approach the plantation. Could you tell how many torches each was carrying."

"It appeared that each man had one torch. They were waving them over their heads as they rode."

"Did you see them leaving?"

"Yes."

"How many torches was each carrying when they left?"

"None of them were carrying anything when they left."

"How many fires were set at the house"

"One torch was thrown through the front door, one through the back door and one through a window at the side. It appeared they were trying to trap the people inside. The back door was closest to the well and we managed to put that fire out. By the time we got the residents to safety, the rest of the house was burning out of control. We had to concentrate on preventing it from spreading to the other houses."

"Your Honour, it appears that all three have set fires at the house," the prosecution lawyer stated bluntly. I suggest the other two be immediately arrested."

George Cutridge bolted for the door but was prevented from leaving by a guard. The deputy found Jimmy Coutts just outside the building. Both young men were brought before the Judge.

"You, George Cutridge, and you, Jimmy Coutts, are both charged with arson. It also appears that there may be some grounds for adding an attempted murder charge. I would suggest that you plead guilty to arson and save the court a lot of trouble."

The young men entered a guilty plea and George added, "As you heard, Oliver was in the field. There weren't nothin' but niggers in that house so we wasn't tryin' to kill nobody."

If a man were to kill another man's slave he may be charged with destruction of property, but that wouldn't be considered murder. If a free black man were killed the courts would not pay much attention. Bobby knew his daughter, Jenny, had been in the building, but the culprits would just have to claim they didn't know and the courts would agree that they weren't trying to kill her. So the arson charge was all they were going to get.

The three men were ordered to pay fines and pay for the destruction of property. Peter Kroft also had a small fine added for perjury. The court determined that three young men were out to have a little fun and got carried away, and since there was no real harm done they were let off easy.

The building was determined to be used mostly as a residence for blacks and therefore was given a value equal to slave quarters that would house as many. The money the three were ordered to pay to Bobby Johnson was very small. They were given time to pay it and each was ordered to pay Bobby Johnson, the person holding the title for the property, ten dollars a month for one year. So the courts estimated the value of the big house to be three hundred and sixty dollars, and that was considered high for slave quarters.

Making Progress

With the court case out of the way, Bobby proceeded to take Krissy and the six workers to Mr. Black's plantation. Samson was making some headway since the workers realized that whipping was not a part of the plan. Cotton picking was just starting and the concept of teamwork was being explained. All the pickers were accustomed to carrying the cotton they had picked to be weighed and being punished if they didn't reach their quota. When Samson had all the cotton loaded onto the wagons, which made continuous trips all day, and didn't keep track of individual production, they were confused. How would Mr. Black know how much each worker had produced? Samson explained that it didn't matter, but the day's production would be tallied to see how they did as a team. He urged each one to do the best he could and to help each other when necessary. Those who were not so fast at picking would be better used by carrying the cotton to the wagon and bringing it to the barns where each load would be weighed and stored. They soon found they could do much better as a team than they had as individuals.

Samson had been devastated when he learned of the destruction of the house at the Lancer plantation but he was very happy to see Krissy when she arrived. Mr. Black gave them a comfortable room in the big house which doubled as an office for Samson.

Much of the initial organizing had been done by the time the workers from the Lancer plantation had arrived. Samson had picked out a few of Black's workers that showed potential and was already training them to take leadership roles. The next morning he called a meeting with the Lancer workers and the potential leaders. They were to work together and observe each other, asking questions and offering advice when appropriate. "What is right for one person may not work for another," Samson stated. "If someone has an idea that will make the job easier and faster, listen to him and allow him to experiment. You may pick up techniques that will make your own production more efficient."

Since they were not being driven by an overseer, many workers felt they were not working hard enough. They were surprised to learn that overall production was better than it ever had been. Mr. Black was delighted and began paying his workers a small amount each Saturday. Samson explained about the profit sharing aspect of his plan and advised Mr. Black to budget for a yearly sharing of profits. "This will be the main incentive for your workers to do well. The greater your profits, the more they will earn. You don't need to pay high wages, but a fair profit sharing program is essential."

The workers from Hamburg bonded with the local workers and they shared many stories during the evening. The recent slaves shared stories of techniques they used in the past to assure they would have just enough cotton each day to satisfy their quota without producing more which would result in their quota being raised. Some told how they would be willing to take an occasional whipping for being short rather than produce too much and have it added to their quota. They were always cautious to leave enough reserve in their abilities so they would be able to meet the new quota in that unfortunate event. They were not really sure how this new system worked. Now it seemed easy to concentrate on picking without worrying about quotas. Once they were assured they would not be punished, they could produce much more than before.

Although the new system was being rapidly applied in Mississippi, the workers that had gone to Louisiana could not believe the efficiency of the operation. They had trouble fitting in at first and were afraid of being punished for not working when they were not sure what they should do, but the lead hands and other workers soon set them at ease. Instead of dreading the horn each morning, they soon looked forward to going to work each day and it was difficult to convince them to take Sundays off. They had comfortable beds to sleep on and good food to eat. They felt like they were in Heaven.

Fear was the driving force behind a slave but fear never got the production that joy did. It is one thing to work out of fear of punishment, it is quite another to work because you enjoy what you are doing and you are good at it. There was singing in the fields, not the singing of a slave to drown his sorrow, but the singing of joy and thanksgiving.

Bobby returned to Hamburg and three reluctant men started paying him monthly visits to bring the ten dollars the courts had ordered. Bobby always greeted them cheerfully and thanked them for bringing the money. He wrote each of them a receipt and closed the transaction with a friendly hand shake.

After working with Black's men for about four months, Samson felt it was time to go home. Bobby and Ruthie came down to return Black's workers and escort Samson and his wife. They again had a meeting with the neighbours. This time they reported the improvements made on Black's plantation, and even though he had lost a portion of his work force, the remaining workers were getting more done in less time. Everyone was much happier and all worked as a team. The extra free time allowed them to get more rest and they worked much more efficiently than they had as slaves.

"Do them niggers still have to do what you tell them to?" Mr. Reid inquired.

"The workers are happy to do a good job. They are encouraged to think for themselves, so they may come up with a better way of doing it, but, yes, they get the job done." Bobby explained carefully. "This does require that we show respect to the workers. They are the force that earns us our money and we need to respect them for that, so we need to be wise in what we ask them to do and not expect them to do stupid and degrading things just because we ask them."

"When I get frustrated I feel I need to hit someone." Mr. Horst explained his feeling. "I don't want to take it out on my wife or kids, so I go out and whip my slaves. It relaxes me and I can get to sleep afterwards. That way no one gets hurt. I don't know what I would do if I couldn't whip my slaves."

"Someone does get hurt," Ruthie stated bluntly. "Your slaves are people. They get hurt, and your plantation suffers since they can't work efficiently when they have pain. Plus you and your family are hurt when you act that way. If you need to hit something, buy yourself a punching bag. That way you can get a workout and no one has to suffer."

Mr. Horst was about to retaliate. He was not the kind of man to take advice from a woman, but his wife put him in his place before he could get his thoughts together. Mrs. Horst said, "I believe that is an excellent idea. I will put a punching bag on our shopping list right now. And, Honey, you are never relaxed after you beat the slaves. You come back in the house in a worse state than when you went out. I think the punching bag would work better."

"The production figures are impressive," Mrs. Reid stated. "I think we should give this system a chance. Do we need to free the slaves all at once or can we implement these ideas a little at a time?"

"The main thing that makes this work is mutual respect," Samson said. "It is virtually impossible to respect someone that you own and even harder for them to respect you. However, on the Johnson plantation we started implementing the ideas a few years before the slaves were freed. Of course we told them that success in our methods would lead to their freedom, so there was always the promise of freedom."

"I found out the hard way that there is a proper way to free your slaves," Mr. Black added. "My workers are so afraid of freedom now that they don't even acknowledge that they are free. They are producing more than they ever did before and I am paying them, but they still consider themselves as slaves. However, I know they are free and that has made me feel free. I think I benefitted more by freeing my slaves than they did."

"Indeed, this is what we find out on a regular basis," Bobby added to the conversation. "Every time an owner frees his slaves he has reported that he felt as though a great burden had been lifted from him. However, the black people can never be truly free so long as the law doesn't treat them equally. We give them as much freedom as we can but there are still many limitations. I wouldn't have had to come down here to escort Samson and Krissy home if the law saw them as equals."

They continued talking as the guests discussed the pros and cons of this new system, but Mrs. Reid had made up her mind, and when she had her mind made up, it didn't matter what her husband thought. They didn't want to make the same mistakes as Mr. Black, so they asked for help. Bobby promised to return in a week. Ruthie indicated that she would like to come along and Mrs. Reid was delighted to invite them as guests of her home. Bobby was concerned that Samson was the brains behind the operation, but Samson had been away from home for a while and was anxious to get back. He assured Bobby that he could manage quite well. "I was your father's slave," he reminded Bobby. "Just look for someone else like me and you will do fine."

A few days after their return to Hamburg the time came for the arsonists to make their payment. Samson was present and Bobby instructed the boys to pay Samson while he was out of town.

"What, we gotta pay a damn nigger now?" George Cutridge was indignant.

"Show some respect," Peter Kroft cut him off. "We caused these men a lot of hardship and Bobby Johnson has been very kind to us. We will do as he says and be happy about it. Bobby, Samson, I am very sorry for what I did. I have seen a glimpse of your operation and I want to learn more. Do you think you could teach me how to run a plantation like yours?"

"You crazy bastard," George was definitely not on the same page. "You's becomin' a nigger lover."

"I think Peter's got a point," Jimmy Coutts added. These guys pay their help and still make more money than our families do. I think we could learn a thing or too."

"Well, I got to be out of town for a bit, but I'm sure Samson could show you around." Bobby's own children could have also done the job but Bobby wanted them to follow the instruction of a black man. "Would that be okay with you, Samson? My boys can help you if you need it."

"I am always glad to show anyone how a slave free operation works," Samson smiled. "Drop by the Lancer plantation any time. Just leave your torches and disguises behind."

George Cutridge stomped off, mounted his horse and rode away. The other two stayed and chatted a while.

Bobby was excited when he reported the incident to his wife. "Seems like we are making progress. We got two more converts in a most unexpected place."

"We should invite their families to dinner and do our presentation like we did at Mr. Black's," Ruthie advised. "If we get the wives on board we have a much better chance."

Bobby remembered his wife's amazing performance at the meetings in Mississippi and readily agreed. "Perhaps we can invite them this Sunday before we go back to Mississippi."

Both Peter and Jimmy were unmarried and living with their parents, so Bobby rode the next day to their plantations to extend the invitation. Peter had spoken to his father about the Johnson and Lancer plantations and they were also interested in how it works, so they readily accepted the invitation. Jimmy's parents were more sceptical and wondered why someone who had their house burnt down would want to socialize with the family of the person responsible. Jimmy wanted to learn more so he accepted, but his parents declined the invitation.

A Late Night Intruder

"Mr. Johnson," Mr. Kroft addressed his host after he and Ruthie had given their presentations. "You have proven yourself to be quite a gentleman. It was extremely kind of you to invite us to your home, especially in light of what my son had done, and your kindness has also had an effect on him. He is quite a different person now and I don't believe he will burn down any more buildings. Ever since that incident I have been having strange feelings. Although I never gave it much thought before, when I'm with my slaves I can't help thinking of how things would be if the roles were reversed and I was the slave. At night when I try to sleep these thoughts weigh heavy on me and I feel like I'm trapped in a bad situation."

"My father," Ruthie piped in, "told us that he felt as though he had freed himself when he emancipated his slaves."

"That's it," Kroft responded. "I feel like, as long as I own slaves, I am a slave. But I'm not so sure your system will work on my plantation. I can't see how I can pay my help and still make a profit. My overseer makes sure my slaves work hard and I can't see how they could work any harder if they were free."

"That's just it," Bobby explained, "They don't have to work harder, just smarter. Once you allow them to use their brains and they are not always looking out for the overseer, it allows them the freedom to do a better job. Plus, giving them proper nutrition and rest makes them stronger so they can work more efficiently. Just think if you were a slave working under the conditions that they do, then think how much better you could do if you weren't always afraid of being whipped. You need to become friends with your workers. Then, when they realize you have their best interest in mind, they will be sure to do well for you. You can start by getting rid of your overseer. Just tell your workers that you are experimenting and if they can show you they can get more done without him, he won't be coming back. You can take steps to make things better for them even before you free them, but you can't truly respect someone you own, so freedom is a necessary step in the long run."

"Well, my overseer has been asking for some holidays. I think I will tell him he can take some time off. If everything goes well, he can make those holidays permanent."

Once he had implemented the new system, Mr. Kroft told his friend about his new way of doing things and Mr. Coutts followed suit. So the conditions of the workers on two more plantations greatly improved.

Bobby reminded his wife of their promise to return to the Reid's in a week, but Ruthie thought it was much too close to Christmas to leave home now, "Besides there won't be much happening there during the holidays. I'll write them a letter to let them know we will come first thing in the New year."

Ruthie wrote that letter stressing that, in the meantime, there should be no whipping and they should assure that their workers get nutritious food.

December and January is when the final picking of the cotton is done. Most plantations would allow up to three days off at Christmas, so it was a more relaxed time of year. Slaves enjoyed a few days of freedom, but their owners were sure to keep them well supplied with liquor and even encouraged excessive drinking. To many slaves, this was the only type of freedom they knew, and the way they suffered from hangovers and sickness, those three days of freedom was all the freedom they could handle. Thus the slave owners instilled in the slaves the idea that freedom was not very pleasant.

Friday evening on December twenty-first, the Johnson's had a late night visitor. Bobby was awakened by the sound of a lone rider and when he looked out the window, the horseman was heading straight for his house with a torch. "Get your guns," Bobby instructed his sons as he grabbed his rifle and went out the door in his bed cloths. With his rifle pointed at the horseman he shouted, "Halt or I'll shoot." John and Harry were soon by their father's side to reinforce him.

The horseman tried to turn and flee, but Bobby fired a warning shot and reiterated his command, "The next one will go through you. Halt."

Reluctantly the man brought his horse to a stop and turned

to face Bobby and his sons. He had disguised himself in a white sheet. "Harry, get that torch." Bobby ordered his son. Harry took the torch and doused it in a water trough. Ruthie came out to the porch with a lamp although the moon and stars were giving a feeble light. "Keep your hands where we can see them and dismount, no sudden moves." Bobby ordered the intruder.

"I thought you were out of town." The intruder spoke and, realizing there was no escape, he drew back the hood of his disguise.

"George Cutridge, well how kind of you to pay us a visit," Bobby said sarcastically. "I suppose, figuring we weren't home you thought we wouldn't be needing our house and you were going to be kind enough to burn it down for us."

"No, I was just coming out to check on things for you. The torch was just so I could see better."

"John, run and get the sheriff," Bobby instructed his older son.

"Ain't no need for that," George Cutridge was squirming. "I see's you's alright now. I'll go peacefully."

"Problem is," Bobby replied, "your story doesn't hold water. You just don't seem to be the type of person that would be so concerned about our well being as to come all this way."

While they waited for the sheriff, George tried many excuses and begged that Bobby let him off. Finally he said, "What if I just get on my horse and ride away, are you going to shoot me in my back?"

"Well the sheriff is coming anyway," Bobby replied. "Suppose it doesn't much matter if he comes to arrest a villain or carries off the dead body of an intruder. That will be your choice." Bobby spoke with such sincerity that the intruder did not dare to challenge him. However, if he did ride away he would have to keep riding for a long time, because, this time he was caught red handed and four witnesses had identified him.

When the sheriff arrived, George repeated his excuses, but

the sheriff did not buy them. "This is a second offence for you. You will not get off so lightly this time." George decided to remain silent as he was handcuffed and hauled away by the sheriff.

It turned out that George Cutridge had about ten years, courtesy of the USA government, to reflect on his actions. He was, from time to time, sent out on a chain gang to do some work. He worked along with other criminals of all colours and, if he didn't feel like working, the sting of a whip would change his mind. Oh yes, in the south in the nineteenth century, criminals didn't have any more rights than "niggers." Only difference was that the criminal was being punished for a crime he had committed and would be set free when his sentence was complete. A slave was punished for being born a slave and he would remain a slave until the day he died.

Chapter Eighteen

Causes and Preparation for War

1850 saw a lot of progress for Bobby and his supporters. As each plantation set its slaves free, friends would want to know why and others became interested in this better and more profitable system. But with each success came more opposition. The pro-slavery components didn't take kindly to having their system undermined. It is a fact in human psychology that those who are made to doubt a long held belief will become very vocal and perhaps militant in their attempt to defend such a false belief. Those who are sure in their belief will not pay much attention to someone who opposes it, but start to show evidence that they are wrong, and there is no measure they will not take to try and disprove you.

This opposition was offset by a growing force of supporters. As more and more plantation owners wanted information about this new system, Bobby and Samson were unable to keep up, so their children stepped up to the plate and did an excellent job at promoting the slave free system. John would often go with Jimmy, Samson's oldest, to visit other plantations to teach the new way. Samson's daughter, Martha, would work with her brother, Harvey, and Bobby's younger son to send out press releases.

The 1840's had begun to show the slave owners the fallacy of their beliefs, however, many more were blind to the incongruent nature of their thinking. Many slaves were escaping to the north each year, but did that keep them from believing their slaves were content? No! If content slaves were running away someone must be to blame. It was those darn abolitionist from the north filling the slaves with this nonsense about freedom. When they tried to have their property returned, those Yankees interfered and helped the slaves reach the land of the free. Secession was the answer. If the government of the United States of America would not enforce the law to return their property, they would separate from the country and form the Confederate States of America.

1850 saw the death of a President of the United States and the slavery issue was a hot topic when the thirteenth president, Millard Fillmore, took office. As an anti-slavery moderate, he supported the compromise of 1850 and the passing of the Fugitive Slave Act. This act greatly strengthened the USA slavery laws and made it illegal to help a slave escape. It had the effect of enforcing slavery throughout the USA. One had only to swear an affidavit that he was the owner of any black person and the law was obliged to arrest the suspected fugitive and turn him over. The black person had no right to testify and no right to ask for a jury trial. Unless some white person was able and willing to prove he was not a slave, he was forced into slavery. Thus the 1850's saw greater numbers of fugitives and free blacks running to Canada. Some of these ended up attending a little chapel on Thames Street in London, Upper Canada. These tougher slave laws were designed to appease the south and keep them in the country, but when northern states opposed the law and passed their own laws that effectively nullified the Fugitive Slave Act, the south became more upset and more militant.

Bobby saw these developments as he struggled to spread the news that slavery was not necessary. The number of plantations that recognized the advantages of the new system was slowly growing. Slavery was slowly being squeezed out and pro slavery activist became more militant. Bobby feared; greatly feared that disaster was coming and worked feverishly to prevent it. In 1850 he and his supporters had trouble keeping up with the plantations that wanted to go slave free. As opposition grew it got more and more difficult to even talk about it.

While Bobby was struggling, Rev. Ichabod Kempler was having limited success. By telling the stories of his dreams and his mule, he gained the support of much of the Christian Community. Many of the pro-slavery preachers were backing off and not stressing their views as they began to have doubts of the system they had grown up with. A very loud minority took the opposite approach and spread venomous lies about the anti-slavery movement. Rev. Kempler visited and prayed with Bobby and Samson often. It was the strength gained by prayer that enabled them to go on. Small victories would come their way but fear of retaliation kept many from upsetting the status quo. Still, many who were afraid to change at least agreed to take a kinder approach and began to see their slaves as more than just work animals.

Christmas of 1850, Edwin Epps from near Marksville invited Bobby and his family to a holiday celebration. He wanted to show Bobby that his slaves were quite content and that they did not desire freedom. He had one slave that could "play a fiddle better than any white man." His name was Platt and he did indeed have an extraordinary talent. Epps also bragged that his boy, Platt, had many other talents. Bobby immediately realized what an asset such a person could be in the free world and tried to have a word with him, but Epps made sure that no private conversation could take place. When Bobby told Epps that he felt all people should be treated equally, Epps readily agreed but added, "Baboons and niggers ain't people."

"You already told me of the extraordinary talent of Platt. Surely you don't think an animal is capable of such things."

"I once saw a baboon at a circus that could do many tricks, but that don't make him human."

It was Monday, January third, 1853 when Epps found out that Platt was actually Solomon Northup, a free black man that had been kidnapped twelve years earlier. Mr. Northup left slavery behind that day and wrote a book about his experiences.

During quiet times, Bobby would gain a few more supporters and many more had a change of heart but did not free their slaves out of fear of the militant pro slavery activists. With dwindling numbers, the pro slavery group had to resort to intimidation and illegal acts, such as arson and assault, to prevent the masses from switching over to the more economic system. Bobby was unaware of many plantations that virtually freed their slaves but kept quiet about it so they wouldn't attract the attention of these enemies. With militant groups becoming more violent, it became dangerous for Bobby to travel far from home and he was forced to post guards around all his properties.

In 1859 the abolitionist, John Brown, marched into a town in Virginia with a few armed men and captured the armouries at Harpers Ferry with the intention of freeing slaves. When the US army arrived, most of his men were captured or killed, and Brown himself was executed after a short trial. As a result, the south had eliminated a criminal and the north had gained a martyr. The already agitated relations became even more volatile and preparations were being made for war. A couple of Brown's men had escaped and when one was located, instead of the local authorities arresting him, they published a notice in the paper that gave him warning and allowed him to escape.

When Abraham Lincoln was elected president in 1860, the agitation grew as he was known to be anti-slavery. Lincoln tried to appease the south but he soon found it was not wise to hand feed a hungry lion. Even before Lincoln took office, Jefferson Davis headed up the government of the Confederate States of America. A Confederate army was formed and war was about to begin. But wait a minute. Wasn't Bobby Johnson supposed to prevent this from happening?

The Nightmare of War

Bobby heard the thundering of countless horses and, before he knew what was happening, some men were pounding at his door. As soon as he opened it, Confederate soldiers burst in. With rifles pointed at Bobby, they informed him that he was under arrest for upsetting the system of the South. The Confederate government also decreed that all free black men or any descendent of a former slave would become their property. Samson, Krissy, Willy, Otis and Ella were brought in with chains binding them together. "We brought your friends so they could thank you personally for the predicament you got them into."

Just then Ruthie ran into the room. "Why do you have free men and women in chains?" she screamed.

"They are now property of the Confederate Government," a soldier informed her.

"No you can't take my brothers, my sister and my friends."

Ruthie found herself very quickly added to the chain gang. "If you are the sister of slaves you must have been born of a slave mother, so you are also property of the government.

Jenny came in screaming, "Mother, what are they doing?"

A soldier quickly detained her and said. "This young one is quite fair skinned, she will fetch a good price. There's a lot of men would like to get their hands on her."

When Samson was young he didn't do very well on slave rations. When he started eating better his body gained strength, but his real strength was in his mind. Now, being forced into slavery by the government he was put back on slave rations and his health failed. He was unable to keep up with the work and suffered many beatings. Otis, having been more recently a slave, faired a little better. The young ones who had never been slaves did not know what was happening to them.

When Ruthie saw Jenny being sold to a very crude looking

man, it was obvious why he wanted her. It was too much for Ruthie to take. She managed to snatch a gun from a soldiers holster and screaming she pointed it at them wildly, forcing the soldiers to gun her down.

Bobby was not allowed the aid of a lawyer. The new Confederate government was making up their own rules, so a lawyer wouldn't have helped him. A soldier was appointed by the court to represent him. Bobby pleaded not guilty but the soldier said he had acted against his advice and recommended he be hanged immediately.

Outside the courthouse a crude gallows had been constructed and Bobby was forced to walk up the shaky steps. He thought the whole structure would collapse, but he made it to the hangman's noose and it was placed around his neck. There was much commotion below as Bobby felt the structure begin to sway, then suddenly he was falling.

Chapter 19

Meeting With the President

Bobby awoke with a start. His uncontrollable shaking awoke Ruthie. "What's wrong?" Ruthie asked.

"I just had the most horrible nightmare." Bobby hugged his wife. "I am so glad that you are okay."

Bobby shuddered as he remembered his dream when a couple confederate soldiers did show up at his door shortly after breakfast. Bobby was cordial with them and invited them for tea. It was Friday March 1st, 1861, and the soldiers had come looking for volunteers to fight in the Confederate army. Bobby, then sixty years old, was too old to serve even if he had wanted to. He informed the soldiers that his sons would not be joining them but then asked how they were doing.

"We got nobody in this area. Seems a lot of folks think they would be better to give up their slaves rather than go to war over it. Somebody has been spreading rumors that more money can be made by paying free labourers."

On April 12th, 1861, a small army of Confederate volunteers marched on Fort Sumter in South Carolina. They were met by the local troops of the US government and they threw down their weapons without firing a shot. The Confederate government could not rally enough support to start a war.

Many years before, Bobby Johnson felt strongly that God did not want him to own slaves. He did things a little differently and it snowballed to change the outcome of history.

Meeting With the President

Bobby was unaware of the effect he was having. Militant groups kept many of his supporters silent, but rumors of a more economic slave free system were being whispered from one plantation to another. Few could be found who would be willing to go to war over the corrupt slavery system. As newspapers reported the buildup of tension between the states, a few reporters latched onto the story of this new system and asked, "Could this prevent war?"

When Bobby freed Samson, he unleashed a power that could change the world. Samson worked out a plan and, with the help of Bobby, Ruthie, and Krissy, the plan was put into action. Slowly the supporters grew into a small army. By the time Bobby turned sixty years old, he had his children and grandchildren to support his efforts. Together with the descendants of Samson and Krissy, they impacted society in a positive way. As more and more joined them they were easily able to defeat a militant minority without resorting to violence.

With rebellion quickly squashed, all eyes turned to the one who had prevented the disaster of war. Bobby Johnson and this slave free system made the news all over the world. Bobby was sixty-one years old when President Lincoln sent him a message. He wanted to meet this hero and learn more about the system that had prevented disaster.

Bobby and his companions were ushered into Lincoln's office by three security guards. The president and his adviser both rose to greet their guests. Once the three arrivals were shown to their seats, Lincoln immediately dismissed the guards.

Lincoln greeted Bobby Johnson and introduced his advisor, Frederick Douglass.

"It is a great honour to meet you in person, Mr. President. I have brought with me my two greatest supporters and advisors, my wife, Mrs. Ruthie Johnson and my best friend, Samson Johnson. Samson is the real brains behind the plan. I would not have even thought it was possible to end slavery, but he had the plan that is doing it." Bobby made his introductions.

"So your all Johnsons." Lincoln appeared interested.

"Yes. Samson was my father's slave and when my father gave him to me I had emancipation papers drawn up immediately." Bobby explained. "That is why he has taken on our last name. I have known him all my life and he really is like a brother to me."

"Samson, could you tell me a little about this program?" Lincoln inquired.

Samson explained about mutual respect and stressed that the freeing of slaves was always done voluntarily. "In some cases they don't free the slaves right away, but they treat them with respect, feed them properly and give them financial incentives."

"Do you find the freed slaves will leave the plantations?"

"Some do," Bobby answered the President. "But many who do come back. We find, with our system, we don't need as many workers, so it all works out. Also, when workers trained in the new system go to work on other plantations, it helps to spread the system faster."

"Mrs. Johnson, had I known you were coming, I would have brought my chief advisor, Mrs. Lincoln. Can you tell me a little about your involvement."

"We find that the wives of the plantation owners usually see the advantages of our system first. By reaching the women, we get our message through to the plantation owners."

"Do you think women should be allowed to vote."

"Oh, yes. Many problems could be resolved if women were involved in all aspects of politics. But the vote should be open to all women and men, regardless of colour."

"Mr. Douglass, any thoughts or questions?" The President turned to his advisor.

"Mr. President, you know I have always advocated for the black population staying where they are and doing what they are trained to do. You are aware of the problems of the migration north and how prejudice begins when the working class in the north accuses the fugitive slaves of stealing their jobs. You also know how I blame the system of slavery, and not the white man, for the problems of the south. But I have one question for our visitors. Would it help your cause if slavery was made illegal?"

Bobby and Ruthie looked to Samson who answered the question. "There is no doubt that slavery is the true villain and the sooner it is done away with, the better. But to force people to give up their slaves would cause bitterness and resentment. Many plantation owners have huge amounts of capital invested in human chattels. It will be difficult for them to see the economic advantage of setting them free. They will not respect their workers if forced to free them. We must educate them so both plantation owners and workers see the advantage of working cooperatively.

"We find the conditions on the plantations vary," Samson continued, "and what will work for one might not work for another. In some cases, we recommend that the slave owners figure out how much they have invested and how many years of work they need to pay off that investment. They can then give their slaves a timeline as to when they will be free. We find the main incentive is the profit sharing and we insist that a share of the profits go to all the workers whether free or slave. This gives them incentive to work hard and efficiently. Improved working conditions and mutual respect along with knowing they will eventually be free is often enough to make dramatic improvements. My recommendation is to concentrate first on education. Once the majority is slave free, the state can vote on it and make it law. Unfortunately, the worst abusers will never give up their slaves voluntarily. These ones don't own slaves for monitory gain, but enjoy the power they have over their subjects and will never give that up unless forced. Eventually slavery must be outlawed, but that should be done by majority vote in each state."

"Bobby, Ruthie, do you have anything to add?" the president inquired.

"When I think of the abuses that are happening, the little girls that are being raped, the men, women and children that are being whipped just because it gives their owners pleasure, I can't stand the thoughts of slavery going on for one more second," Bobby commented. "However, Samson has been a good adviser and I agree, to force people to free their slaves, at this point, would cause more problems. We first have to educate people that the black population are humans. Unfortunately, the slavery system has blinded them to that obvious fact. As humans, they deserve the respect and rights of every other human. Perhaps laws could be introduced gradually to give the blacks more rights. We could start with the right to education as that is what is holding them back the most. Then the rights to a fair trial and the right to testify in a court of law would be next on the list. No one should be punished indiscriminately without first being proven guilty of an offence."

"Mr. President," Ruthie took her turn. "I have a great deal of respect for your position and can imagine the difficulties in making decisions that affect a country. There is no doubt that slavery is wrong and damaging to all of society. I saw the damage it did to my own father and, had Bobby not rescued me, it could have done the same to me. There is no question as to if it should end, but only in how to end it. My father, being a slave owner, was enslaved by that system most of his life. After he freed his slaves he finally enjoyed freedom himself. If Bobby had not come along when he did, my father would never have enjoyed the happiness he felt during the last few months of his life. We desperately need to get this word out. My father was a horrible abusive man, but it was all because the slavery system had taught him that this was how he should be. When he realized that slavery was wrong he became a completely different person. My plea, Mr. President, is please, please, please end this evil system. How I wish it could just be turned off, but I believe the advice of Bobby and Samson are correct and, if we can get most people to do it voluntarily, then it will be easier to rid the world of the true villains."

"Impressive speech," the President responded. "I'm sure glad I never had to run against you. Mr. Douglass. Your thoughts please."

"Mr. President. This is a very new concept, but one I wish I'd thought of. You already know my opinion; that everyone should have equal rights in the location where they are living. If freedom was available in the south, the workers would not run, in fact many former fugitive slaves would go back to their friends, family and old masters. I think we should investigate further and see if the government can be of any assistance in this program. I suggest we put together a few experts to go to these plantations and see firsthand what they are doing. I would love to be on that panel myself."

"I thought it was risky for you to travel in the south, but not to worry. I think I should like to go along and I am quite sure you will not get kidnapped in the presence of the President of the United States."

Suddenly the plan Bobby and Samson had worked on for about forty years had the backing of the US government. From that point, things progressed very quickly. Laws were passed that would lead to the eventual end of slavery. No more was anyone born a slave and the governments of the slave states were given the task of finding the best way to end slavery in each state. No state was allowed to have laws preventing the education of any citizen and all people, slave or free, were, from that point, considered citizens. A mass of literature was printed about the system Samson had devised and he, along with his children, sat on panels of experts to further refine it and find ways to implement it. One by one the slave states became free while social and economic conditions greatly improved. Cooperation and profit sharing began to spread beyond the former slave states. Soon, every university in the country taught the principles that Bobby and Samson had initiated.

By 1875 equal rights was firmly established, the vote was given to all men and women once they reached the age of twenty one, and no one paid any more attention to the colour of one's skin than they would to the colour of their hair or eyes. Not only war had been averted, but a century of hatred and prejudice were avoided. As a system of mutual respect, friendship and cooperation spread around the world, the standard of living improved immensely. Government no longer had to worry about things such as unemployment. Everyone took on the responsibility of assuring all others had meaningful employment regardless of their abilities. With everyone working, crime rates dropped and a minimal police force was required to keep the peace. With the country at peace, the whole world was affected. Armaments were reduced to a minimum. Unstressful living conditions coupled with the fact that food producers cared about the well being of their customers meant that overall health improved. Lower health care costs, less strain on law enforcement and a very low defence budget resulted in lower taxes and much happiness for all.

Bobby and Samson enjoyed a peaceful retirement as their children took up the challenges ahead of them. Each generation advanced and refined the plan that Samson started. When all learned that cooperation led to more affluence than competition ever could, society advanced at a rate never before imagined.

Epilogue

I fully admit that the preceding has been pure fiction. I don't blame anyone if they find it unbelievable, but consider this, is it not more believable than thinking that a nation could cause more destruction and loss of life to its own people than any outside force has ever done? The history of the USA is filled with wars, yet no war took more American lives than the civil war. It took until the 1970's before US casualties in all other wars exceeded the lives lost in this most devastating war.

The horrible destruction of this war was not its only drawback. Reconstruction took more than one hundred years and still prejudice lingers between the white race and the race they formerly enslaved. The bitterness of losing a war and being forced into a value system that they did not agree with meant that the former slave owners did all in their power to assure the ones they had held as chattels could not prosper. There is times when injustice must be stopped no matter the cost. The horrendous system of North American slavery was very evil and the cost of stopping it was very high.

Through changing laws, we prevent outward acts of slavery from being manifested, but until the heart changes, the spirit of slavery will remain. Slavery was a legal way for one group of people to exploit another and exploitation of others is not yet against the law. Indeed those inflicted with the disease of greed will continue to find ways around the laws so that they may exploit and take advantage of those less fortunate. Not until they realize that these practices are not only hurting their victims but are holding back all of society, including themselves, will they have a change of heart. Once one experiences the joy of cooperation and helping others succeed, he will never again resort to greed.

The Sowing Peace initiative was started by George McNeish to promote peace throughout the world.

More information at

www.sowingpeace.ca

Front cover photographs by George McNeish.

The picture of the cannon was adapted from a picture taken at Victoria Park, London, ON

The mansion is actually the O'Neil funeral home on William Street in London, ON

The people pictured are the author, George McNeish and his wife Delta.

Made in the USA
Charleston, SC
14 January 2016